CLAIMED BY THE ALIEN BODYGUARD

ALIENS AMONG US #3

TIFFANY ROBERTS

A retired alien bodyguard. A luscious human female he craves. He'll do whatever it takes to make her his by Christmas.

Gabriela Romero is a single mother struggling to make ends meet. With Christmas fast approaching, she's lost work, she's late on rent, and the zeroes in her bank account are on the wrong side of the decimal point. Fortunately, she has a couple bright spots in her life—her amazing daughter, Ana, and her brief interactions with her gorgeous neighbor from across the street, Mason Lee.

He's big, strong, kind, and he's great with Ana. Plus, he looks at Gabriela like he wants to devour her. How could a man like him be real? When he finally asks her out—and an unexpected job comes her way—it seems Gabriela's luck is finally turning around.

Until the universe decides to give her a reality check and disaster strikes.

In Gabriela's most desperate moments, Mason rushes to the rescue. But her savior isn't what he seems. He's a seven-foot-tall alien with horns and glowing violet eyes. Did she run into the arms of an otherworldly demon or will this unusual being save Christmas—and claim Gabriela's heart in the process?

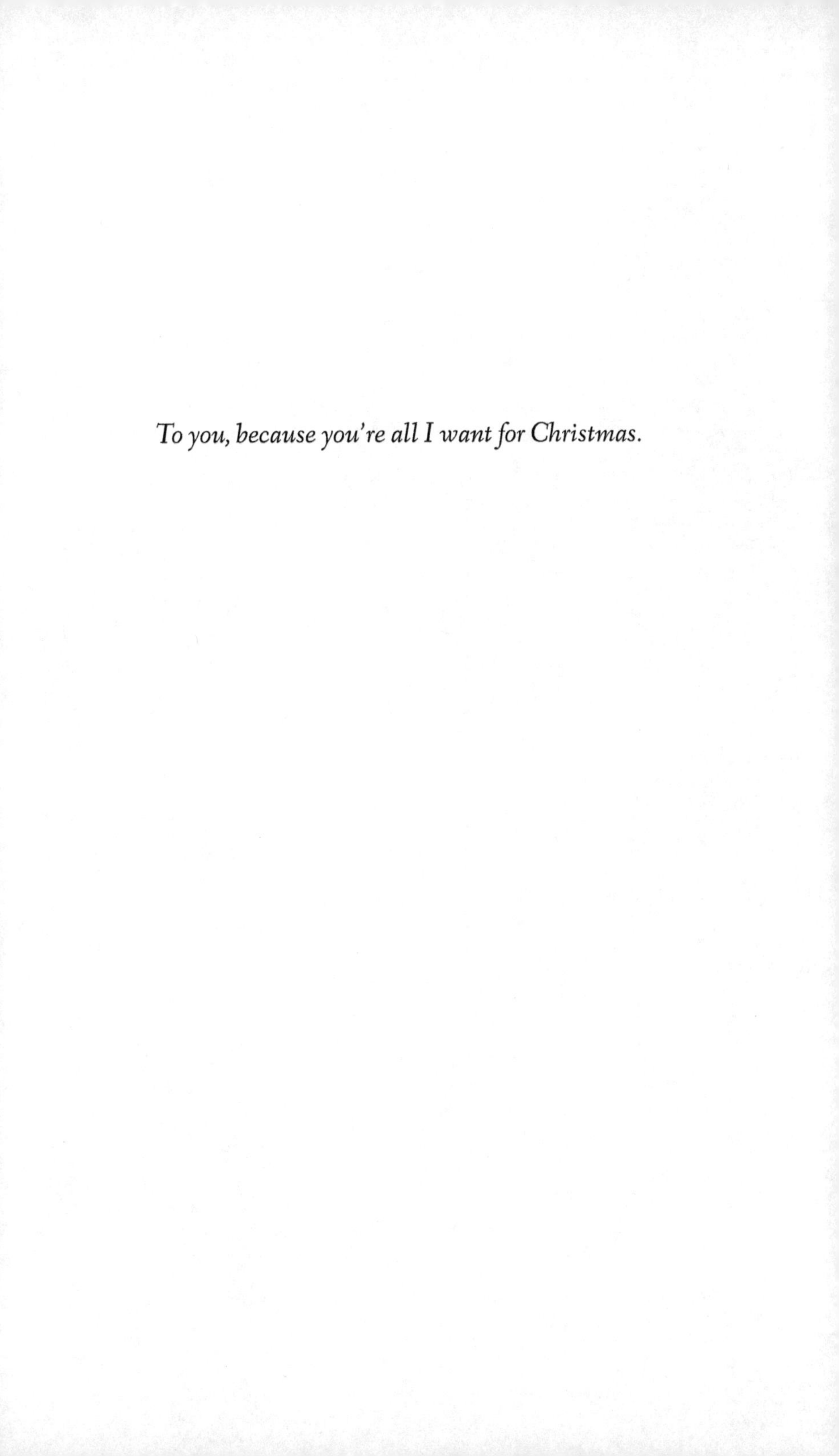

To you, because you're all I want for Christmas.

ONE

Gabriela Romero stood in front of the big block of gray mailboxes with her key in the keyhole of her box. She drew in a shaky breath, shoved aside the knots twisting in her belly, and opened the door. Atop a pile of bills and junk mail lay a plain white envelope. It had no postmark, no address or return address; just Gabriela's name and that stupid stamp her landlord loved to use so much—*URGENT* in red ink.

She had known the notice would come. Hell, it had probably been sitting in her mailbox for a week by now.

It didn't matter how much she'd hoped that envelope wouldn't arrive, it didn't matter that she'd prayed her landlord would show an ounce of compassion and understanding so close to Christmas and cut her a break. That had all been nothing more than wishful thinking. She didn't have that kind of luck.

That wasn't how real life worked. Problems didn't just disappear, they didn't just resolve themselves. If anything, ignoring them only made things worse.

And it wasn't even like she was always late paying rent.

She'd been getting those payments in on time for years. But this past year had been rough, and money was tighter and tighter every month. She'd cut expenses every way she could just to make sure she and her daughter had the essentials.

She knew exactly the unhelpful advice many people would've offered her—that she should just find a new job or move to a more affordable area if she was struggling so much. But high-paying jobs weren't exactly abundant in areas that thrived on tourism, and it wasn't exactly easy to move when you had no money in your bank account to cover first month's rent and security deposits.

This house had been a steal when she'd started renting it, but when Allen Jensen, her current landlord, had bought it from the old owner a few years ago he'd immediately raised the rent. He'd bumped it up a little more every year since. And the ridiculous thing was that her rent was still considered cheap for this town.

Gabriela reached into her mailbox, removed the envelope, and quickly tore it open, just like ripping off a band aid. She removed the letter from within and unfolded it. Tears filled her eyes as she read. Though there were many words, only one, written in bold letters, stood out to her—*eviction*.

This was her fault. Rather than scrimping and saving for just in case, like she'd known she should have, she'd made a decision based on money she had expected to earn. Buying a Christmas tree and a few decorations should've been no big deal. It should've fit into her budget.

But then a property management company had cut a deal with one of Gabby's clients and taken management of four vacation homes she normally cleaned—switching those proper-ties to their own housekeeping service. The blow to her income had been too much. Had nothing changed, she would've been able to cover her bills, buy the Christmas stuff, and have a tiny bit left over. Now she was a hundred dollars short on rent, and Allen Jensen had made it clear that he would not accept partial payments.

All Gabriela wanted was for her daughter to have a good Christmas. Ana rarely asked for anything. She was an amazing little girl; bright, sweet, funny, and so compassionate. Gabby wanted to give her *something* more than the few small presents she'd purchased during the fall, but she didn't know how she was going to accomplish that with Christmas only a week away.

Gabriela sniffled, chest constricted as tears spilled down her cheeks. The cold winter air made those tears burn.

"You okay?" someone asked in a deep, gruff, familiar voice.

Gabriela started, keeping her face forward.

"Oh! Yeah," she said as she hurriedly wiped her cheeks and eyes with her coat sleeve. She forced a laugh. "It's the cold. Kind of burns my eyes sometimes, you know?"

She took in a deep breath that stung more than her tears had and she turned toward Mason Lee, her sexy neighbor from across the street.

He stood several feet away from her, but that distance couldn't disguise how big the man was. At five foot two, Gabriela was used to looking up at people, but Mason towered over her. She swore he was over six and a half feet tall. Though he'd lived across the street for a year, and she saw him on a regular basis, she was always stunned by his size.

Mason wasn't simply a tall man—he was big and broad all over, like a bear. And he was beautiful in an otherworldly kind of way. Long black hair framed his masculine face, hanging well past his square jaw. Dark, thick brows rested above his unique violet eyes, and he had full, sculpted lips that Gabby had dreamed of kissing.

Those lips were currently turned down in a frown so slight that it had no right seeming as severe as it did, and those eyes were fixed on her with an unmasked blend of skepticism and concern.

He was going to press her, was going to pry, and Gabriela wasn't sure if she had the emotional energy to pretend for much longer. The last thing she needed right now was to break down in front of her gorgeous neighbor.

But Mason just grunted and said, "Good weather for a hot drink."

Though his English was excellent, he had a noticeable accent. Gabriela had never been able to place it; to her, it had a hint of Russian or Eastern European, but there a touch of something in it that just couldn't be identified.

Gabriela smiled. "Hot chocolate does sound pretty good."

He stepped closer, close enough that Gabriela could almost feel the heat radiating from his big body, close enough that she had to tip her head back to maintain eye contact. For a few seconds, he looked into her eyes. A thousand crazy thoughts tumbled through her mind—a thousand desires that seemed wholly inappropriate given the circumstances.

Is it so wrong to just want to be held by a big, brawny man?

Except she didn't want it to stop at that. She wanted more. It'd been a long, long, *long* time since she'd been intimate with a man.

And this man had taken part in many of her most recent fantasies.

Mason lifted a hand, and Gabby's breath caught. But instead of cupping her cheek or slipping his long, strong fingers into her hair, he proceeded to insert his key into the keyhole of his mailbox, unlocking the little door and swinging it open.

"Sorry," she said, grabbing the stack of mail from her box, closing the door, and removing her key. She stepped back, giving him some space to retrieve his mail as she shoved her keys and her mail—including the late payment letter—into her purse.

He turned his gaze to his mailbox as he reached inside. "There's a place on Third that's supposed to be good."

Gabriela's brow creased, and she tilted her head. "Good for what?"

"Hot chocolate."

"Ohhh. I...I'll have to take Ana there sometime."

Mason closed the door on his mailbox, the sound of it loud enough to echo in the winter sky, and winced. "I, uh, meant that I could take you."

For a moment, everything went quiet and still. Gabriela stared at him, unsure if she'd heard him correctly, but his words kept replaying inside her head.

Is he...is he asking me out?

Well, don't just stand there and stare at him!

Heat flooded her face. Gabby ducked her head, dropping her gaze to the snow piled around the mailboxes' posts. She shuffled her feet, nudging aside a chunk of snow with the toe of her boot, and peeked up at him with a smile. "Are you...asking me out, Mason?"

He tugged back some of his long hair and released a heavy breath that emerged in thick cloud. "Yeah."

"I would like that."

His eyebrows rose, and his oddly entrancing eyes widened. "Really?"

She chuckled. "Really."

Mason waved back toward his home with the stack of mail in his hand, lowering his other hand to stuff it in his pocket. "We can take my truck."

Gabriela looked toward his blue pickup, and something clicked in her mind. Her eyes rounded as she returned them to Mason. "Wait, you mean now?"

"You're cold now."

She laughed. "Yeah, I am, but I need to pick up my daughter from school in..." Reaching into her purse, she dug around the seemingly bottomless pit until she found her phone. She pressed the side button to check the time and gasped. "Shit! I'm late. I was supposed to leave ten minutes ago."

How long had she stood there staring at her mailbox?

Gabriela looked up at Mason as she walked toward her house, turning to keep her eyes on him. "I am so, so sorry. Thank you for the offer. We'll....we'll have to plan for it another time, yeah?"

He remained in place, his expression taut with lips slightly downturned, his hand still in his pocket. "Yeah. Another time."

"Thank you!"

She spun around and ran the rest of the distance. Her car was sitting in the driveway. It was a small, bronze Honda Accord, a little beat up but dependable. The best part? It was hers, something she'd paid off in full.

Gabriela opened the driver side door and got into the car, tossing her purse onto the passenger seat. It wasn't until she'd shut the door and placed a hand on the wheel that she registered what she'd just done.

I turned Mason down.

She looked back toward him. He was already across the road, walking to his front door with his jeans hugging his tree trunk-like thighs and sculpted ass.

I turned Mason down...for a date.

"*Jueputa!*" Gabriela clutched the steering wheel in both hands and banged the back of her head against the head rest.

The first man—a damn fine man, at that—to show real interest in years, a man who'd asked her out, and she'd left him hanging.

"You didn't turn him down, Gabriela, you just...rain-checked it. You didn't say no. You just have responsibilities and a kid. He understands."

Except he'd looked like a man who'd been rejected.

That tightness seized her chest again. Gabby buckled her seatbelt, pulled her keys out of her purse, and stuck them into the ignition. She took in a deep breath to calm herself before starting the car. Cold air blasted from the dashboard vents. She reached forward and switched the dial to defrost, shivering.

As she backed out of the driveway, she once more glanced toward Mason's house. He was no longer in sight.

"Way to go, Gabby," she muttered as she faced forward, put the car into drive, and followed the private street out onto the main road, which was thankfully well maintained and clear of snow and ice. Though it snowed a lot in McCall, Idaho, the city did a great job keeping the roads safe.

When she reached her daughter's school, the pick-up lane was already empty, allowing Gabriela to pull right up to the main doors where Ana was waiting with a couple other students. As soon as Ana caught sight of Gabby, she turned to her teacher, waved, and ran to the car.

Gabriela snatched up her purse and tucked it between the two seats, atop the parking brake.

"Hi, Mom!" Ana said as she pulled open the door and dropped into the passenger seat. After a brief struggle make sure her backpack and coat were fully inside the cab, she pulled the door shut.

"Hey, *mija.*" Gabriela reached out, tugged her daughter close, and pressed a kiss to her head. "How was school?"

"Boring," Ana said, shoving her backpack onto the floor between her legs before turning up the radio.

Gabriela laughed as she pulled away from the curb. "You always say that."

Ana flashed a big smile, revealing the same dimples in her

cheeks that Gabriela had, as well as the gaps between her teeth where her canines had yet to grow in. "Because it's always boring."

"You're just not being challenged enough, that's all. You're too smart."

Ana blew on her fingernails and rubbed them against her chest. "Damn right, I am."

"Ana! Language!"

Ana laughed. "Mom, damn isn't a bad word."

"It is under my roof."

"But you say it all the time."

Gabriela chuckled, glancing at her daughter. "Is this where I tell you *do as I say, not as I do*?" She shook her head. "Are you excited for tomorrow at least? Last day of school before Christmas break?"

"Yes! Mrs. Connelly said we're going to watch a movie and have snacks. We get to wear our pajamas to school and bring blankets, too. Julie said she has an amazing Pegasus onesie she's going to wear to match me better."

"That sounds fun."

"Can I bring a snack for the class?"

Gabby's smile died, and she squeezed the steering wheel. "Ana..."

"It's okay if I don't. Just thought I'd ask. I...know we don't have much money."

Gabriela curled her lips in and bit them. Her eyes burned, and it took a lot of effort to blink away the blur of tears without crying. She felt like a failure as a mother. Ana went without so many of the things her classmates had, things Gabriela just couldn't afford—even things as simple as treats for the class.

"I'm sorry, baby," she said softly, throat tight.

"It's okay, Mom. Really. I understand."

And Ana did understand. Even on those rare occasions

when she asked for something, she never whined, begged, or threw a tantrum when Gabriela said no. The little girl just accepted it, often graciously. Though things had never been easy, Gabriela wouldn't give her daughter up for anything. She was proud of the young lady Ana was becoming.

Gabby only wished she could give her daughter more.

The rest of the fifteen-minute drive was quiet save for the music. Ana sang along to the radio as she watched the snowy, wooded landscape pass by through the window. When they arrived home, Gabriela pulled into the driveway and killed the engine, handing the keys to Ana.

"We're home!" Ana unbuckled her seatbelt, threw open her door, and hopped out, slinging her backpack over her shoulder as she ran toward the house.

"Ana, you forgot something," Gabriela called.

Her daughter came to an abrupt halt, did a one-eighty, and hurried back to the car to shut the passenger door.

Gabby shook her head and smiled to herself. Unbuckling her own seatbelt, she picked up her purse, opened her door, and stepped out of the car. She stood up just in time to see Ana unlock the front door and disappear inside the house.

"Homework before TV!" Gabriela shouted.

"I know!" Ana's muffled voice said from inside.

Gabriela locked the car, and just as she was closing her door, she glanced toward Mason's house. The corners of her lips turned down.

Maybe I should have said something more? Something to reassure him that I am interested in him?

That she'd been interested in him for months.

Gabriela sighed, turned, and walked toward her house.

The blaring of a high-pitched ringtone broke the peaceful mountain quiet.

Stopping, she dug her phone out of the black hole that was

her purse. The incoming call was from Paige, one of her long-time clients. Gabriela accepted the call and lifted the phone to her ear.

"Hi, Paige. How are you today?"

"Gabriela! Yes! So glad you picked up. I know this is last minute, but I have an emergency and I was wondering if you were free tomorrow. Turns out I'm going to be hosting a big Christmas dinner party this weekend, and my house is a mess. A total wreck! Please, please, please tell me you're free. I will totally pay double for the inconvenience."

Gabriela's heart quickened. "I-I... Yes! I'm free."

Paige's breath whooshed out in a sigh. "Oh, thank you. Thank you! I swear, Gabriela, without you, my house would be a pigsty. You'd think I raised these kids in a barn."

Gabby chuckled. "Kids will be kids. I can be there at eight, right after I drop my daughter off at school if that works?"

"That'd be perfect. You're a life saver! Our kids will be at school, and my husband and I will be at work, so just come on in like normal. You'll have the place to yourself."

"Thank you, Paige. You have no idea how much this means to me."

"No, thank *you*. I hope you have a great night!"

"You, too."

Once the call was disconnected, Gabriela let out a little squeal. This was exactly what she'd needed—a break. Paige's house was big, and it'd take Gabby most of the day to clean, but the pay would push her beyond what she needed for rent with a bit left over to pick up some food and a couple more Christmas gifts for Ana.

Clutching her phone to her chest, she closed her eyes and took in a deep breath, releasing it in a small, relieved, "Thank you."

TWO

Broxen kor'Stygos had spent countless hours of his life waiting. Waiting for opportunities, waiting for threats, waiting for word to act. If nothing else, he'd shown a talent for waiting. Some would've called it patience, though that wasn't quite right —it was more a matter of quieting his conscious mind and shifting fully to sensory input and instinct.

He'd once waited beside a beaten-up blast door in a dark alley for three cycles—almost two full Earth days—while his boss at the time, Astius's father, had conducted *business* in the back room of a club. Though that experience hadn't been pleasant thanks to hunger and the alley's lingering stench, Broxen hadn't once been bored or restless. He'd simply done what he was good at. He'd watched and waited.

Astius would've called that being reactive instead of proactive or some *kruk* like that, but the ability to simply wait while remaining fully alert for such long periods had served Broxen well. When he was a kit, it had often been the difference between going hungry and getting some food in his belly.

So why was this wait so unbearable?

It was routine; he'd done this almost every weekday in the spring, fall, and winter over the last year. And because it was routine, he knew it was short. Just over thirty minutes most days, closer to forty every now and again. Compared to the cycles he'd spent in that alley, this was nothing.

Another fifteen or twenty minutes, and the wait would be over. He was halfway through already.

And yet he could barely keep himself still. He'd changed positions several times, as though the angle from which he was looking out the window made any difference. He'd adjusted the blind slats twice, as though their tilt would somehow change the fact that the driveway across the street was still empty. He'd lifted his hand several times to tuck rogue strands of hair behind his pointed ear, and each time, he'd scraped the tips of his claws over the bases of his horns.

It was fortunate that he was alone—any human would've wondered why there was a bone-scratching sound whenever he combed his fingers through his hair. The holographic projection created by his holoshroud could mask his inhuman features, like his red skin and fangs, but it couldn't hide all evidence of their existence. He still had to duck going through doorways to avoid striking not only his head but his horns. He still had to take care how he touched things so as not to produce damage with his claws.

He released a huff through his nostrils, plunged his spoon into the ice cream carton, and shoved a chunk of chocolate and peanut butter ice cream into his mouth. The end of his tail curled against his calf, as stiff and restless as always having spent another day hidden away in his pants.

What was he doing?

Gabriela would be back soon, and he'd hear her car on the road like he had every other time. He didn't need to stand here like a hormonal human adolescent or a beast desperate for the return of its master. And he certainly didn't need to be eating this ice cream.

He shoveled another bite into his mouth before even finishing the last. Maybe he didn't need to be eating it, but he wanted to. If there was anything in the universe as delicious as chocolate and peanut butter ice cream, he'd never tasted it.

Hot chocolate, with Gabriela. That would taste better.

And he'd made a mess of that, hadn't he?

He'd known as he walked to mailbox that Gabriela had been due to go pick up Ana. He'd known that she was running late as he'd looked upon her face and seen the tears brimming in her big, entrancing eyes, as he'd seen the defeat and sadness take hold of her expression.

He'd known she had to leave, until he'd asked if she wanted to go get some hot chocolate right then—apparently, the knowledge had fled him in that moment. As though he'd not been awkward enough before then. All he'd wanted to do was ease her sadness, was make her smile so he could see her eyes shine, so he could see those endearing dimples on her cheeks.

Broxen knew what Astius would've said—something about making opportunities instead of awaiting them. But Astius had never had to deal with humans. These people were confusing by nature, and every aspect of them was somehow contradictory. Broxen had yet to figure them out. He wasn't even sure if they could be figured out.

But...he wanted to figure out Gabriela. Even if he never understood a single other human on this planet, he wanted to understand her.

She hadn't refused him. He needed to keep that in mind. She'd simply said they could go out another time. That was good, right?

And he wasn't eating this ice cream because he felt

rejected. He was eating it because it was good. He was only having a few bites.

He glanced down at the carton—which had been full when he'd opened it fifteen minutes ago—and frowned. About half of the one point five quarts of ice cream was gone. Unbidden, his tail coiled around his leg and squeezed.

Clenching his jaw, he turned away from the window, crossed the living room, and entered the kitchen, battling his urge to look back with every step. It was too soon for her to be home. Her car wasn't going to suddenly appear in her driveway; he wasn't going to miss out on a chance to see her again.

Besides, this ice cream thing was more concerning, wasn't it? He'd seen this phenomenon in human movies and television shows. The only people who seemed to eat ice cream like this were humans—often female—who had just been *broken up with*. Humans who had been spurned by their mates. It seemed to be a treatment for what humans sometimes called a broken heart.

He placed the ice cream on the counter, slipped the spoon into his mouth to suck off the lingering ice cream and peanut butter, and put the lid on the carton.

"Not rejected," he mumbled around the spoon. "Not sad."

His heart didn't even hurt—though there was a tightness in his chest that had persisted since he'd approached Gabriela earlier.

Broxen returned the ice cream to the freezer and stepped to the sink to clean the spoon, shaking his head at himself along the way. After everything he'd been through in his life, after everything he'd endured, everything he'd done, his time here on Earth should've been the easiest. This planet—or at least this region of it—was the calmest, quietest place he'd ever been. The humans were largely oblivious to the universe at large.

They were oblivious to the non-humans living amongst them.

But apparently the threat of being pummeled, bludgeoned, stabbed, or shot in his old life had been much easier for Broxen to face than the chance of being rejected by a tiny female human, or else he would've tried to approach Gabriela much sooner.

Tiny female. Kind, passionate, beautiful female.

He dried his hands on the dish towel hanging under the sink and returned to the front window, taking his customary place on the right side.

The ground outside was blanketed in thick snow, making the black asphalt of the road stand out starkly; that road had felt like an uncrossable chasm for so long.

And that was ridiculous.

Broxen had spent most of his life in the service of one of the most powerful crime families on Turata. He'd done bad things. He'd stolen, he'd hurt people. He'd killed. He'd been wounded more times than he could count, and he had caused far more wounds than he'd received. Why should he feel this way about a fucking road?

Zorak akai, he'd walked across that road many times during the year he'd lived here. He'd helped clear out Gabriela's driveway and unbury her car after snowstorms, had helped her tear down and chop up a dead tree in her back yard last spring, had given Gabriela her mail that had been mistakenly put in his box. He'd even helped little Ana fix the chain on her bike a few times this past summer.

Every time he'd gone over there, he'd wanted to tell Gabriela of his interest in her. He'd wanted to express his desires. He'd wanted to do what he'd done today—but he'd never known how. Apparently, he still didn't know.

He tugged his phone from his back pocket and checked the

time. Gabriela had left twenty-two minutes ago. She'd be back soon.

What was troubling her?

In his old life, long before he'd become a bodyguard in a dangerous underworld, Broxen had learned to assess threats. That often came down to knowing how to read people—not so easy when he was always dealing with varied alien species. In his experience so far, human emotions were often quite easy to read, but their motivations never were.

Though he knew Gabriela was upset, he had no idea why, and he didn't know how to even begin guessing.

Returning the phone to his pocket, he clasped his hands behind his back, leaned his shoulder against the wall beside the window, and shoved his thoughts aside. He forced his tail to unfurl, easing its tip to rest just above his ankle. It was time to just wait. No more racing mind, no more worries, no more doubt.

At least not for a little while.

When he finally heard the whisper of tires on the wet road, it seemed too soon. He checked his phone again; Gabriela had been gone for exactly thirty minutes. Her previous best time was thirty-two.

She left late today. Missed the rush.

He turned his attention back to Gabriela's home just as her car pulled into the driveway. The brake lights flared for a moment before going dark. Broxen eased aside slightly, hiding as much of his body behind the window frame as possible.

Broxen doubted anyone would be able to see in through the window from outside, but the extra caution couldn't hurt. He had plenty to hide, and from what he understood, humans didn't like being watched.

The passenger door of Gabriela's car swung open.

Broxen clenched his fists, pressing his claws into his palms.

Ana darted out of the car first, rushing toward the house until a call from her mother stopped her in her tracks. The little girl spun on her heel, hurried back to the car, and slammed the door shut. She was already running to the house again by the time Gabriela climbed out of the car.

Gabriela glanced toward Broxen's home, and his heart stuttered. That look lasted only an instant, but it affected him in ways he couldn't describe—and she hadn't even looked directly at him.

As Gabriela was walking toward the front door, she paused abruptly, opened her purse, and pulled out her phone. Within the first few seconds of her conversation, all the upset and sadness that had been on her face vanished. It was replaced first by shock, and then by a big, bright smile that made her eyes sparkle. She was far more animated for the duration of the call, nodding and grinning.

After dropping her phone back into her purse, she let out an excited squeal that he heard despite the distance and the closed window. Broxen couldn't help but smile, too.

Composing herself, she straightened her coat, adjusted the strap of her purse a little higher on her shoulder, and tucked a few dangling strands of her long, black hair behind her ear. She turned her gaze toward Broxen's home again.

It might've been a trick of the distance between them, but it looked like her smile widened just a little.

The tightness in Broxen's chest intensified. No female, whether human or any other species, had caught his interest like Gabriela had. His past encounters with females had been brief, fueled by mutual lust and a desire for release. It was different with Gabriela. It was something...deeper, unlike anything he'd ever experienced.

And he might never have found her had things gone different. He hadn't known this planet even existed until overhearing something in a seedy bar on the other side of the galaxy—that Earth, apparently, was a good place for a someone to go if they needed to disappear.

That had been exactly what Broxen needed to do.

Astius had been dead for two years by the time Broxen had arrived on Earth. Broxen had spent his first year and a half in New York City, refining the English language that had been loaded into the neural transceiver implanted in his brain. Attempting to absorb an alien culture. But he'd been without direction, without purpose, left on a strange world with strange people and their bizarre mannerisms. Between a mix of unofficial currency conversion and hacking, he'd been set up with more Earth money than he could ever spend, and yet...he hadn't known what to do with himself.

Eventually, the crowds, the noise, the huge buildings, and the overwhelming smells had all become too much. He didn't want to be reminded of his home city back on Turata—Nakonin—any longer. So, he'd wandered, trekking across the country until he'd finally found McCall, Idaho—a place where he could have quiet, if nothing else.

And it was only here, unexpectedly, that he'd found a reason to carry on, a purpose.

Watching over Gabriela and Ana, even if only from afar, had given him meaning. It had eased the disorientation of being on an alien world where he felt like he understood so little even if his neural transceiver could translate every word in any human language.

Gabriela turned her gaze forward and walked to the front door, which Ana had left open.

Broxen willed Gabriela to look toward him again. He wanted one last glimpse of her face, one last look into her eyes, before he'd have to wait until tomorrow to see her again.

Though the view from behind...he'd be lying if he were to

say it was unappealing. It made him long for warmer weather, when she wouldn't be wearing her big coat and boots. During the summer, she'd often gone outside in sleeveless shirts and shorts that showed off her shapely legs. A few times, she'd worn only a swimsuit that revealed every contour of her body as she lay in the sun, basking in its warmth while Ana played in a sprinkler on the grass.

Zorak akai, the way that material had hugged her full breasts, the way it had revealed her ass...

He groaned and gritted his teeth as his cock swelled, pressing against his jeans to produce a deep, throbbing ache.

Gabriela didn't look back. She simply stepped across the threshold and nudged the door closed with her boot.

Broxen released a heavy breath through his nostrils. For several seconds, he stared at that closed door. Maybe she'd forgotten something in the car and would have to come back out. Maybe she would come over to set a time to get hot chocolate with him, or to say they should go now.

Those seconds stretched into minutes, and her door did not open again. The gloomy sky would soon be darkening, the temperature would begin dropping, and the chances of her coming out would only shrink.

Astius would've laughed about this—big, bad Broxen staring longingly at a female's home, too uncertain to go and talk to her again. And that thought...it hurt. It hurt because Broxen would never hear Astius's laughter again. He would never again be dragged into those painfully intellectual conversations Astius had been so fond of, he would never be forced to question beliefs he didn't even know he held, he would never be challenged to be more than what he was.

No. That's not true. By being here, by looking out for her...I am being more. I'm not who I was.

Yet Broxen knew he could stand here telling himself that

until he died of starvation and the thought wouldn't be true for merely thinking it. He knew better than anyone that actions were what ultimately counted. Wanting to change didn't mean he had.

He shoved away from the window with a grunt and walked to the dining table, which was positioned between the kitchen and living room. The cardboard box containing his latest haul from the local thrift stores was still atop the table, and this was as good a time as any to start digging in. He needed a distraction now more than ever to stop himself from staring at Gabriela's house all damned night.

Broxen opened the box, revealing the books it contained. Most of them had faded covers, yellowed pages, and creased spines; they'd been well-read, and he would eventually contribute to that wear by reading them himself.

Astius had spent years trying to convince Broxen to read in his free time. Broxen had never understood the appeal—not until Astius was dead and Broxen had found himself on Earth with nothing but time to fill. He'd followed Astius's example of reading anything; any genre, any subject, whether it was made-up or factual.

He lifted hand, sweeping back his hair. His thumb claw scraped along his right horn.

If Gabriela saw him as he really was—if she saw him as Broxen kor'Stygos rather than Mason Lee—would she still be kind to him? Or would she be frightened, disgusted? Even though the holoshroud made him look like a male human, she would still feel his backswept horns if she combed her fingers through his hair. She would still feel his tail tucked along his leg if she bumped into him from the right angle. She would still feel his claws if he trailed his fingertips over her skin.

"Bah," he grumbled before reaching into the box and grabbing a book at random. He flicked on the kitchen light and carried the book over to the recliner he had positioned near the front living room window.

Placing his phone on the armrest, Broxen clicked on the nearby floor lamp, sat down, and flipped up the footrest. Only then did he look at the book.

There was a red rose at the top, resting over large, flowing white letters that dominated the majority of the cover. *Johanna Lindsey*. The title was written in pink text toward the bottom —*Prisoner of My Desire*.

Broxen lifted his gaze for a moment, glancing through the blinds toward Gabriela's house. Another human saying came to mind, one that had taken him quite some time to puzzle out; the title almost seemed *too on the nose*. Broxen longingly staring out through these blinds wasn't unlike the image he'd seen time and again in human entertainment—a prisoner looking out through the bars of his cell.

Muttering another curse, he opened the book to the first chapter and read. Though the neural transceiver provided translations for everything, he had to use his phone to research more context on a few of the terms. It didn't take long to determine that this was what the humans called a *romance*.

He enjoyed such stories. They spoke to his own desires, to wants he wasn't sure how to articulate, and gave him some sense of hope that those things could come to be. It didn't matter if these stories were fiction; there had to be some semblance of truth at their cores, right?

Through those books, he'd learned about human females— about their bodies, about their desires, about their pleasure. And for months, he'd yearned to apply those lessons to Gabriela. He yearned to satisfy her, to please her, to give her *everything* and hear her cry out his name while she soared at the heights of ecstasy.

He could be the male for her. He could be...her mate. She

and Ana would want for nothing if they were his. He would protect them and provide for them, he would show them the support, compassion, and respect they deserved. Were Gabriela his mate and Ana his kit, he would give his all to ensure they had reason to smile every day.

By the time he marked his place with a finger and lowered the book, it was dark outside. The display on his phone said it was six fifteen. His stomach decided then that it wasn't satisfied with the half-carton of ice cream he'd eaten a few hours earlier; it demanded sustenance.

Pushing the footrest down, he stood up and strode to the dining room table, shifting around unused placemats and finally lifting the cardboard box to find the Payette Lake bookmark he'd purchased from a local giftshop. He slipped it between the pages, closed the book, and set it down before continuing into the kitchen.

Broxen opened the refrigerator and freezer. Cold air flowed over him as he stared at the fridge's contents. He had frozen meat on hand; beef was a particular favorite, though he was also fond of many of the species of fish he'd tasted. It wouldn't take much to cook a steak or a salmon filet. He could even fry some pork chops. He'd bookmarked a few new recipes on his phone that he'd been meaning to try.

Steaming a bag of frozen vegetables would be easy, too, and would pair well no matter what meat he chose, but...

With a sigh, he reached into the freezer and grabbed one of the frozen microwaveable meals. Meatloaf and potatoes or something like that—*for brawny men with big appetites!*

Closing the fridge and freezer, he stepped to the microwave, opening the package as he walked. He poked holes in the plastic covering with a claw and put the tray in the microwave, punching in the recommended time.

He braced a hand on the counter as the microwave

hummed. His eyes itched, desperate to shift toward the front window again even though the reflection of the interior lights on the glass would make it impossible to see Gabriela's house. That he knew it was there was enough, right? That he knew *she* was there.

Instead of looking toward the window, he dropped his gaze to his hand and drummed his fingers on the countertop, counting the microwave timer in his head. His claws clicked against the surface. He stilled his fingers when he reached zero and awaited the beep.

Brow furrowed, he glanced at the microwave. It still had six seconds.

Even after two and a half years, Broxen hadn't quite synched with the human tracking of time.

He pressed the end button at the microwave's first beep, popped the door open, and removed his tray of food. The plastic was fogged with steam and condensation. He peeled it back, stirred the mushy potatoes—*mashed* potatoes—and placed the tray in the microwave to finish heating. As soon as it was done, he tossed the plastic film in the trash and carried his meal to the couch.

Broxen sat down and turned on the television, switching it to a random channel. While he'd never been disappointed by selecting a random book, the TV had proven far less reliable. It felt like half of it was advertising and the rest was often watered-down. For all their vices, humans seemed to recoil from their own true nature, finding it distasteful to depict on the screen.

Still, he left this movie—something about stealing cars, apparently—on as he ate the microwaveable meal. Within a minute, he'd burned his tongue on the potatoes despite gently blowing on them and stirring them thoroughly to release the excess heat.

Were Gabriela and Ana eating their own dinner now? Was Gabriela truly feeling better, or was it just the joy of being around her daughter that had uplifted her?

Should he drive into town and pick up some hot chocolate to bring to the two humans? He wasn't sure if such a gesture would be considered kind or creepy; it was surprisingly difficult to tell the difference between the two a lot of the time.

What would it be like to have Gabriela and Ana here with him now? To have cooked dinner for them, to be sharing it with them? What would it be like to watch TV with them? Perhaps even this outlandish movie, which seemed to have little regard for the laws of physics, would be entertaining if he had Gabriela sitting beside him.

"Ah, fuck." He shoveled the last few bites of food into his mouth, stood up, and brought the empty tray into the kitchen to throw it away.

He attempted to continue the movie afterward, but found his attention constantly straying to the window; he could just make out the glow of Gabriela's porch lights through the reflections on the glass. So he did all he could think to do—picked up *Prisoner of My Desire*, returned to the recliner, and continued reading.

By ten o'clock, he was more than halfway through the book. He put the bookmark in place, tipped his head back onto the recliner's headrest, and stared up at the ceiling. The situation in the book was...complicated, to say the least. Kidnapping, nonconsensual sex, a controlling and cruel relative. Broxen couldn't guess how the two main characters would overcome the obstacles set in their path—would overcome what they'd done to each other—to reach their happy ending.

Yet no matter how wild the circumstances, reading about a blossoming relationship between two made-up characters only turned his mind back toward Gabriela. If Rowena and Warrick could overcome their circumstances, that had to mean Broxen and Gabriela could overcome their own, didn't it?

Broxen wasn't sure how to approach her. He wasn't sure how to tell her what he felt, what he wanted. That was nothing compared to the things these fictional characters were facing.

There was some way to make it work. There had to be.

He had to believe that. A few years ago, he would've thought it was all a load of what the humans called *bullshit*, but now...

What else was there for him to do but hope?

Releasing a heavy breath, he pushed himself out of the chair, turned off the lamp, and went to the kitchen for a glass of water.

His house was quiet. Still. Empty despite all the furnishings. He scanned his surroundings slowly, wondering what would be different if he shared this place. Humans were fond of decorating; how would Gabriela decorate Broxen's home?

He gulped down the water, wiped his mouth with the back of his hand, rinsed the glass and placed it in the drainboard. The gentle clink of glass on metal was amplified by the relative quiet. Broxen didn't know this world, didn't know its people, didn't even really know where Earth was other than unfathomably far from the place he'd been born. There were other nonhumans on this planet, but they were undoubtedly in situations like his own—they were here to hide.

But there was something like seven billion humans on Earth. How was it possible to feel so alone among so many people?

Broxen flicked off the kitchen light and headed for his bedroom. His bed, though barely long enough to fit his tall frame, looked huge and empty now, seemed cold despite the heavy blankets atop it.

He unfastened his belt and unbuttoned his pants, finally

letting his tail free and stretching it out behind him, but he dared not deactivate the holoshroud. He couldn't allow himself to get that complacent. The safest thing was to assume he was always in sight of someone or something.

"Need a shower," he muttered as he kicked off his pants and tore off his shirt. A hot shower, and then bed.

Because even though so much was uncertain, even though so many things were beyond his knowledge, Broxen knew that Gabriela would come out to start her car at about seven twenty tomorrow morning. At seven thirty-five, she would leave to bring Ana to school. For that precious fifteen-minute window, he'd have a chance to glimpse her two or three more times.

And he wouldn't miss that for anything in this world or any other.

THREE

Gabriela's back ached, her feet and hands were sore, and she was exhausted after a day of rigorous house cleaning. On top of that, the line of cars filled with impatient parents waiting to pick up their kids at the elementary school was even longer than usual. But Gabriela didn't care. None of that could quell the excitement thrumming inside her. Today had been a good day, and it would be even better once she picked up Ana.

Before arriving at the school, Gabriela had dropped off the rent money—paid in full—and purchased some groceries and a couple more Christmas gifts for her daughter. All her worries had evaporated with that call from Paige yesterday. Now, Gabby could enjoy a stress-free Christmas with her daughter.

Gabriela pulled the car up into the pick-up zone. She grinned at the sight of her daughter in her rainbow unicorn onesie pajamas. The fluffy pink tail swayed as Ana rocked back and forth while talking to her friends, and the golden horn on the hood bobbed.

Ana turned her head, and her face lit up when she saw Gabriela. She hurriedly waved to her friends, Julie and Max, and raced toward the car, carrying a small bag decorated with cartoon candy canes in one hand. She opened the door, tugged off her backpack, and slipped into the car.

"Today was so much fun!" Ana was already opening the little cellophane bag as she slammed the passenger door. She pulled out a mini cupcake with squished green icing, holding it out to Gabriela. "I saved this for you."

Gabriela's heart clenched. How she'd ended up so blessed with such an amazingly thoughtful daughter, she didn't know. "Oh, *nena*, thank you. Tell you what, how about you split it in half, and we'll share?"

Ana smiled big. "Sounds good."

"Get that seatbelt on first, though," Gabriela said as she drove away from the curb. "Tell me about your day."

Holding the cupcake up high in one hand, Ana used the other to reach behind her and grab the seatbelt, pulling it across her body and snapping it in.

"We did a little bit of work in the morning, but after lunch everyone passed out their snacks and drinks and we all snuggled in our blankets and watched Finding Dori." She tore the cupcake in half and held the bigger piece out to Gabriela. "Me, Julie, and Max all laid together on the floor. Julie had this *huge* pillow that we all got to share."

Gabriela accepted the offering, her thumb landing in the dark green icing. "That sounds fun." She glanced to the left, making sure the road was clear before exiting of the school parking lot. "Maybe we should have a movie slumber party in the living room during Christmas break."

Ana perked, brows shooting up. "Can we? Please? Please? Please?"

"Yes. And I'll even let you choose the movies."

Ana pumped her fist. "Yes!"

Gabriela chuckled and popped the cupcake chunk into her

mouth, making sure to lick the icing off her thumb. It was almost too sweet, but it was delicious.

"I'm so excited for Christmas break," Ana said around the cupcake in her mouth. "Oh, I got something else for you, but you can't open it until Christmas."

Gabriela glanced at Ana, who unzipped her backpack and pulled something out. It was a small bundle, no bigger than her palm, wrapped in red tissue paper with a white bow on top.

"Aw, I can't wait to open it, Ana. Thank you."

"I made it in class. You're going to *love* it!"

"I know I will because you made it."

Somehow, Ana's smile grew larger, and she carefully tucked the gift in her backpack.

"I have a surprise, too," Gabriela said.

"Really? For Christmas?"

"Well, that too, but this surprise is for when we get home."

"What is it? Tell meeeee!"

"We're going to bake Christmas cookies."

"Yay!" Ana bounced in her seat. "The kind that I like, with the icing?"

"Yep."

"You are the best!"

They chatted some more as Gabriela drove home, making plans for Christmas break to go sledding and ice skating, to watch movies, and to build snowmen. By the time the car was in the driveway, Ana was so hyped that she couldn't sit still.

Gabriela turned off the engine and handed the keys to Ana. "I need you to open the door and go to your room."

"How come?"

"Because...I have gifts I don't want you to see yet. And I need to hide them from prying little eyes."

Ana laughed. "I don't pry!"

Gabriela snorted. "That's what they all say."

"Okay, fiiiiiine." Ana unbuckled, wrapped her hand around the strap of her backpack, and opened her car door. "And then we'll make cookies?"

"And then we'll make cookies."

"Sweet." She jumped out of the car.

"Ana, wait," Gabriela said before Ana could close the door. She reached into the back seat and grabbed her coat, holding it out to her daughter. "Can you take this in for me?"

Ana took it. "Sure."

"Thank you."

Her daughter closed the car door and took off toward the house.

Gabriela picked up her purse and exited the car. The chilled air touching her bare arms made her skin prickle with goosebumps. "And remember, no peeking!"

"I won't!" Ana called over her shoulder as she slipped the key into the lock.

Reaching down, Gabriela pressed the button to pop the trunk. After making sure the car was locked, she closed the door and walked to the back, lifting the trunk lid.

She listened as the house door opened and Ana's boots thumped into the house, waiting until the girl had enough time to get to her room before scooping up the grocery bags in the trunk one by one and hanging them over her forearm. She had three of the bags on when she heard heavy footsteps on the pavement behind her.

Gabby turned, and her breath caught in her throat when she saw Mason walking toward her. He wasn't wearing a coat, and his long-sleeved, knitted gray shirt clung to his torso, accentuating his wide shoulders and broad chest. The three buttons at the collar were undone, affording her a glimpse of the muscle beneath. His long black hair hung loose around his shoulders, wisps of it flowing in the wintry breeze. Her eyes dipped. He wore a pair of faded jeans that hugged his thick, muscular legs, tucked over a pair of black boots.

This was a man who didn't skip leg day. He clearly didn't skip arm day and chest day, either—or *any* day, really.

Something sparked in her core, something hot and thrilling that made her pussy clench in sudden need. Her nipples tightened into hard points, and it had nothing to do with the cold.

She had never felt this kind of immediate desire for any man before. Not even for James, her ex-boyfriend and Ana's father, the last man Gabriela had been intimate with ten years ago. No, this sort of attraction seemed like a once-in-a-lifetime kind of thing, and she only felt it when she saw Mason.

Unfortunately, she was sure her predicament was quite noticeable through her sports bra and the snug t-shirt she'd worn to clean Paige's house. She moved to lift her arm and cover her chest, but it caught on the three heavy bags attached to it.

Gabriela smiled regardless. "Hi, Mason."

"Hi," he said, pausing a few feet away with his hands in his pockets. "I was just..." Mason frowned, brow furrowing. "I was going to ask you, uh... Need help carrying those?"

"I've hauled much more than this, plus a car seat with a baby, many times before." She grinned and slipped her arm free of the bags. "But the help would be wonderful. Thank you."

He stepped forward, stopping beside her. Warmth radiated from him, and the air was suddenly laden with his scent—pine, cedar, and moss, like the very mountains in which they lived, and something entirely unique to him, something warm, spicy, and manly. She leaned toward him to take a deeper breath. That ache between her legs intensified.

I need to get laid.

Gabriela's eyes widened, and she jerked back, pressing her lips together, afraid she might have said those words out loud.

But Mason made no indication that he'd heard anything as he reached down to pluck the bags of out the trunk, catching the handles in his big hand smoothly and effortlessly. No indication but for the faintest smirk on his lips, anyway—which was so infinitesimal that she couldn't be sure whether it was there or not.

"Those too?" he asked, gesturing to the bags she'd tucked away at the very back of the trunk.

"Oh, I'll get those." She bent forward, her hip brushing his thigh as she leaned in to reach for the bags, making her breath hitch. "They're...Christmas gifts for Ana. She's hiding in her room so I can run these to mine to wrap later."

She straightened and placed her hand on the trunk lid, closing it. She looked back up to meet Mason's violet gaze. Her heart thumped.

He has such beautiful eyes...

"Um, Mason... About your offer to get hot chocolate together..."

He looked away, lifting a hand to rub the back of his neck. "I understand if you don't want to. No prob—"

Gabriela settled her hand upon his chest. "No! No, no. That's not what I was going to say. I want to. I really, *really* want to. I was worried you might've thought I was just making an excuse to run off and get out of it yesterday, and I wanted to just reassure you that I wasn't. I want to go out with you, Mason. In fact, I'd love to. It's just...it might need to wait until after Christmas break since Ana's home, and I'm sure you'd rather not have a kid tagging—"

The words died on her lips when she realized that Mason was staring down at her hand—her hand that was currently flat against his strong, solid, warm chest. His pulse accelerated beneath her palm.

He lowered his arm slowly, moving like a man in a daze, his expression uncertain.

Annnnd just like that, Gabby, you screwed it up.

Her fingers tensed, and she withdrew her hand—or at least tried to. Before it had moved even an inch, Mason covered it with his own, pressing it back into place.

"She like hot chocolate?" he asked, finally returning his gaze to hers.

Gabriela stared up at him, stunned. "She...she loves hot chocolate."

"So she can come, too. Right?"

"Really? You want Ana to join us?"

Mason tilted his head aside slightly, his eyebrows falling. "Don't you?"

"No. I mean, yes. I do. It's just that...some men would rather not have a kid around on a date, you know? This...is a date, right?"

"Yes."

Gabriela smiled. "And you want Ana to come with us?"

His hand tightened over hers just a bit. "Yes. She is your kit."

Her smile slowly widened, and her fingers curled against his chest. He wasn't bothered that she was a single mom, that she had a nearly ten-year-old daughter. And something about that made this man impossibly sexier.

He wants me and *Ana.*

"Then it's a date. Tomorrow?" she asked.

Mason held her gaze as he lifted his hand away from hers and reached forward. The tip of his finger brushed over the dimple at the side of her mouth with surprising gentleness, but she felt something more—a feather-light scrape on her cheek.

One corner of his mouth rose in a smile that was at once warm and enticingly devilish. "Tomorrow."

"Mooooooooom! Hurry up," Ana called. "Oh. Hi, Mr. Lee."

Gabriela started, pulling away from Mason, and turned to see her daughter standing at the open front door, waving at him with a smile.

Mason waved back with a hand that had only an instant before been tenderly touching Gabby's face. "Hi, Ana."

"We're coming in now," Gabriela said. "Go hide again."

"You sure?" Ana asked.

Gabriela laughed. "Yes. I've been forcing Mason to stand here holding the bags long enough."

"Hurry! I want to make cookies." Ana disappeared into the house again.

"You sure you want her to tag along?" Gabriela asked Mason with a smirk.

"Feels like you're warning me. Am I putting myself in danger?"

"The only danger you'll be in is getting your ears talked off."

Mason's eyes dipped, sweeping over Gabriela down to her feet before swinging back up. "I'm willing to risk it." He raised the bags slightly, gesturing toward the house. "After you."

Heat flooded her body, suffusing her cheeks. Did he...did he just check her out without even trying to hide it? She ducked her head, unable to suppress her smile as she led him toward her front door. She felt his gaze on her, caressing her as though it were a physical thing, every step of the way.

As she walked into her home, she was met with the spicy-sweet fragrance of apple cinnamon. "You can just set those on the island counter in the kitchen. I just need to run these bags to my room. I'll be right back."

Gabriela glanced to the right, making sure Ana's bedroom door was closed, before heading to her own room, which was on the opposite side of the split-bedroom home. She took the bags to her closet and hid them under a spare comforter.

When Gabriela stepped out of her room, Mason was standing in the living room, looking at the Christmas tree and the framed pictures on the small table beside it. There were several photos of Gabriela and Ana, a few with Gabriela's parents, and even one that had her parents, grandparents, and Gabby with little baby Ana together when they'd taken a trip to her grandparents' hometown in Colombia.

For a few moments, she simply took him in. Though the living room and kitchen were a big, open space, Broxen seemed to fill it completely. He was tall enough that she doubted he'd even need to fully extend his arm to touch the ceiling. She'd need a stepladder and a jump to manage that.

Though Gabriela had been born and raised in these mountains, she'd never once considered taking up mountain climbing —but she'd gladly climb Mason Lee.

"Thank you for carrying the bags in for me," she said.

He turned his attention to her and smiled. "Glad to help."

"So, we'll see you tomorrow morning. Shall we say...ten?"

Mason nodded. "I'll try not to be late. Long commute to get here."

Gabby laughed. "Sure is."

His smile widened. He stood there, watching her for a few seconds, before seeming to jolt out of a daze. "Oh. Well, I'll, uh"—his smile faded, and his brow furrowed as though he were trying to remember something—"get out of your hair."

She chuckled and walked toward the front door. "You're not a bother, Mason." She looked back to find that he'd followed her. Her smile softened. "I can't wait for tomorrow."

"What are we doing tomorrow?" Ana asked from her bedroom doorway.

"Mason's going to take us out for hot chocolate," Gabriela said.

Ana turned her big, hopeful brown eyes toward Mason. "Really?"

"Really. As big as you want," he replied, glancing at Gabriela. "Or, uh, big as your mother says is okay?"

Ana danced in place, her unicorn tail swaying. "This is going to be the best Christmas break ever! Thank you, Mr. Lee."

Gabriela reached out to brush her fingertips along Mason's arm. "Thank you," she said softly. "For inviting her, too. It... means a lot to me."

He gifted her with another warm smile. "Can't wait, Gabriela." He offered Ana another wave and stepped through the door, ducking his head low to fit through.

"Good night, Mason."

"Good night," he said over his shoulder as he set off down her walkway.

Gabriela watched him go, her gaze dipping to his ass; she couldn't resist given the way the jeans molded to his ass.

"Mom, are you looking at his butt?"

Gabriela snapped her face toward her daughter. "Ana!"

Ana grinned. "Well? Were you?"

Gabby smirked as she slowly closed the door. "And if I was?"

Her daughter's face screwed up in disgust. "Ewwww!"

Gabriela laughed. "Who is ready to make some Christmas cookies?"

"*Finally!*"

Ana helped Gabriela put away the groceries and clear the island counter before they set out everything they needed to make the butter cookies. While Ana was measuring out the dry ingredients, Gabriela focused on the wet and let her daughter slowly spoon the flour mixture into the mixer.

They took a break to eat an easy dinner of ham and swiss sandwiches while the cookie dough chilled in the refrigerator. When they were finished, they rolled the dough out and used Christmas cookie cutters to cut out the shapes. The big bear was Ana's favorite.

Once the cookies were cooked and cooled, Gabby put on some music—a mix of Pentatonix's Christmas albums—and she and Ana sang as they made several different colors of icing and decorated the cookies.

This had always been something Gabriela loved to do with her daughter every Christmas since Ana was a little girl. It had become a tradition. Their tradition.

Gabriela had tried to keep up on the Christmas traditions passed down from her family, but she hadn't done the best job of it over the last several years. She knew that if her *abuelita* were still alive, the woman would've been calling to scold Gabriela every day lately for not praying faithfully during *La Novena de Aguinaldos*.

"So…is Mr. Lee your boyfriend now?" Ana asked.

Gabriela started, making the red icing stripe spill over the edge of the candy cane cookie she was decorating, and looked up at her daughter. Ana was focused on her cookie, her tongue sticking out as she covered the bear in white icing. She'd asked that question so nonchalantly, as though seeing her mother and a man touching each other wasn't a big deal.

Those touches were as innocent as can be, anyway.

"He's not," Gabriela said. "We're all just going out for hot chocolate tomorrow."

"On a date."

"Well…yeah, I guess so. But that doesn't mean we're together yet."

Ana lifted her head and looked at Gabriela. Her unicorn hood had fallen back, and her hair, pulled back into a ponytail, rested over her shoulder. "It's okay if you want to date him, Mom. I...would like to have a dad, and Mr. Lee is really, really nice."

"Whoa! Whoa, whoa, *whoa*. Hold up a minute, *nena*." Gabriela lowered the bottle of icing and stood up straight. "Don't you think we're getting a little ahead of ourselves? This is the first time we'll be going out together. Yeah, we've talked and waved to each other here and there over the last year, but we don't really *know* anything about each another. These things...they take time, Ana."

"I know, I know. Just like in Frozen, when Ana thought she was in love with the prince she just met."

The corners of Gabriela's lips rose in a small smile. "Yeah. You can't marry someone you just met."

"But Mr. Lee *is* nice. He's not like that nasty Prince Hans. He wouldn't hurt you."

Warmth filled Gabriela's chest, sparked by Ana's concern for her mother's wellbeing—but also by the memory of Mason's gentle touch. He was such a big, strong man, a real-life goliath, and yet he'd been so tender with Gabriela.

She tilted her head as she watched her daughter meticulously decorate her bear cookie.

How long had Ana been yearning for a father, how had Gabriela missed the signs? Was this a failure on her part for not noticing? Despite the lack of a father figure in her life, Ana had always been a happy child. It had always been just the two of them since Ana was born, and Gabby had done everything she could to fill the roles of both parents.

Why had Ana never said anything before now?

"How long have you been wanting a dad?" Gabriela asked.

Ana shrugged, looking a little shy as a crease appeared between her brows. "I don't know. A while? I just hear all this stuff from Max and Julie, and the things they've done with their moms and dads. I just...wondered what it would be like. To be a whole family."

Pain and grief struck Gabriela's heart. "Ana, we're still a whole family. Your family is who you make it."

"We could make it bigger." Ana peeked up at Gabriela. "I know you're lonely, too, Mom."

"Oh, baby, I'm not lonely. I have you."

"But it's not the same...is it?"

No, it isn't.

And it killed her knowing that even her nine-year-old daughter could tell the difference.

Gabby glanced down at her unfinished cookie before turning her gaze toward the window that faced Mason's house. What was he doing right now? He was over there, by himself, all day, every day. She'd never seen any visitors, had never seen anyone stop by to stay with him, had never seen him with any other woman, with any friends or family. Was he as lonely as Gabriela? Or was he even lonelier because he didn't have *anyone*, whereas Gabby had Ana?

"I like him," Ana said.

Gabriela looked back at her daughter and smiled. She knew Mason had talked to and helped Ana on many occasions, doing things that a father might normally do while Gabriela was busy inside the house. He'd always kept an eye on Ana, always made sure she was safe.

Mason was a good man, a kind man.

An incredibly sexy man.

"Yeah, I do, too," Gabriela said softly.

"Then you should make him your boyfriend." Ana wrinkled her nose. "But *please* stop staring at his butt, okay?"

Gabriela laughed. "That kind of comes with being boyfriend and girlfriend, so you'll have to get used to it."

"*Bleck.*"

"Just wait till we *kiss.*"

"Mooooooooom."

Grinning, Gabby stepped toward the cupboard where she kept her dishes, unable to stop herself from imagining what Mason's lips would feel like against her own. Would his kiss be tentative, soft, and seductive? Or would he devour her in a heated, passionate kiss that would steal the very air from her lungs?

Either way, she knew her toes would be curling.

She opened the cupboard, took down one of the plates, and turned back to Ana. "Here. Why don't you pick a few of the best cookies and take them over to Mason."

"Okay! I'm going to give him the bear I made him."

Gabriela looked down at the bear as Ana delicately picked it up and set it on the plate. She bit back her laughter.

No one was perfect. Not even her beautiful, perfect little girl.

But Ana was perfect to her.

FOUR

On any other evening, Broxen might have pondered the nature of mashed potatoes. They were an oddity to him. Humans seemed to largely consider mashed foods suitable only for infants, but potatoes were an exception—so much so that every frozen meal he'd seen that was marketed toward *males with appetites* contained mashed potatoes.

Why? Did mashed potatoes possess some masculine quality that made it acceptable for adult males to eat them when any other pulped food was only for babies?

Tonight, however, his thoughts did not wander such paths, not even as he scooped another forkful of overcooked mashed potatoes into his mouth. He barely registered the taste. In fact, he'd barely tasted any of his dinner, though the tray was nearly empty now. And he didn't care.

He had a date with Gabriela tomorrow.

To humans, that meant a mutual interest in becoming mates—or at least in exploring that possibility. He'd told himself several times that it was best not to grow too hopeful. His understanding of humans and their ways was limited at best, and he couldn't be sure that Gabriela thought of this date on the same terms as him, but...

He had a date with her tomorrow, and she'd *touched* him.

Broxen speared the last chunk of chicken fried steak—a name so confusing he dared not think too hard about it—with his fork and ate it. There'd been the accidental bump of her hip against his leg, which had been thrilling in its own way, but when she'd deliberately placed her hand on his chest, Broxen had nearly exploded with heat and excitement.

It had been a long while since any female had touched him intimately, and he couldn't recall anyone having ever done so with such tenderness and affection. It was a sort of intimacy he'd never experienced but had always longed for. He knew there was no other female in the universe who could've made him feel that way with such a simple bit of contact.

He laid his left arm on the table and turned his palm up, staring at it as he slowly flexed and relaxed his fingers—fingers that still appeared so very foreign to him. When he'd settled that hand over Gabriela's, she hadn't pulled away. She hadn't recoiled or widened her eyes in alarm. Her hand had fit so perfectly beneath his, and her skin had been so warm, smooth, and soft. He'd never felt its like.

Her scent had filled his nose; soft, sweet, and fresh, reminding him of coconuts but with another fragrance beneath that was undeniably unique and feminine, something that was purely Gabriela. Just the memory of her scent made his tail curl tight against his leg.

Delightful tingles had coursed across his chest and up his arm while he and Gabriela had stood like that, and he'd wondered what it would have felt like to have her hands on other parts of his body with no barrier between them. To have her palm slide across his back, down his tail...up his thigh.

To have her hand on his cock.

Broxen's blood heated, flowing down to his groin to make his shaft throb. He dropped his left hand to his lap, clamping it over his swelling erection as though he could somehow relieve that sudden pressure, as though he could hold back this flood of desire.

He'd wanted Gabriela for so long now. Why hadn't he acted sooner? Why had he wasted so much time?

She agreed to a date, to some hot chocolate. That's all.

Gritting his teeth, Broxen growled, placed both hands on the edge of the table, and pushed his chair out. His cock continued to pulse, but he had to accept that there was nothing he could do about it—nothing fulfilling, anyway. His own hand couldn't give him the release he needed.

As he stood, his jeans pulled taut over his shaft, triggering a wave of discomfort and pleasure that almost made him shudder. He released a strained breath and collected his fork and the empty freezer meal tray, carrying them into the kitchen. His gaze wandered around the house as he walked.

Almost everything in Broxen's home had either been left behind by the prior owners or purchased second hand, whether at thrift stores, from private sellers, or at the flea market down in Cascade. The dining table's wood bore more than a dozen scratches and stains from its previous owners, most of which weren't visible at a glance. Only two of the four chairs around it matched the adornments carved on the lip under the tabletop. The couch's floral-patterned upholstery was a different color on the back as it was elsewhere, likely thanks to years of being exposed to the sun, and the leather recliner was cracked and worn.

The blankets he'd draped over the backrests of the couch and recliner were also faded. One was a rough sort of wool that cycled through a variety of colors from top to bottom with patterns interspersed through it, while the other was red and black plaid that was slightly frayed on one end. The four-foot-tall carved black bear standing in the corner had clearly spent a good part of its existence outdoors.

The little pieces of décor he'd collected over the last year were simply objects he'd found intriguing. He was unsure about the different styles humans used in furnishing their homes, but he thought his house had a slight rustic feel to it, like so many other places in the area.

He dropped the plastic tray in the trashcan and washed his fork at the sink. Though he'd been the one to choose the furniture and decorations, though most of it was old and worn, though he was comfortable here, none of it felt quite right. Everything here had history, even if he didn't know any of it. The furniture had seen years of use, had been part of people's lives.

But Broxen had contributed so little to that history. The faint red stain on the right side of the dining table might've been left by a child coloring something atop it, or from some sugary drink spilling, or any number of sources—no matter its source, it had been left there because someone had been living.

Being inside Gabriela's home for the first time had only made him more aware of his situation. Where were the pictures of happy times here? Where were the truly personal touches that made this place his own? Where were the children's toys on the floor, or the incomplete puzzle on the table, the cozy blanket crumpled on the couch after being used to keep a male and his mate warm?

There were no holiday decorations here, no tree or lights. Gabriela had a small fir tree inside her home, adorned with multicolored lights and small ornaments of different shapes and colors and thin, shimmering silver strands. He knew it was a Christmas tree, though he understood little about the holiday or the traditions surrounding it.

But he didn't have to know much about it to have picked up the sense of festivity. There were subtle green, red, and white decorations sprinkled around Gabriela's home, the same sort he'd seen in town lately, or adorning people's homes. She'd even had a small scene arranged on her fireplace mantle with tiny figurines, some sort of shelter with people dressed in robes and a tiny baby at the center. There'd been something almost reverent about it. Something oddly wholesome.

Where was the feeling that someone had been *living* in this place?

Broxen had simply been...surviving.

Astius had tried to make Broxen understand that for years. He'd tried to make Broxen see that the existence he'd always known, the path he'd always walked, wasn't the only one. It hadn't been the only way. That Broxen didn't have to be what he thought circumstance had forced him to become. And it was all about the small things.

Broxen might have come to Earth to hide, but he didn't have to settle for it being nothing but a hideaway. No one knew he was here. This could be a fresh start. A new life...a better life.

He turned and glanced toward the front window. He'd closed the blinds, but he could see Gabriela's house in his mind's eye. Maybe he didn't deserve happiness after the things he'd done. Maybe he didn't deserve the female who he desired above all else, maybe he didn't deserve to feel good. But he couldn't deny that he wanted all those things—*craved* those things. Happiness and a mate had been unimaginable for him a year ago.

Now, having those things seemed possible. Maybe not likely, but possible.

The doorbell chimed. Broxen started, reflexively reaching for a weapon he wasn't carrying as he was jarred from his thoughts. He clenched his jaw and growled a curse, pushing away from the kitchen sink to walk to the front door. He'd never been the sort of person to be so easily caught off-guard. He'd never been the sort of person to lose himself so deeply in contemplation.

Zorak akai, he probably hadn't known what contemplation even meant until recently.

He wasn't sure yet if that was a good thing or a bad thing.

Broxen unlatched the deadbolt, grasped the knob, and opened the front door. His brow furrowed in confusion as he stared out into empty evening air. The street was dark but for the exterior lights of the houses along it, and the only sound was from the wind rustling the nearby trees. His confusion vanished when he lowered his gaze.

Ana stood before him, smiling broadly, wearing the same, strange animal clothing he'd seen her in earlier with the horned hood on her head and her pant legs tucked into a pair of pink snow boots. In front of her, she held a round plate topped with various shapes colored red, green, white, and blue.

"Hi, Mr. Lee!" She lifted the plate. "My mom told me to bring you some of the Christmas cookies we made."

"Oh." He reached down and accepted the plate on one hand, tilting his head as he studied the cookies. He realized the shapes were familiar—a sock, a pine tree, a cane.

No, a candy *cane.*

Those treats had become quite commonplace in the stores lately. They must've had something to do with the upcoming holiday.

Ana stepped closer, rose on her tip toes, and pointed to the large bear in the center of the plate. "I made that one special for you. It's my best one."

The corner of Broxen's mouth quirked up. The bear-shaped cookie was decorated in white icing with blue eyes of two different sizes, a crooked smile, and what must've been a red scarf around its neck. It was the strangest bear he'd ever seen, but it was charming...and no one had ever made anything like this, just for him.

"Thank you," he said, meeting Ana's gaze. "I like bears. And this one is the best."

If possible, her smile only grew wider.

"So, are you going to be Mom's boyfriend?" she asked.

Damn, this kit was right to the point.

Yet he couldn't deny a rumbling of irritation. He knew how that word, boyfriend, was commonly used, and he understood what it meant to humans, but he didn't care for it. Nothing about him was boyish; he was a full-grown, powerful male who would do all he could to protect his female. And he longed to be far more than friends with Gabriela. *Mate* was the more fitting word. The right word.

Broxen grunted and shrugged with one shoulder. "Hopefully."

She turned her head to the side slightly and narrowed her eyes. "You won't hurt her, right?"

"Never."

Ana nodded. "My dad hurt her, but he's not really my *dad*. He left when I was in Mom's belly. He didn't want us."

Broxen frowned, eyebrows falling low. "You're better off without that kind of male in your life. You and your mother are the best. Even better than this bear cookie."

She smiled again. "That is the best cookie, and she is the *best* mom." Dipping her head, she slid a foot forward, grinding the toe of her boot on the ground. "And...I think you'd make a good dad. Cause you're nice, and you helped fixed my bike. And dads do that stuff, right, Mr. Lee?"

"I..."

Ana's words hit him harder than he could ever have

guessed they would. The trust in her expression, the rawness of what she'd said, the hopefulness behind it... How could he ever respond to all that? He didn't know what it meant to be a father, and he definitely didn't know how to be a good one. He didn't even know where things would go between himself and Gabriela from this point.

But he knew what he wanted. He wanted Gabriela in his life. He wanted Ana in his life. And he couldn't deny, as foolish as it might have been, that he was as hopeful for that as Ana.

Keeping the plate of cookies balanced on his palm, he sank into a crouch, putting him closer to Ana's eye level. "Whatever happens, Ana, I'm going to look out for you and your mom. I promise I'll keep you both safe."

Those big brown eyes, so much like her mother's, met his. "Truly?"

Broxen nodded. "Truly. And any time your bike breaks, just come to me. I'll help."

"Thank you, Mr. Lee."

"Call me Brox—" He snapped his mouth shut, cutting himself off before he could stupidly utter that name. "Mason. Not Mr. Lee, okay?"

Ana beamed at him. "Okay."

"It's late. You should get home, and I have cookies to eat. Thank your mom for me."

"I will."

She stepped back, hesitated for a moment, then ran forward, throwing her arms around his neck and squeezing him. The embrace was over before Broxen could register what she had done, leaving him to stare after her in stunned silence as she ran toward her house.

As she reached the end of his walkway, Ana turned and waved. "Good night, Mason. See you tomorrow!"

Broxen lifted his hand and waved back. He stood upright

and watched as she raced across the road and back to her home, his heart thumping a little louder, a little faster, as she reached her front door. He held his breath, hoping for a glimpse of Gabriela when Ana threw the door open and darted inside.

"Mom, Mom," Ana shouted, and then the door slammed shut behind her.

Blowing out the breath he'd been holding, Broxen stepped back and closed his own door, though he did so softly. He couldn't ignore the ridiculousness of this situation—that he was so crushed, so disappointed, to have missed out on seeing Gabriela for what wouldn't have been more than a second or two.

Zorak akai, those romance books and romantic comedy movies were beginning to make sense. This was what the humans called *falling hard*.

But he wondered if that was the right term as he carried the plate of cookies to the table and placed it down in the same spot his microwaved dinner had occupied minutes before. Falls usually came with pain, with a jolt. What he felt now...well, it seemed more like floating than falling. Or maybe it *was* like falling—like falling forever, with no ground in sight.

Broxen sat down, propped his arms on the table, and stared down at the cookies. The little white bear stared back up at him unblinkingly, its smile never fading.

The cookie bear wasn't judging Broxen. It didn't know about his past, it didn't know his true form, and it didn't care. Neither did Ana. Somehow, she'd looked at Broxen and had seen a good man. A potential parent, a potential father. She hadn't seen a former street thug, an enforcer, a bodyguard who'd protected some dangerous people—and had failed to protect the one person he'd known who might've done some good.

And that quick hug she'd given him before running off...

That little girl had placed her trust in him. She'd placed her hope in him. That had to mean something, didn't it? That had to mean that maybe, just maybe, Astius had been right—that Broxen could be more than his past. That he could choose a different path and succeed.

Maybe it meant that Gabriela had seen something like that in him, too.

He shifted a hand, reaching toward the bear cookie, but stopped himself. Something about it gave him pause.

Saving the best for last.

That was a human thing, wasn't it? There was no harm in it. How often was he gifted homemade bear cookies, anyway? He'd keep that bear aside for a little while.

He picked up a striped candy cane cookie instead, holding it delicately between his forefinger and thumb. The red, white, and green icing stripes were neat and relatively even, with only one spot where a tiny trickle of white had mixed with the red. That small imperfection made him smile. This cookie had undoubtedly been decorated by Gabriela.

When he lifted it to his nose and inhaled, he was hit by a pair of appetizing scents—the cookie and its icing, each smell unique but complementing one another. Broxen opened his mouth and took a small bite.

"Mmm," was all he could manage as he chewed. He'd tasted pre-packaged cookies from the grocery store, and they were fine, but this was something entirely different. Sweet and buttery but not overly so, the icing and the cookie in perfect balance.

The rest of the candy cane vanished in one more bite. Broxen hadn't quite finished chewing it before he made his next selection, the green tree with red, blue, and yellow dots all over it and a star on the top. A Christmas tree. His smile widened as he turned the cookie to look it over. The dots were haphazard and uneven, and the green icing had run off one side of the cookie. Another of Ana's creations.

Broxen devoured the cookie and picked up the next one. His mind was overwhelmed by the flavor, the sweetness, the surprise of having been gifted them. Perhaps that was why they tasted so good.

Or, perhaps, Gabriela was simply a good baker.

By the time he stopped himself, only one cookie remained on the plate, surrounded by crumbs and a few flecks of icing. The bear continued to stare up at Broxen, happy despite its companions having been devoured before its very eyes.

He still couldn't bring himself to eat it. This one was special, just for him. He'd save it for a more special time.

Broxen stood up, picked up the plate, and walked into the kitchen. He put the bear cookie into a plastic sandwich bag and set it on the counter. As he washed Gabriela's plate, he was struck by the kindness of her gesture.

He knew Gabriela had struggled. He knew she was tight on money, that she often cut it close paying her bills. In the fall, while the weather was still nice enough for windows to be open during the day, he'd heard her on the phone with debt collectors and credit companies. He knew she had little to spare most of the time. But she'd still shared this with Broxen.

Perhaps a few cookies wasn't much, but he knew from experience that value was relative. The less you had, the more you valued those things. For her to have thought of him, to have shared with him, to have made him a small part of something she and her daughter had done together, meant a lot to him.

He set the plate in the drainboard and glanced around his house again. The living room, kitchen, and dining room were all connected in one large, open space. What would it be like to have that space full of life? To have Gabriela and Ana here, laughing and talking, to have music playing and the fire crackling?

Maybe if he had someone to cook for, he'd finally take out those steaks.

Broxen could almost imagine this home with Gabriela's touch applied to it. He could almost imagine the door opening and little Ana bounding through, offering a big smile to her mother and Broxen. He could almost hear her tell them about her day at school.

And he could almost feel Gabriela's hips between his hands as the Broxen in his imagining walked up to her from behind and swept her into a kiss after Ana had raced into the spare bedroom. He could almost taste those full, enticing lips. He could almost smell her scent and feel her warmth as she turned toward him and wrapped her arms around him, pressing her soft, sensuous body against his.

His heart sped and his breath grew ragged as blood rushed to his groin again. Coiled heat dominated his chest. Planting his fists on the counter, he bowed his head, and strands of his long hair fell around the sides of his face. This desire was becoming so strong that it hurt, and that wasn't dissuading him at all.

There was no doubt in his mind now—he wanted Gabriela and Ana to be his. To be his family. And tomorrow at ten o'clock, he would begin working toward that.

He would seize every opportunity to make Gabriela his mate.

FIVE

"Did you brush your teeth?" Gabriela asked as she placed the large glass mixing bowl in the dishwasher.

"Yeah," Ana called from her bedroom.

Gabriela added soap to the dishwasher, closed the door, and started it. She turned to look at the rest of the kitchen. Everything had been tidied. The dirty dishes were all in the dishwasher; the flour, powdered sugar, and smeared icing had been cleaned from the island counter; and the cookies were spread out on parchment paper so their icing could finish hardening overnight.

She smiled as she ran her eyes over the cookies. Each one was uniquely decorated.

It had been a good day. A *better* than good day.

Gabby pushed away from the sink and headed for Ana's bedroom, stopping in front of the Christmas tree along the way. There were five gifts for Ana under the tree, including the couple Gabby had wrapped while her daughter was in the shower earlier, and the little tissue-paper-wrapped bundle Ana had made at school sat in front of them.

Ana had been so proud and excited when she'd placed it there.

Smile widening, Gabriela continued to her daughter's room.

Ana was lying on her stomach on her bed, drawing in a sketchbook, a rainbow of markers spread on the blanket beside her. She had changed into a blue long-sleeved shirt and pajama pants with little sloths on them. The overhead light cast a warm glow on the room, which was filled with so many pinks, purples, and blues that you'd think a unicorn had farted in it.

That probably wasn't too far from the truth considering all the unicorn décor. There were unicorn posters and drawings hanging on the walls, a rainbow unicorn rug on the floor, a unicorn lamp on the small corner desk, a glowing unicorn nightlight on the pink plastic storage cart Ana used as a nightstand, and stuffed unicorns and unicorn pillows on the bed. Ana was obsessed with them.

"What are you drawing?" Gabriela asked as she entered the room.

Ana hurriedly flipped over her sketch book and smiled sheepishly up at Gabriela. "Nothing."

"Sure didn't look like nothing."

"It's a secret." Ana closed the sketchbook and gathered the markers.

Gabriela sat on the edge of the bed, grinning as Ana slipped off the other side. "I see."

"No looking, Mom." She set the sketchbook on her little desk and put the markers away in the top drawer.

"I wouldn't dream of it."

"Better not. It's called *privacy*."

Laughter spilled from Gabby. "I'm twenty-nine years old. I believe I know what privacy is."

Ana put her hands on her hips. "And you better not forget it."

Shaking her head but still grinning, Gabriela pulled down Ana's blanket. "I won't. Now come get into bed."

Ana climbed onto the mattress, slipped her feet beneath the covers, and lay down. She raised her arms, allowing Gabriela to draw the blanket over her before folding her hands atop her chest.

Gabriela was going to miss these moments when Ana was older. She brushed her fingers over her daughter's forehead, smoothing her hair back. "Did you have a good day today?"

Ana smiled. "It was the best."

"It was, wasn't it?"

"And tomorrow is going to be even better. Can we build snowmen with Mason after we have hot chocolate?"

Gabriela arched a brow. "Mason? What happened to calling him Mr. Lee?"

"He said I could call him Mason."

"That was nice of him. And you'll have to ask him about the snowmen, but no pestering or begging if he says no, got it?"

Ana nodded. "Got it."

Gabriela leaned down and pressed a kiss to Ana's forehead. "Goodnight, Ana."

Ana hugged Gabriela. "Night, Mom."

Once Gabby was free, she straightened and walked to the door, glancing back in time to see her daughter roll onto her side to face the window. Gabriela flicked off the light, leaving only the gentle blue glow of the unicorn nightlight. She closed the door as she stepped out.

She cleaned up the living room, returning the television remote to the coffee table, stacking the coasters, folding the blankets and draping them over the back of the sofa. The carpet needed a good vacuuming, but that could wait until tomorrow.

After checking the front door locks and making sure her cellphone was plugged into the charger on the kitchen counter, Gabriela turned off all the lights except for those on the Christmas tree. That colorful glow drew her eye naturally to the nativity scene upon the mantle.

It'd been a Christmas gift from her mother, after eighteen-year-old Gabby had moved out. Even when other traditions had been set aside or forgotten, Gabriela had put out this nativity scene faithfully every year. Looking at it always reminded her of her parents.

Looking at it now reminded her of how much she *missed* her mom and dad.

Money had been especially tight this year, for Gabby and her parents, too. She hadn't been able to make the trip to Arizona to visit them with Ana, and they'd been unable to travel to Idaho. Hopefully, they'd see each other next year.

And perhaps...she'd have Mason to introduce them to.

Gabby, getting way ahead of yourself here.

Yet she couldn't help but grin at the thought of Mason meeting her mother and father as she made her way into her bedroom. She turned on the light and closed the door behind her.

Gabriela's room was sparsely decorated compared to Ana's. With the exception of a few paintings of flowers, the walls were bare. The queen-size bed with its blue and white comforter and matching pillows took up most of the room. The nightstand behind the bed had her alarm clock perched atop it, and the tall dresser was tucked in the corner, a basket for dirty clothes beside it.

Walking to the dresser, Gabby grabbed underwear and a pair of oversized, fuzzy socks from the top drawer and pajamas from the next drawer down. She carried the clothing into the adjoining bathroom, flicked on the lights and fan, and set her clothes on the counter.

Gabriela paused and stared at herself in the mirror. There were small, dark circles under her eyes, and wisps of hair had fallen from the bun atop her head. She looked...tired. And she was. She'd barely had a moment to sit down all day, and her entire body felt it.

Is this what Mason saw?

If that weren't bad enough, she'd likely smelled of sweat and cleaning chemicals when he'd been so close to her earlier.

She wrinkled her nose at her reflection.

But...they were still on for their date tomorrow. So, he must have seen something he liked.

Gabriela smiled. "It was an amazing day."

And as Ana had said, tomorrow would be even better. Gabriela couldn't wait for morning to come so she could see Mason again, so she could spend time with him and learn more about him. He hadn't lived across the street for long, and he was always such a quiet, reserved man, but he'd always been kind.

He was also alone.

Her mind turned back to what Ana had said, about how it would be okay for Gabby to open herself up to someone—to Mason. About how much she longed for a father.

For a whole family.

Had Gabriela failed in some way?

No. It wasn't her fault—it was her ex's fault. He'd been a selfish coward. He hadn't wanted to be tied down so young in such a small town, hadn't wanted a baby, so he'd left, leaving Gabriela alone and pregnant at nineteen to raise her daughter by herself. She hadn't even had the help of her parents because they'd moved to Arizona a year prior, and Gabriela had decided to stay behind in Donnelly with James.

And Gabby had been too prideful to ask for money, to move back in with them. To ask for help. Her parents hadn't liked James from the start, and she'd been too headstrong, too *in love* to listen to their warnings. She had made her bed, and she would lie in it no matter what it took.

Despite all the heartache, despite the hardship, she wouldn't have changed anything. Ana was worth it all.

Gabriela had accepted state assistance when she could—she wasn't stupid—but she'd still worked hard to earn a living without sacrificing time to bond with her daughter. Cleaning homes had been a natural fit, as it had allowed her to bring Ana along and had saved a ton on daycare. Things had become easier once Ana started attending school.

Over the years, Gabby had built enough of a client base that she and Ana had been able to move out of the old trailer and into this little home, and they'd lived comfortably on her income for a time.

Gabriela had done *everything* she possibly could for Ana, and she'd always do more, but she simply couldn't fill the role of a father. Ana deserved to have a dad, a man who would love her unconditionally, protect her, and treat her as his own.

And...Mason could be that man.

He could be *Gabriela's* man.

"Again, getting way ahead of yourself there, Gabby. You haven't even gone out with him yet."

But now that the thought had presented itself, she found that she wanted it, craved it with every fiber in her being. She desired Mason. A simple touch of his fingers had lit her body up like striking a match. She could only imagine what it would be like to have those big, strong, calloused hands all over her body, caressing her skin, stroking her between her thighs until she succumbed to the burning passion locked within her.

Gabriela caught her lip between her teeth and clutched the

hem of her shirt as her core tightened, and her clit throbbed with arousal.

It had been so long—too long—since she'd been with a man, since she'd had any kind of intimacy.

She breathed in deep and let out a slow breath through her mouth. There wasn't much to be done about it now. Using her own fingers to get herself off would feel as empty as it had the last time she'd done it weeks ago. She'd be left as unsatisfied now as she was then, and the time before that, and the time before that.

Not to mention, she was simply too tired to bother putting in the effort to give herself little more than a few seconds of empty pleasure.

Closing her eyes, she placed her hands on the counter and let her head drop in defeat.

"Let's just see where things go between me and Mason. Today...today was a start."

But God, she wanted him. Badly.

Gabriela opened her eyes, picked up her toothbrush and toothpaste, and brushed her teeth. Once she'd finished, she flossed and rinsed out her mouth before turning on the shower. As the water heated up, she peeled off her clothes, tossing them in a pile on the floor. It was so nice to finally be out of that damp, smelly bra.

She stepped into the shower, turned, and tilted her head back, groaning as the hot water sluiced down her body and warmed her chilled skin. The scent of her coconut shampoo filled the air as she washed and conditioned her hair, and she breathed deep the calming aroma.

Despite her weariness, she found just enough energy to run a razor under her arms and legs. It was winter, and normally she'd just let her legs go—who was around to care?—but now that she had a date with Mason, well... If things happened to take that turn, she wanted to be prepared.

Body clean and muscles relaxed, Gabriela turned off the water and reached for her towel. She dried quickly and stepped onto the mat, running the towel through her hair, absorbing as much of the moisture as possible. When she was done, she tossed the towel atop her dirty clothes on the floor, got dressed, and ran a comb through her hair before plugging in the hairdryer and turning it on.

Warm air blew into her face, making her squint—and striking her with a whiff of smoke. Gabriela frowned and flicked the hairdryer off, lowering the appliance to examine it. There was no smoke coming from the hairdryer. She touched it with her free hand; it wasn't even hot yet.

Turning the hairdryer back on, she resumed drying her hair.

But the smoke smell grew stronger and acrider as the minutes passed. The steam from her shower was still thick—so thick that it made her cough as she breathed it in. She waved her hand in front of her, trying to clear some the air. Should that steam have dissipated by now, or at least made the mirror so foggy it was impossible to use?

Yet mirror was fogged only along its uppermost edge.

Brows furrowing, she turned her head and glanced through the open doorway. Gabriela's eyes widened. Shutting off the hairdryer again, she set it down and walked into her room, coughing again. The steam was even thicker in the bedroom— and the stench of smoke even stronger.

It's not steam at all.

"Oh, my God."

Rushing to the bedroom door, she yanked it open and stepped out into a blazing inferno that had once been her living room and kitchen.

Her heart ceased to beat. For several moments—they felt like eternity but couldn't have been more than a few seconds—all she could do was stand there and stare as roaring flames roiled from floor to ceiling, blasting her with unbearable heat. The air was hazy with smoke, the worst of which was gathering in a thick, impenetrable black cloud on the ceiling. The pops and cracks of everything being consumed by fire were almost deafening.

This...this couldn't be happening. It *couldn't*. If there was a fire, surely the smoke detector would have gone off, right? That damned detector went off at the slightest hint of smoke from the oven when she was cooking.

As though on cue, a shrill alarm blared.

It was like being woken from a nightmare only to find yourself still dreaming. Worse...this was *real*.

And the raging fire was between Gabriela and Ana.

Gabriela sucked in a stinging breath that sent her into a coughing fit. Her throat and eyes burned, and tears streamed down her cheeks.

She blinked away those tears and screamed, "Ana!" Her voice was raw, ragged, desperate, and the blaze seemed to swallow it up.

"Mom!"

Though the response was muffled and competing with far more aggressive sounds, Gabriela knew it was from her daughter.

"Go to your window, *mija*," Gabriela yelled before she was overtaken by more coughing. She bent forward and lifted her forearm to cover her mouth and nose, sweeping her gaze from side to side to seek a path to her daughter's room. But between the smoke, the bright flames, and the tears in her eyes, she couldn't even see the door to Ana's bedroom. The front and back doors were likewise obscured.

Heart pounding, Gabriela turned away and stumbled back into her own room, slamming the door shut behind her. The smoke was noticeably thicker now. The burning in her throat had burrowed down into her lungs, making every breath painful. But that didn't matter.

Only Ana mattered. That was all.

Gabby vaulted onto her bed, crawled across it, and leapt down on the other side, catching herself with her hands against the wall beside the window. She hurriedly threw open the curtains and tugged on the string to raise the blinds so hard that something snapped overhead. She didn't bother checking the damage.

Her fingers felt clumsy and weak as she fumbled with the window locks.

"Come on, please. Come on!"

Finally, she had both locks undone, and she didn't waste a second in thrusting the window up and shoving out the screen. Frigid air blasted her, made all the worse by the withering heat she'd just faced.

Grasping both sides of the window frame, Gabriela pulled herself through, swinging a leg over the windowsill. She dropped down into the snow below, landing on her feet and sinking to her knees before she lost her balance and fell on her backside.

"Help!" she shouted into the night as she scrambled upright. "Help!"

Her breath was ragged as she fought her way through the two-foot-deep snow to get to the front of the house, crawling on hands and knees where she had to. She cried out for help—and called her daughter's name—the entire way.

The snow in front of the house was bathed in the orange glow of the growing flames when Gabriela finally neared Ana's window.

"Oh, God," she gasped.

Ana was at the window, with terror gleaming in her wide, tear-filled eyes. She banged on the windowpane. "Mom!"

Gabriela braced herself against the window frame and met her daughter's gaze. The bedroom was hazy, and darker smoke was creeping in through the cracks around the door, though Ana had stuffed a blanket along the door's base.

Gabby flattened her palms on the glass and pushed up. The window shifted slightly but didn't open even a bit. "Open the window, baby!"

Ana had her hands on the window, too, her face strained as she also pushed. "It's stuck, Mom!"

"Unlock it," Gabriela cried, spreading her feet to solidify her stance and put more strength into her effort.

"I did!"

The fear in Ana's voice shattered Gabriela's heart, but she did not let the pieces fall apart. Not yet.

She'd told the landlord about this window several times—that it had been sticking, that it didn't slide right on its tracks. She'd *told* him again and again, and the bastard had never fixed it.

"Someone help!" Gabriela's scream tore from her throat like it had been made of glass shards. She dropped onto her knees and dug into the snow, throwing aside handfuls of it as fast as she could in her search for something, for *anything*, buried beneath that could break the glass. "Help, please!"

Her fingers, somehow numb and burning at the same time, brushed something hard and heavy. She grasped the object immediately, dragging it out of the snow as she rose. "Stand back, baby."

Ana backed away from the window, coughing, and Gabby swung the rock in her hand. It struck the double-paned glass with a dull *thunk* and a high crack. But only a tiny chip was left in the glass.

The smoke in Ana's room was even denser now, and licks of flame were creeping in through the tiny gap at the top of the door. The paint around the edges was starting to blacken and peel. Ana was kneeling on her floor with a hand over her mouth, coughing over and over again.

"No," Gabriela whispered, drawing back her arm for another blow. "No, no, no!"

She hit the window again, and again, putting a couple more chips in the glass. Her heart somehow sped further, pounding hard enough that it seemed likely to burst out of her chest. She raised the rock for another swing, and her foot slid in the snow. She pitched forward.

Big, strong arms banded around her middle, catching her before she could fall. Gabriela barely understood what was happening in her panic and desperation; she could only think of Ana, of getting to her little girl. She felt herself being lifted off the ground, felt her feet pulled free from the snow, and the next thing she knew she was sitting on her butt, staring up at Mason's hulking form.

She caught a flash of reflected light in his eyes just before he turned to face the window.

"Ana," she shouted, struggling to get to her feet.

Before she could fully rise, before she could even get the two syllables of her daughter's name fully past her lips, Mason braced his hands on either side of the window frame, tipped his head back, and snapped it forward.

The sound of the window breaking echoed through the night, briefly rising above the growing roar of the flames. Gabriela was vaguely aware of falling shards of glass clinking together as they landed.

Mason tore off his shirt—Gabriela actually heard the fabric

rip—and quickly wrapped it around his arm. He swept that arm around the inside of the window frame, clearing away the remaining shards.

"Throw your pillow over the glass," he said to Ana in a booming voice as he tugged the ruined shirt off his arm and dropped it. He leaned into the open window, slipping his arms inside.

The light from Ana's room had taken on an orange cast now, and smoke was pouring out through the broken window. Gabby held her breath, oblivious to the burning in her lungs and throat, to the numbing cold that had seized her feet and legs, and lifted her hands to her still-damp hair, sweeping it back before squeezing the strands between her fingers. She couldn't see around Mason. She couldn't see her daughter.

But she could hear Ana's coughs, could hear her baby suffering.

Little arms wrapped around Mason's neck. He withdrew from the window and spun to face Gabriela, holding Ana to his chest with one arm.

"Oh, God, thank you," Gabriela breathed, knees suddenly weak.

Mason stepped over to her, and Gabriella threw her arms around Ana, who twisted to return her mother's embrace with one arm. Ana was talking quickly, frantically, and Gabriela realized she was doing the same, but she couldn't make out anything either of them were saying—and she didn't care. Her little girl was safe.

"Need to move," Mason said. He looped his free arm around Gabriela's waist and guided her away from the house.

She clutched at her daughter and Mason, but only made it a few steps in the deep snow before stumbling. He easily accepted her weight, dropping his arm down around her back-side to lift her, and carried her forward. He was strong, solid, warm. Her savior, her guardian angel. She held him and her child tight, unwilling to let go even after Mason lowered her and she felt the cold, hard pavement of the road under her nearly numb feet.

Mason sank into a crouch, setting Ana down gently. He released his hold on Gabriela at the same time. She swayed slightly before her legs decided to fully support her weight.

"My baby, oh my baby girl," Gabriela sobbed as she clutched her daughter close, smoothing her hands down the girl's hair, unable to stop trembling. "I love you, *nena*. I love you so much."

"Is everyone all right?" a someone asked, their familiar voice winded and worried.

Gabriela turned her head to see Austin Stevens, one of their older neighbors down the street, jogging toward them. She pulled back slightly and looked down at Ana. "Ana, are you okay?"

"My hand hurts," Ana said.

"Let me see, baby."

Ana lifted her hand with her palm up. There were patches of red and what appeared to be the beginning of a few blisters. "The doorknob was hot."

Mason grunted and twisted aside. He extended his arm and scooped up a handful of snow before turning back to Ana. He placed the snow on her palm and, with his other hand, curled her fingers over it carefully. "Hold this."

Ana nodded, keeping her fingers closed around the snow.

"I called nine-one-one. Hopefully the fire department will be here soon," Austin said with a deep frown as he turned his face toward the fire.

Gabriela looked at the burning house. The flames had spread into Ana's room, lighting it up and flickering through the broken window. Fire consumed everything—Ana's unicorn stuffed animals, her posters, her bed, her sketchbook, and her clothes—just as it had destroyed so much else. The nativity scene, the Christmas tree, the gifts and framed pictures. Even the photo albums stored in the living room bookcase containing all the photos of Ana from her birth.

Everything Gabriela and her daughter owned was turning to ash.

A sob caught in Gabby's throat. The fire danced above the roof, and something crashed inside the house. She turned back to her daughter, pulling her close. She was unable to hold in her cries as she listened to the fire roaring behind her and faint sounds of sirens in the distance.

All that mattered right now was that Ana was *alive*.

Nothing was more important to Gabby than her daughter.

SIX

Broxen's jaw muscles ticked as he watched the firefighters across the road. They were working through the ruins of Gabriela's home with flashlights and spotlights, seeking out any lingering flames and embers, knocking down crumbling beams and opening blackened, half-collapsed walls. From Broxen's vantage in his driveway, there were no visible fires, but thick smoke still poured from the rubble to drift away in the wintry night sky—especially from the blackened husk of her car, which had been near enough to the house to catch fire, as well.

The angry orange glow that had been cast on the surrounding snow earlier had been replaced by the red and white flashing lights of the firetrucks parked along the road. Somehow, those lights were both less intense and more severe than the light that had radiated from the hungry flames.

Releasing a short, harsh breath through his nostrils, Broxen turned his head to look at Gabriela and Ana.

The females were huddled together on the lowered tailgate of his pickup truck with their legs dangling, wrapped in the biggest, warmest blankets he owned. They were mere feet away from him, but that distance felt so immense now. Gabriela's eyes glistened with unshed tears.

What could he say to them? What could he do to make any of this better?

He wanted to put his arms around them, wanted to hold them, to share his warmth. To tell them everything would be all right. But would it? Could he really promise that?

Icy cold and searing heat coiled in his chest, constricting his heart and lungs. His breath caught in his throat, and something hot, sour, and heavy sank in his gut. He'd almost lost Gabriela and Ana tonight. He'd almost lost them before ever truly claiming them as his own.

He'd almost failed again to protect the ones he'd sworn to safeguard. He'd endured that once, but he couldn't bear it again. Especially not when it came to these two females.

If nothing else, tonight's events were a sign that there was no time to waste. That nothing was guaranteed, that every moment was precious. It didn't matter if he was uncertain of how to woo a human female. He couldn't learn, couldn't figure out what Gabriela needed, if he always kept himself at a distance.

Shifting closer, Broxen slid his hand toward Gabriela and settled it on her thigh, giving it a gentle squeeze through the thick blanket covering her.

She looked up at him, and her lower lip quivered. The tears that had gathered in her eyes spilled down her cheeks as she blinked. She turned her attention back the remains of her home.

"We didn't have renter's insurance," she said softly, brokenly. "It was an expense I let go, at least until things picked up, but they never did, and I...I just forgot about it. I never thought anything like this would happen. But we lost...everything. I don't know what I'm going to do."

Ana tilted her head to look at her mother. "It's okay, Mommy. It's just stuff." She laid her head down against Gabriela's shoulder and hugged her mother tight. "I don't need any presents. I have you."

"I know, baby. I know." Gabriela turned her head away, but not before Broxen saw her features crumple in anguish. She covered her face with a hand as her shoulders shook with her quiet sobs.

Broxen couldn't stand seeing her like this, and he couldn't keep silent. He took hold of the hand she'd raised and, gently as he could, guided it back down. Leaning closer, he captured her chin with his finger and thumb and tilted her face toward his. "We will figure it out, Gabriela. I am here for you."

Her watery eyes searched his, and her bottom lip quivered again before she wrapped her arm around his neck and hugged him close, burying her face against his throat.

Putting his arms around Gabriela was the most natural thing in the universe for Broxen. He felt her lips, so soft, so enticing, on his skin, but he also felt her warm, wet tears. Her sweet scent teased his nostrils, but it was nearly overpowered by the stench of smoke clinging to her. His tail twitched with the need to touch her, to twine around her and secure his hold on her.

When he'd longed to hold her, this hadn't been what he'd envisioned—but that wasn't important. The female he wanted to claim as his was reaching out to him for comfort now. She needed him.

And *sul'kalor vir sul'astal*—by sun or by stars—he was going to be there for her and Ana both.

He would do *anything* to help them. He would do anything to see those tears in Gabriela's eyes dry up, to see her smile again.

After a time, the sound of tires on the road caught his attention. He lifted his head and turned it to look at the approaching vehicle just as the car's brakes squealed faintly and it drew to a stop.

Broxen narrowed his eyes. They'd already had a few of the permanent residents come gawk at the flames. A couple, like Austin, had been helpful and sympathetic. A few others had treated it merely as a spectacle and had seemed to pity Gabriela rather than sympathize with her.

The car door opened, and a middle-aged male human climbed out and slammed the door shut behind him. His eyes were fixed on the smoldering remains of Gabriela's home. "What the hell... What happened?"

"House fire, sir," said one of the nearby firefighters.

"Yeah, so I was told when one of you called me. I'm the owner of that damn house. What happened?"

Gabriela lifted her head and sniffled, but she didn't release Broxen.

Another firefighter—the one who'd introduced himself as the captain to Gabriela earlier—strode over to the newcomer. "Sorry we had to wake you with a call like that, Mr. Jensen. I'm Captain Walker of McCall Fire."

"So? What'd she do?"

"What do you mean, sir?"

"Gabriela. The lowlife I was renting this place to."

Gabriela stiffened, and her fingernails bit into Broxen's back.

"That's the first thing you're asking about her?" The captain frowned. "Not if she and her kid are okay, it's *what'd she do?*"

"She's been late on her rent two of the last four months," Mr. Jensen snapped. "I had grounds to evict her this time. For all I know, she burned the place down just to get back at me."

Gabriela drew back, placed her hands upon Broxen's chest,

and gently but firmly pushed him aside. He could have easily resisted, could've held her in place without any effort, but he was not going to deny her the right to defend herself. And he was not going to stand by idly while this worm—this *vakalgis*— spoke about Broxen's female that way.

"You *asshole!*" Gabriela tore away her blanket, draping it over Ana's lap, and leapt down from the truck. She stumbled slightly but caught herself before Broxen needed to steady her.

Mr. Jensen and Captain Walker turned toward her. She marched toward them, her wet socks leaving footprints upon the pavement.

Broxen scowled. For a tiny female in her sleepwear, she projected a surprising air of threat, but he could not ignore Gabriela's state—her pajama pants were soaked from the knees down and along the backs of her thighs and ass, and her shirt was too thin to provide any protection from the cold. It didn't matter that she displayed not an ounce of her discomfort; he knew she was freezing. He knew her trembling earlier had been due just as much to the cold as it had been to her traumatic experience.

And that made something stir deep inside him, like a beast roused from age-old slumber—an ancient instinct. It demanded he march forward, scoop her up in his arms, and bring her into the house to warm her, soothe her, tend to her. To shield her from anything that would do her harm, be it a person like Mr. Jensen or an insurmountable force like the weather.

He'd take on *any* foe for the good of his mate and her kit.

"What's happening?" Ana asked in a small voice. She was wrapped up snugly in her blanket with her freshly bandaged hand sticking out near her chest, fingers bent slightly.

"Stay here, Ana," Broxen muttered. "Your mother needs to have a talk with that man."

He pushed away from the truck and followed Gabriela, his

scowl deepening. *Talk*...humans liked to talk, but Broxen found he had no patience for it right now. The longer Gabriela had to deal with Mr. Jensen, the longer she'd be exposed to the cold, and the more frustrated Broxen would become.

Need to care for her.

His fingers itched to take hold of her, if only just to lift her soaked feet off the freezing pavement. If only to draw her into the shelter of his body—both to warm her and make it clear to this angry newcomer that she was under Broxen's protection.

Gabriela stopped in front of Mr. Jensen. "I was living in that house for years before you took ownership. And I just paid the rent *today*. Why the hell would I even pay you at all if I had some malicious intent?"

Mr. Jensen glared down at her. "Don't you talk to me that way, missy." He thrust a finger out toward the remains of the house. "This is your damned fault. I could sue you for—"

"You can take your threats and shove them up your ass, *caremonda!*"

His eyes rounded, and his jaw dropped.

"You'll get your insurance money," Gabriela continued, "but I lost *everything* tonight—everything except my daughter. Though I nearly lost her, too, because you never fixed that *fucking window!*"

The captain seemed to be trying to interject, but neither Gabriela nor Mr. Jensen paid him any attention. The latter was far too occupied gaping at the former.

"That's not true, you little liar," he spat. "I should've known not to rent out to a hisp—"

"Don't you fucking dare say it," Gabriela grated through bared teeth.

"You're trying to slander me, making up lies about that window."

"*Por Dios*, I won't stand here and listen to this! I told you about it three times over the summer and again in October, and you never fixed it. She was trapped in that room, you heartless bastard." Her voice was getting dangerously low and tight, taking on a tone that Broxen was familiar with.

It was the way people of many species talked before they started throwing punches—or shooting.

"It's not my fault that you're an irresponsible mother who—"

Broxen stalked forward, placing his hands on Gabriela's hips and gently tugging to guide her back. When she didn't budge, he simply lifted her off the ground, twisted, and deposited her behind him, ignoring her startled gasp.

He turned to face Mr. Jensen.

The human male tilted his head back to look up, eyes widening and skin paling. His voice was small and thin when he asked, "Who are you?"

"The one who had to break the window open to save that little girl," Broxen growled and bent toward the man. "And maybe I'm not done breaking things tonight."

"Hold on, please," the captain said, hands raised. "Hasn't enough happened here tonight?"

"Just having a chat," Broxen said without looking away from Mr. Jensen. "He was about to apologize."

"I-I will do no such thing," Mr. Jensen stammered, lifting his chin, "especially not to—"

Broxen's hand darted out, catching a fistful of the man's coat. He lifted Mr. Jensen off the ground with one arm until the man's feet were dangling more than a foot in the air. Broxen's gums throbbed, and he felt his fangs extend, reflexively preparing to be turned upon his prey.

The *vakalgis* screamed, grabbing Broxen's arms with both hands. "Call the police! This is a-assault! Get him off me!"

A gentle hand settled on Broxen's back, and he saw Gabriela lean toward him from his peripheral vision.

"Mason, put him down," she urged softly.

He clenched his jaw and bared his teeth, tightening his grip on the man's jacket. "There's something he needs to say first."

Several of the firefighters had gathered around, looking on with uncertainty. Broxen felt something he hadn't felt in a long while—the rush of energy that preceded a fight. He used to love that feeling, used to thrill in it. But he didn't want it now. He wanted this filth to apologize to his mate so he could take her and Ana home and get them warm.

"He will," Gabriela said with utter confidence.

Broxen grunted, glared at Mr. Jensen for a couple more seconds, and dropped the man onto his feet.

Mr. Jensen staggered backward, bumping into the door of his car—likely the only thing that kept the *vakalgis* upright. With large, rounded eyes, he looked to the firefighters. "Aren't you idiots going to do anything?"

The captain's eyebrows fell low, and he shook his head. "No. No, I don't think so."

"That man put his hands on me! He threatened me!"

"I didn't see anything," one of the other firefighters said with a shrug.

Mr. Jensen reached into his coat pocket and pulled out a phone, fumbling to unlock it with shaking hands. "I'm calling the police. He's spending the night in a cell, and the rest of you are going to have formal complaints filed against you!"

"Put the phone away," Gabriela said.

"I don't take orders from *you*," the man sneered.

"Put the phone away, or I promise that I will take you to court over that window. You put my child's life in direct danger with your negligence."

Impossibly, Mr. Jensen's skin paled further. "You don't have any proof about the damned window."

"I have the e-mails I sent you. The dates are all there."

"She's not even hurt," the man said. There was fear in his eyes, an unmistakable gleam that was common throughout so many of the universe's species.

"Burned hand, smoke inhalation," said the captain. "A few more minutes..."

Broxen's chest constricted. He wasn't the best at picking up the meanings humans were so fond of implying, but that one was simple. A few more minutes, and there'd be no more Ana.

"Put the phone away," Gabriela said. Her voice was calm, even, and cold.

Trembling, Mr. Jensen obeyed.

"Did you have something to say?" she asked.

"I...I'm..."

"What's that?" Broxen demanded, leaning forward.

"Sorry! I'm sorry!" Looking to the firefighters for help that wasn't going to come, Mr. Jensen spun around, yanked his car door open, and leapt into the driver's seat, nearly closing the door on his foot.

Several of the firefighters chuckled.

In that moment, all the tension fled Gabriela, and Broxen could tell immediately by the way her posture changed that she was on the verge of collapse. He slipped his arm around her shoulders and drew her against him. Her entire body trembled.

She leaned against him and let out a shaky breath.

The captain stepped closer to Gabriela, shaking his head. "Listen, Miss Romero, it's going to be a little while before the official investigation is done, but...for what it's worth, this wasn't your fault. There are always fires like this around this time of year. Usually faulty lights on Christmas trees or bad surge protectors. You did everything right. You got your daughter out of there, and you're both safe. That's all that matters."

Gabriela nodded. "Thank you, Captain."

"Do...you have anywhere to go?" His eyes briefly flicked to Broxen. "Someone to stay with?"

"I..."

"With me," Broxen said. "They will stay with me."

Under my protection.

Gabriela gasped and looked up at him. "You want us to stay with you? Are...are you sure?"

He met her gaze and nodded. "I am."

Tears filled her eyes, turning them into deep, dark pools.

Captain Walker cleared his throat. "You have my card, and there's no use staying out here in the cold. Why don't you all go on ahead and get warm and settled in. If you need anything, give me a call. Otherwise, I'll be in touch soon."

"Okay. Thank you, Captain," Gabriela said. "Good night."

Broxen followed Gabriela as she returned to Ana; by the time she'd crossed that short distance, she was visibly shivering, and his teeth were clenched in frustration. It took everything within him not to reach for her.

"Are you okay, Mom?" Ana asked.

"Yeah, baby. I'm okay," Gabriela responded, helping her daughter down from the truck.

Broxen grabbed the extra blanket that had been draped over Ana's lap, lifted the tailgate into place, and gestured toward the front door. "Come. Let's get inside."

Ana looked toward the house before turning her face back toward her mother in confusion.

"Mason offered to let us stay with him tonight," Gabriela said.

"Oh." Ana tipped her head back and met Mason's gaze. There were bits of ash in her hair, just as there were in

Gabriela's, and tears had left streaks upon her cheeks. "Thank you, Mason."

For a moment, Broxen had a powerful urge to stalk across the road, pull Mr. Jensen out of his car, and pummel him, just because he knew the man had caused these females pain and distress. But he also knew it wouldn't ease his aggression—and that it would only cause more trouble for his female.

Revenge wouldn't help anything. That was a lesson Broxen had learned firsthand.

He offered Ana a nod and the best smile he could manage, placed a hand on Gabriela's back, and gently nudged her toward the house. "You're freezing. Let's go."

The females walked to the door with him. Broxen opened it wide, stood aside, and gestured for them to go in ahead of him. They moved to stand in the living room, where they gazed around. Having seen the warmth and coziness, the...the hominess of their house, Broxen couldn't help but feel oddly self-conscious now. He closed the door behind himself and strode past his guests.

"Sorry. I, uh... I know it's not much."

Gabriela placed her hand upon his arm and met his gaze. "It's fine, Mason. It's...everything to us right now."

He smiled at her. He couldn't help it, couldn't do anything but that for a few seconds. When he was finally able to move, he covered her hand with his.

Her skin was cold as ice. Broxen's smile fell.

"Both of you, come with me." He led them into his bedroom, grateful that he usually kept things neat. "You can take the bed. I'll get some clean bedding on it, and, uh..."

He walked to the dresser, tugged open a drawer, and rummaged through it until he found a few t-shirts, a pair of drawstring sweatpants, and a couple pairs of basketball shorts.

"I know they won't fit well, but I don't have anything smaller," Broxen said as he held the clothing out to Gabriela. He tilted his head toward the bathroom door. "You can shower in there. Clean towels in the closet."

"Thank you." Gabriela took the clothing and turned toward Ana. She handed her daughter a shirt and a pair of shorts. "Go ahead and shower, Ana. Try not to get your bandage wet. We'll get some sleep after, okay?"

Ana nodded, clutched the clothes to her chest with one hand, and entered the bathroom, closing the door behind her.

Gabriela stared at the door for a moment before turning to face Broxen again. "I...can't thank you enough. For what you did." Her eyes watered. "You...you saved my baby girl."

She was still trembling, and her skin was paler than usual. While he knew how it felt to be cold, he couldn't begin to understand the emotions she must've been experiencing—couldn't begin to guess at what she was thinking.

Or...perhaps he could.

There was something in her voice that he recognized, something he knew well after what had happened to Astius. Something he'd felt tonight, when he'd heard Gabriela scream and he'd run outside to see flames rising from the roof of her house and the sky filled with smoke.

Helplessness.

Broxen would've given his life to protect Astius not because it was his job, but because of the friendship they'd developed. In some ways, he had—because this was nothing like the life he'd known. That relationship had taken years to form. He already knew after this short while that he'd lay down his life for Gabriela and Ana, but more importantly, that he would sacrifice anything to make them happy, to ensure they never felt so hopeless, so terrified, so broken again.

"You don't need to thank me," Broxen said. He stepped

closer to Gabriela and placed his hands on her shoulders, gently steering her toward the bed. "Sit."

She stiffened, holding herself in place, and tears spilled down her cheeks. "But you saved her, Mason. You got her out of there. Without you, she—"

"Sit, Gabriela." He pushed a little more firmly, trying to remain mindful of how small she was, of the immense strength disparity between them. He never wanted to hurt her; he wouldn't be able to forgive himself even if he were to harm her by accident.

She offered no resistance this time, and when the backs of her legs bumped the bed, she dropped down to sit on its edge. She stared at him the whole time with big, dark, beautiful eyes that were currently red and bloodshot.

Broxen frowned down at her pants. There were ice crystals clinging to the fabric around the hems and over her shins, and smears of ash on her thighs. Kneeling down, he cupped her calf with one hand, lifted her foot off the floor, and peeled her sock —which was soaking wet and partially frosted itself—off her dainty foot. The skin beneath was pale and damp and freezing.

"She's safe," he said as he repeated the process with her other foot. "You are safe. Don't think about what could have happened. She's still here. You're still here." He lowered his hands to her ice-cold feet and wrapped his fingers around them. He slowly massaged them, willing warmth back into her flesh. "You would have found a way...but you didn't have to. I was there for you. For Ana."

Taking care with his claws, he rubbed her soles with his thumbs, working his way up from her arches to her small toes and then back down to her heels. He'd never seen such delicate feet before; each of hers was smaller than his hand. Were he not careful, were he not gentle, he could easily crush them. It once again reaffirmed how much larger and stronger Broxen was than his female—his female who was currently freezing.

She needed to get out of her wet clothing before she could truly warm up, but he could not go that far. Not yet. He brought her feet together, covered them with his hands as fully as possible, and leaned down, releasing a deep, warm breath onto them. He glanced up and stilled when his gaze met hers.

Gabriela's eyes were wide, and she was clutching the bedding on either side of her, the blanket wadded between her fingers. Her breath had quickened, causing her chest to rise and fall with her rapid breaths. Broxen's gaze dipped. The outlines of her nipples were visible through the thin fabric of her pajama shirt.

The muscles low in his belly tightened, and his cock pulsed. That quickly, he remembered his hunger for her. His craving. His lust. And the way she was looking down at him, with that mix of surprise and anticipation, only made him want her more.

Yet as arousing as this moment was—as sensual as him kneeling before her, caressing her bare feet was—he could allow himself no enjoyment of it. His female had suffered greatly tonight in more ways than one. He would not take advantage of that suffering. He *would* claim Gabriela as his own, but it would be when she was of clear mind.

"Mason…" Gabriela whispered.

The door to the bathroom opened, and Ana stepped out, startling Broxen and Gabriela. They turned toward her. Broxen's shirt dwarfed the kit, hanging well past her knees, and his shorts were as long as pants to her. Her hair was wet, hanging around her shoulders, and her face was clean of the soot.

She raised her bandaged hand. "I accidently got it wet when I was washing my hair."

"Oh." Gabriela frowned. "Um, we could—"

"I'll take care of it," Broxen said, gently setting Gabriela's feet on the floor. His fingers briefly lingered on her skin. He longed to touch her more, to caress her, hold her... But he knew he couldn't. That time hadn't yet come. And right now, Ana needed him. "Take your shower, Gabriela. I will help Ana, and she can help me change the bedding."

Gabriela stared down at him, a crease forming between her brows. "Are you sure? You can just set the bedding out and I can change it. You've already done so much."

Broxen curled a finger beneath her chin. "Let me do this, Gabriela. Let me...care for you."

A soft breath fled her, and once again, tears shone in her eyes. She pulled her lips in and nodded. "Thank you."

When was the last time someone had taken care of her? How long had it been since the weight of responsibility had been lifted off her shoulders, even for just a little while?

She reached up, grasped his wrist, and brought his hand up to her cheek. Broxen's chest constricted, and unbidden, his cock twitched. She closed her eyes, turned her face into his palm, and pressed her lips there, whispering another quiet thank you before she swallowed thickly and released him, pushing herself to her feet.

He stood up and took a step backward to give her some space, though all he really wanted to do was take her in his arms and feel her body against his, to capture her lips and feel their softness, to taste the depths of her mouth with his tongue. Broxen wanted her to depend on him. He wanted her to lean on him whenever she was in need. He wanted to be close to her always. He wanted to be her protector, her mate. But this was not how he'd wanted it to occur, and he would've spared her all this if could have.

She offered him a shaky smile, brushed the backs of her hands over her eyes, and turned, rounding the bed to make her way toward her daughter. She drew Ana into a hug, which the girl returned.

"I'll be quick, baby. Mason will fix your bandage, and once the bed is made, you can get some sleep, okay?"

"Okay," Ana replied, finishing the word with a little yawn.

Gabriela pressed a kiss to Ana's cheek. "I love you."

Ana smiled. "I love you, too, Mom."

That brief, simple exchange made the entire house feel different to Broxen. He'd known little about love before coming to Earth; it was a concept on the edges of his awareness, something that had existed around him but had never truly been a part of his life. He'd never had the sort of relationship Ana and Gabriela shared. He'd never had anyone who really cared for him, not until Astius had befriended him.

And this taste of what he'd missed, this taste of what he'd craved even before he'd known what it was, only intensified his yearning. To be part of something, to be part of a family...

To have a mate and a kit, whether or not that kit was his by blood, would be sublime. More than he ever could've imagined, more than he deserved.

Gabriela pulled away from Ana, cast Broxen one more small smile and walked into the bathroom.

For a few moments, he stared at that closed door. He knew he was on the verge of imagining what was happening on the other side. Imagining Gabriela peeling off her wet clothing, baring her skin, stepping into the stream of hot water to run her hands over her body and—

Zorak akai, *you have Ana standing right here. Not the time.*

Shaking away those thoughts, he looked at Ana and smiled as sincerely as he could. He held his hand out to her. "There's a first aid kit in the kitchen. Let's get your bandages changed."

There was still some *calathas* with the human supplies, a medical ointment he'd brought to Earth with him. Ana was young enough that she wasn't likely to question what it was, and it would heal her wounds far faster than anything the humans currently had access to.

She placed her tiny, uninjured hand in his, tipping her head back to meet his gaze. "Is there candy in the kitchen, too?"

Broxen chuckled. "Guess we'll have to check. I think you've earned some for being so brave tonight."

"As long as we save some for Mom," Ana said, walking alongside him as he moved toward the door. "She deserves *lots* of candy."

"She does. As much as we can find."

She deserves...everything.

SEVEN

Sleep eluded Broxen. That was nothing new for him; he'd endured many sleepless nights, a good number of which had been spent in places far less pleasant than his living room here on Earth. And he had adequate reason to be awake tonight—so much had happened, so much had changed, so much remained uncertain.

He stared up at the ceiling, which had unfamiliar shadows and a patch of dim yellow light cast across it, the result of the light over the stove being turned on for the first time since he'd moved into this house. It was the best he'd been able to do without any nightlights on hand; should little Ana wander out of the bedroom during the night, at least she wouldn't be in the dark.

Though that light seemed much brighter to him than it did to his humans, he didn't find it bothersome—especially compared to the flashing lights of the firetrucks, which even the blinds hadn't been able to completely block out. Fortunately, the trucks had left a couple hours ago.

And as strange as it was to be lying on his couch trying to

sleep, he was comfortable. Even having to keep his legs draped over the armrest, dangling in the air. His tail was free for the first time all day, finally stretched out alongside his leg rather than wrapped around it, and its tip was swaying back and forth lazily. All was quiet in the house but for the gentle creaking of the building in the winter wind and the dulled drone of a fan in the bedroom. In so many respects, this was just another night on an alien world.

Gabriela is in my bed.

He quickly reminded himself that these weren't the circumstances under which he'd wanted her there—and she was in that bed with her daughter. But he couldn't deny the tiny spark of satisfaction in his chest, couldn't ignore the flutter of excitement in his stomach.

When Gabriela had emerged from the bedroom earlier, she'd been wearing the clothes he'd given her. The hem of his shirt had hung past her knees, and she'd had the legs of the sweatpants rolled up to keep them from dragging on the floor. Seeing her in his clothing had felt *right*. He couldn't deny that he'd enjoyed it, that he'd...loved it. She'd accepted his protection by staying with him, but she'd accepted something more by using his clothes. She'd accepted him.

Part of Broxen knew that probably wasn't how she was thinking about all this, that humans didn't view things in the same way, but that couldn't change how he felt. Gabriela in his clothes had been attractive, sensual, arousing. Knowing that a bit of his scent was on her beautiful tan skin now, marking her as his, threatened to drive him wild. He longed to mark her properly. To claim her fully. And he'd seen a glimmer of longing in her eyes when she'd looked at him, had seen what couldn't have been anything but desire.

He'd barely stopped himself from stalking up to her and taking her in his arms, from slamming his mouth over hers, from tearing his clothing off her enticing little body, pinning her against the wall, and taking her.

Just thinking about it now made his cock stiffen, and he balled his hands into fists, digging the tips of his claws into his palms. His tail twisted and coiled around his calf, and a low growl sounded deep in his chest.

Those yearnings were stronger by far than any he'd ever experienced. His struggle in those moments had been immense.

But the heat had faded from Gabriela's eyes with the gathering of fresh, glistening tears. She'd apologized for crying so much before wishing him goodnight and retreating into the bedroom to get some rest.

Broxen wasn't great at this introspection stuff, but he was fairly certain that it was Gabriela's tears, even more than his unfulfilled cravings, that were keeping him awake now.

Gabriela and Ana had lost everything but each other tonight. All their belongings were gone, all the items that had made their home feel so warm and inviting, all the objects they'd cherished. Broxen knew Gabriela had worked hard for everything she'd owned—and that many of those objects could never be replaced. Worst of all, she'd faced the terror of almost losing the thing she cherished above all else. Her daughter.

It was wrong for Broxen to feel this sense of pride, this flare of contentment and satisfaction. It was wrong for him to feel like Gabriela and Ana were right where they belonged. It was wrong of him to view this situation as his best opportunity to make them his forever.

If he could've spared them these experiences, he would have, even if it meant never having them.

So where was his guilt? Where was his self-loathing, his remorse?

His females' tears, their sadness, their fear and grief, were like knives plunged into his chest over and over again. Their suffering had become his. But...Gabriela and Ana were here. They were with him. That meant he could better protect them. That meant he could ensure they had all they needed, that they'd never have to worry about anything again.

Protector. Provider. Mate...and father?

Broxen sat up, casting aside the blanket, and swung his feet onto the floor. He propped his elbows on his thighs, bowed his head, and ran his hands back over his horns, dragging his hair out of his face.

"I could've waited," he rasped.

He'd never wanted Gabriela and Ana to lose everything to become his. He'd wanted it to be a natural—if inevitable—process. But fate, or the universe, or whatever damned unseen force it was that called the shots had done this instead. Without having had any time to prepare, Broxen had two females in his house.

Catching his hair in his fists, he tugged on it, barely noticing the sting in his scalp. "*Kruk.*"

There were two *humans* in his house.

His mind raced, and his tail lashed across the couch cushions, striking with dull thumps. Was everything hidden? Had he left anything in plain sight that Gabriela and Ana might recognize as alien in origin?

How the hell had he failed to think about that before inviting them into his home, before giving them use of his bedroom? It would've taken two or three minutes to do a quick sweep and ensure everything was in order—to ensure everything looked human.

He stood up and strode toward the bedroom, heart pounding and tail flicking back and forth stiffly. He hadn't brought much to Earth. The most important device—the neural transceiver with its connected holoshroud—was inside his brain, and the *calathas* in the first aid kit could be explained away, but he also had a few advanced weapons and a hacking device that didn't look like anything he'd seen on Earth in his stockpile. Though he usually kept everything hidden in the crawlspace, he sometimes took the items out for maintenance...

But he'd been in an odd mood lately, and he couldn't fully trust that he'd taken the necessary precautions. If his females found something, if they discovered that he wasn't human...

Broxen would lose them.

Sure, being exposed had other consequences. Human entertainment hadn't exactly instilled him with confidence that Earth's governments would treat him well if they discovered what he was. Then there was the matter of this planet having been declared off-limits by intergalactic law, and the fact that there was a price on his head back on Turata. News of a lone omnyrian hiding out on Earth could catch the attention of the enemies he'd left behind.

Holding his breath, he grasped the bedroom doorknob and cracked open the door as slowly and quietly as he could, wincing at the faint click of the latch. The sound of the fan in the bedroom became more immediate.

He braced a hand on the doorframe and leaned forward to peer through the gap.

His eyes fell on the bed immediately, where Gabriela was curled up in the heavy blanket, holding Ana close. Only their heads were visible, and they were motionless save for the slow rise and fall of the blanket with their breathing. Gabriela was holding Ana as though the little girl were the most precious thing in the universe.

Not long ago, Broxen wouldn't have understood that. Maybe he still didn't, not entirely...but he was coming to understand.

He opened the door a little more so he could get a better

look at Gabriela. In sleep, her worries had faded, and her expression had eased in a way he'd never seen. Even when she'd smiled and been kind, even when she'd seemed happy, there'd always been that tiny flicker in her eyes—there'd always been a hint of the weight she carried. There was none of it now.

Whatever his reasons for opening the bedroom door had been, Broxen forgot them in that moment. Gabriela was beautiful, and Ana was...what was the word? Adorable? Cute? Even with a dictionary implanted in his brain, it was often difficult to find out the right words to say in this convoluted language humans called English, but that didn't matter.

Because he was looking at his reasons right now—he was looking at his purpose. He wanted to lie in that bed at night, holding Gabriela in his arms, her body tucked against his. He wanted to breathe in air that was perfumed only by her scent. He wanted to feel her warmth, her softness, her breath on his skin. He wanted to see her smile and hear her laugh.

He wanted Ana to have stability, to have the joyous childhood so often depicted in human media. He wanted to keep these females safe from a harsh, cold universe in every way he could.

They were his. There was no question about it, there were no doubts to be had. Gabriela was his mate, and Ana was his kit. He would give them everything he could. He would take their burdens when possible, and when he couldn't, he would do everything possible to share them.

His claws dug into the wood of the doorframe. How best could he show Gabriela that she wasn't alone in this, that she never had to be alone again? That he was here for her and Ana in every way? That she could rely on him...even if she didn't know what he was.

One day, he'd have to reveal the truth. He'd have to tell Gabriela about his past, would have to tell her he wasn't human. That was a secret he could not keep from someone he was coming to care for so deeply, so quickly.

It was not a secret to keep from one's mate.

But for now, all his focus would be on them. On their needs, on their wants, on their comfort and satisfaction. His own could wait.

For a little while at least.

He might easily have stood there until dawn, but he had a faint notion that, were one of the females to wake, they'd not appreciate seeing him staring at them through the doorway. They were at peace for now, getting rest they desperately needed. He would not disturb them.

With the greatest care he could muster, Broxen eased the door shut. He needed sleep, himself, if he was to provide for them tomorrow.

And he'd need to start doing some research. Christmas was coming up soon, and he'd have to learn more about it if he wanted to make this the best possible holiday for his females.

EIGHT

Broxen groaned. He wasn't sure if the sound of it had woken him or if he'd made it because he'd woken, but he knew it was too damned early in the morning to care. Releasing a heavy breath through his nostrils, he straightened his legs, stretching them out with his tail beside them. His feet were sticking out of the blanket, which was bunched and twisted around his waist, and his hair was in his face. But he felt...good despite sleeping on a couch that was too short for him.

That feeling was complicated a moment later when his grogginess faded just enough for the events of the prior night to rush to mind.

"*Gur'osh brakhan,*" he muttered.

"What does *gurush brakkin* mean?"

He opened his eyes and snapped his head up. Through the dark curtain of his hair, he saw a tiny human sitting on the floor in front of the couch, staring up at him. The shirt she was wearing looked big enough for her to use as a tent.

"What language is it?" Ana asked. "Is it Russian? Are you from Russia? My *abuelita* is from Colombia, and she speaks

Spanish. So does my mom, but not very often. She taught me how, too."

With a grunt, Broxen propped himself up on an elbow and scooted his ass back to sit up. He lifted his hand, meaning to sweep his hair back from his face, but froze with his palm upon the root of his horn. Clenching his jaw, he lowered his hand to glance at it; his skin appeared that pale color common to so many humans, and his claws were invisible.

He let out a relieved sigh and tucked his hair back. His holoshroud had deactivated during his sleep a couple times when he'd first been growing accustomed to it, and he'd been concerned about it happening again ever since.

It would've been especially troublesome had it deactivated last night.

If she'd seen the real me, she wouldn't be calmly sitting on the floor.

Ana tilted her head to the side. "Are you okay?"

Broxen's brow furrowed. "I'm fine. Just..."

"Still waking up? Mom says she's not awake until she has her coffee. Did you know you growl sometimes in your sleep?"

Broxen swung his feet onto the floor and leaned forward with his elbows on his knees. He shifted his tail—which was still rendered invisible by the holoshroud—slowly, wrapping it around his waist so it was out of the way. "Don't a lot of people snore?"

"Yeah, but you weren't snoring. Snoring sounds like this." She breathed in, making a loud, rattling, snorting sound.

The corner of Broxen's mouth tilted up. "And what'd I sound like?"

"Kiiiind of like a wolf. Like this." She bared her teeth, scrunched her nose, and let loose a rolling growl from the back of her throat. Her expression was made more adorable by the gaps where her mini, human fangs should've been.

Broxen laughed and shook his head. "I don't sound like that."

"Yeah, you do," she replied, brows falling low. "Just, you know, deeper and quieter."

Amusing as this was, he couldn't ignore the implication of her being there—he'd lost his edge. In the past, he never would've slept deeply enough for anyone, especially this little girl, to get so close to him without waking. He never would've been caught off guard. He needed to do better now that he had these females under his protection.

He ran his tongue over his teeth and glanced up at the clock on the wall. It was one of those circular clocks with arms, leftover from the previous owners of the house, and he'd seen no reason to take it down—but he still wasn't accustomed to using it. His lips moved as he soundlessly counted off the tick marks between the numbers. Seven sixteen. That explained the faint gray light outside that was struggling to penetrate the blinds.

Were it a school day—and were things normal—Broxen would've been waiting at that window now to get a glimpse of Gabriela as she went out to start her car.

"Where is your mother, Ana?"

"She's still sleeping."

My mate is in my bed.

A growl built deep in his chest at that reminder, but he held it back. Instead, he cleared his throat, looking down at Ana. "You hungry?"

She sagged. "*Starving.*"

He chuckled, flattened his hands on his knees, and pushed himself up. "I'm sure you are. Give me a minute and we'll get some breakfast going."

Ana stood up and tilted her head back to keep her eyes on him. "Can I help?"

"Can you make toast without burning it?"

Ana gave him a flat look. "I'm nine and a half. I know how to use the toaster."

Broxen lifted his hands, displaying his palms in surrender. "My mistake. I shouldn't doubt your toasting skills. I'll be back."

"You sound like the robot in that movie when you say that," she said with a smirk.

"What robot in what movie?"

"The Terminator. It's a *very* grown-up movie, and I've seen it. Mom let me watch it. It's one of her favorite movies. I love it, too."

Broxen walked toward the guest bathroom in the hallway. "Oh? Guess I'll have to watch it sometime."

"I should warn you. It has kissing."

He paused as he opened the bathroom door and looked back at Ana, lifting his brows high and widening his eyes. "But it's *still* a good movie?"

"It's awesome!"

Smiling, he stepped into the bathroom, flicked on the light, and closed the door. He unwound his tail, letting it flow freely behind him. This was likely the last time he could have it out until tonight. After emptying his bladder, he washed his hands and glanced at himself in the mirror.

His hair was a tangled mess. Not unusual for having just woken, but with his mate in the house, he couldn't leave it like that. He ran his claws through it quickly, tugging it all back and working out the knots. The result was still a bit unruly, but it was decidedly better than how it had started.

He would've preferred to brush both his hair and his teeth, but his toiletries were in his bathroom, and he dared not disturb Gabriela. If anyone needed rest, it was her.

Broxen washed his face with cool water before seeing to his

tail, tucking it into his sweatpants and coiling it around his leg. Though the position was never comfortable, it was necessary, and he'd grown accustomed to having to do it all the time.

Someday I won't have to hide it. When she knows what I am. When she accepts it—when she accepts me.

For now, he needed to prepare food and feed his humans.

He rejoined Ana, who was more than eager to follow him into the kitchen and get to work on breakfast, practically skipping along behind him.

"Hand first," Broxen said as he took the first aid kit down off the fridge and set it on the counter. "How is it?"

"Doesn't hurt anymore," Ana replied.

Broxen crouched before her, holding one of his hands out to her, palm up. She placed her bandaged hand atop his, and he delicately peeled away the bandages. When her hand was exposed, he lifted it toward his face, examining her wounds.

Last night, her palm had been blistered and red—almost as red as his natural skin color. But the *calathas* had done its job. All that remained of her wounds were a few tiny bumps and a little patch of flesh that looked pink and slightly raw.

After applying a bit more *calathas*, Broxen bandaged her palm, able to use a few smaller adhesive bandages instead of a full-hand wrap. "It'll be healed, soon, kit."

Ana smiled at him. "*Muchas gracias*, Mason."

He couldn't help but return that smile. "Ah, so you do speak Spanish."

Her smile only seemed to widen. "Do you?"

Broxen stood upright and closed the first aid kit. "I...understand it. Don't think it'd sound good coming from me, though."

"It's easy. Someone says *gracias*, and you say *con mucho gusto*."

With much pleasure.

Now it was Broxen's smile that widened. He returned the

first aid kit to its place, faced her fully, and said, "*Con mucho gusto, Ana.*"

"See, you got it. We'll have to work on your accent a little, but you show promise."

Laughing, he plucked the loaf of bread off the counter and handed it to her before taking some plates from the cupboard and setting them on the counter next to the toaster.

"Do you have strawberry jam?" she asked while opening the bag.

"I have jelly," he replied as he opened the fridge.

"What kind?"

"Jelly." Broxen grabbed the jar from inside the refrigerator and placed it on the counter before grabbing the carton of eggs on the top shelf.

Ana peered closer at the jar and nodded. "Grape. That'll do."

Broxen arched a brow at her. "That'll do?"

She grinned as she put four slices of bread into the toaster. "I approve of your taste."

He set the eggs on the counter beside the stove and opened the cabinet where he kept his pots and pans. "Because I have grape jelly?"

"Yes. Strawberry's better, but grape is still good. But the *best* kind is Mom's homemade huckleberry jam. We go and pick the berries every year to make it."

Broxen hummed thoughtfully and dug out one of his frying pans. He'd seen signs in town about huckleberries, and was aware they were popular in the region, but he hadn't tasted anything made with them yet. "Hopefully I get to try it some time."

"You can pick them with us next year!"

"Maybe."

He'd make sure of it. Next year, and the year after that, and the year after that.

He slid open one of the drawers and dug out his spatula. He'd slacked in cooking other things, but breakfast foods, especially eggs, were something simple to make, versatile, and delicious. "How do you like your eggs?"

The toaster popped.

"Scrambled." Ana carefully plucked the toast out of the toaster one slice at a time to place them delicately atop a plate.

Broxen turned on the burner and set to work. Though it was easy to cook a bunch of scrambled eggs, he was nonetheless grateful for Ana's help; he hadn't mastered multitasking in the kitchen, even when all he had to do was turn on the toaster and make sure the eggs didn't burn.

"Did you like the cookies?" Ana asked a little while later.

Broxen flipped the semi-cooked eggs with the spatula. "Best cookies I ever had."

"You didn't want to eat the bear?"

Broxen glanced over his shoulder to see her standing next to the bag with the lone cookie—the bear with its mismatched eyes and friendly grin. "Wanted to, but I couldn't. I just liked it too much to do that. But now that you're here, you can have it."

She looked up at him. "Can we save it for Mom?"

He smiled. "Maybe we can all share it?"

She returned his smile. "Okay."

Broxen and Ana chatted—mostly Ana—as they cooked. She talked about school, about her best friends, Max and Julie, about unicorns, about her favorite arts and crafts. She spoke easily and openly, as though she and Broxen had spent countless mornings like this, as though he weren't an omnyrian in disguise who would've terrified her had she seen his true appearance.

She spoke to him as though they were already family.

It wasn't until he'd cracked the last of the eggs into the pan that his bedroom door opened. His heart quickened, and he turned to see Gabriela stepping out of the hallway. She was still wearing his clothing, and her hair was tousled, with strands of it dangling on the sides of her face—just the way he imagined she'd look after being well pleasured. She wasn't wearing any of the makeup she normally had on when he saw her most days; it was just her skin, just her eyelashes, just her lips. And she was even more beautiful to him like this than ever before.

"I'm *so* sorry," Gabriela said as she walked into the kitchen. "I didn't mean to oversleep."

"You didn't," Broxen replied, hoping he didn't look like a damned fool—or worse, a creep—as he stared at her. "It's your, uh...day off. You had a rough night. Think you earned sleeping until seven forty-five."

Ana looked up from the piece of toast she was currently slathering with jelly. "Morning, Mom! We're making breakfast."

Gabriela smiled at her. "I see that, *mija*." She turned her face toward Broxen. "Anything I can help with?"

Broxen wasn't deceived by the smile Gabriela had put on for her daughter—a smile that was meant to maintain the illusion that everything was okay. He could see the despair and helplessness deep in her eyes. He vowed he'd do everything he could to take those feelings away from her, to eradicate them, to make sure she'd never have to force a reassuring smile again.

"No." He nodded toward the table. "Sit."

Looking a little unsure, Gabriela walked to the dining table, pulled a chair out, and took a seat. "How long has Ana been up?"

Broxen offered Ana what he hoped was a meaningful glance before turning his attention back to the eggs. "Longer than me."

"I woke up at six fifty-five," Ana said. "I was too hungry to go back to sleep."

Brows falling low, Broxen frowned down at the sizzling eggs. Had the kit spent that whole twenty minutes watching him sleep?

Gabriela frowned. "Why didn't you wake me?"

Ana shrugged and carried the plate with the jellied toast to the table, setting it down in the middle before seating herself. "You were tired."

"Did she wake you, Mason?"

Chuckling, he lifted the pan off the burner and dumped the eggs onto the last plate. "No, but she was there to greet me when I woke."

She narrowed her eyes on Ana.

"What?" Ana asked. "I was quiet. I heard Mason growling, so I wanted to check on him. I think he was dreaming that he was a wolf."

This time when Gabriela smiled, it was genuine. She turned her eyes back up to Mason as he took three forks out of the utensil drawer, picked up all three egg-laden plates, and approached the table.

"Mason was growling?" she asked.

"Yeah. Like this." Ana demonstrated the same growl she'd done for him earlier.

"Still don't think that's accurate," he grumbled before setting the plates down and pulling out a chair, sitting across from Gabriela.

Ana picked up her fork and began shoveling eggs into her mouth.

"She does tend to exaggerate things," Gabriela said.

"Do not," Ana said around a mouthful.

"Don't talk with food in your mouth."

Ana moved the food to one side of her mouth, making her cheek stick out. "Sorry."

Shaking her head with a smile, Gabriela turned her eyes back to Broxen. "Thank you for breakfast."

He paused with a forkful of eggs halfway up to his mouth—which was already filled with eggs—and looked up at Gabriela. He lowered the fork and quickly chewed and swallowed before replying. "No problem. Can take you to the store afterward. Get whatever you two need."

Her smile faltered, and she dropped her gaze to her plate. "Do you...have a computer I could use? I need to let my parents know what happened, and...check my bank account, but my phone is gone."

Based on what she'd said yesterday—and the look on her face now—Broxen guessed she knew exactly what was in her account.

Nothing, or damn near close to it.

"I'll get my laptop when we're done," he said. He dipped his chin toward her untouched plate. "Eat, female."

Her brows creased as she looked at him questioningly; only then did he realize what he'd said.

Female. That wasn't how humans talked.

"Are we still getting hot chocolate?" Ana asked.

Gabriela's eyes widened. "Ana!"

That interjection was convenient enough to nearly make him thank the kit. "Yes. We had a date."

"Mason, you've already done so much. I...I don't expect you to—"

"Are you...cancelling our date?" he asked, putting on an exaggerated frown. He wouldn't have been surprised if it was a tactic Ana had used many times during her young life.

It was called a *guilt trip.*

"What? No! I just thought with... I wouldn't cancel. I want

to"—she glanced between him and Ana—"go on a date with you."

"I knew it! He's your boyfriend." Grinning, Ana looked at Broxen. "I saw her staring at your butt."

"Oh, God." Gabriela buried her face in her hands.

The corner of Broxen's mouth quirked up as he reached across the table with both arms, taking hold of her wrists. She struggled a little when he tried to guide her hands down, but finally gave in. Her cheeks had darkened; that natural hint of blush was more tantalizing than any makeup she could ever have worn.

"I'm taking you for hot chocolate," he said when she met his gaze. "I will do that, and so much more. And don't worry. You have my permission."

Her brows knitted. "Permission for what?"

"To stare at my butt whenever you want."

And I will continue to stare at yours in turn, my mate.

Gabriela laughed even as her cheeks grew darker. "Is it possible to die from embarrassment? Because I think I might."

"You will not. Now"—he released one of her wrists and picked up her fork, placing it within her hand—"eat."

She caught her bottom lip with her teeth as she held his gaze. Lowering her fork, she poked a piece of egg and slowly brought it to her mouth. "Yes, Sir."

Watching her slip the eggs past her plump lips sent a rush of desire straight to his groin. For a moment, he imagined those lips wrapping around his cock, imagined those dark eyes staring up to meet his half-lidded gaze as she pleasured him with her mouth and tongue.

He dropped his hand to his thigh, curled in into a fist, and gritted his teeth as his shaft twitched and hardened. The ache was bearable. For now.

Soon.

Soon he would have Gabriela in his bed, her body bared and spread to receive him. He'd cover her with his mouth first, would lick her and taste her, would drink of her essence as she cried out in rapture. Then he would claim her as his own.

She'd be *his*.

Soon.

NINE

Seventy-two dollars.

That was all Gabriela had left to her name. A measly seventy-two dollars. She didn't even have that on her person currently—it was in her checking account, and her debit card had been in her purse, which had been turned to ash along with everything else she owned. She'd have to get that replaced, along with her driver's license, their birth certificates, and social security cards, none of which she could afford right now.

A few house cleaning jobs would've brought in money to cover the bare essentials, but she had nothing scheduled until after Christmas—and even if she'd had something sooner, Gabriela had no way to get anywhere. Her car had been totaled thanks to its proximity to the house. Her liability insurance sure as hell wasn't going to cover that.

Maybe she could call her clients and offer a housecleaning special?

And then what? Have Mason drive me all over the county like he's my chauffeur/personal taxi service while I clean houses?

Gabriela clutched the shopping cart's handlebar, trying hard to keep her eyes from blurring with tears as she walked toward the toiletries section of the grocery store. That sense of helplessness she'd felt since first seeing the fire in her living room hadn't diminished. She drew in a quiet, shaky breath.

She didn't even have shoes to wear—at least not any that fit. She and Ana had used some of Mason's spare boots to walk outside, but they hadn't even been inside the store for a minute before they'd both removed the oversized footwear and set it on the cart's bottom rack. Traveling through the grocery store in their socks was embarrassing, but clomping along in big, noisy boots that slid and flopped around was even more so, especially when those boots fell off every couple steps.

Ana was walking beside the cart, holding it with her hand—a habit left over from when she was a little girl and Gabby had insisted Ana always stay close. Gabriela studied her daughter, and her chest constricted. The changes in Ana were subtle, and oftentimes Gabriela was oblivious to them, but every now and then she'd notice everything in a rush and it'd be almost too much to take. Ana was nine and a half, and she was already showing hints of the woman she'd too soon become.

Where was the time going?

Gabriela turned the cart into the aisle containing oral hygiene products.

Mason followed her, his steps heavy upon the floor. His entire demeanor had changed the moment they'd left his truck. He'd grown quiet and more watchful, remaining behind her as though he were her shadow. Every time she glanced over her shoulder, he'd look her way and offer her an encouraging, friendly smile.

Gabriela brought the cart to a stop in front of the toothbrushes. She skimmed the choices, seeking out the cheapest ones until she finally plucked up a pack of two that was priced under two dollars. She selected a tube of the store brand of toothpaste next.

The deodorant was a little farther down the aisle. She chose two sticks of the cheapest brand—one for her, one for Ana—and continued on to grab a bottle of body wash, a bottle of two-in-one shampoo, and a hairbrush, keeping a metal tally of the prices. For her face cream, she picked one of the travel-sized tubes. It wasn't cost effective, but it was marked cheaper than a full-size container, and it was all she could afford right now.

She glanced at the cosmetics as they passed. Though she'd owned various shades of eyeshadow and lip gloss for those rare special occasions, she didn't normally wear makeup other a little coverup and mascara. There wasn't much of a reason for her to primp when all she did was work and hang out at home with her daughter. Makeup was something she could do without.

On the far side of the store was the clothing department. Most of the items catered to tourists—t-shirts, hoodies, coats, and even socks with *McCall* printed on them with various fonts and designs.

Gabriela almost blanched when she looked at the price tags. "Ana, see if you can find anything that'll fit that's been marked down."

"Okay, Mom."

As Ana proceed on to the girls' clothing, Gabriela sought the intimates section. She found a small package of underwear and socks for Ana, which she tossed into the cart, and added two pairs of underwear, a bra, and a two-pack of socks for herself. She'd have to ask Mason to take them to a thrift store for everything else; her money would go a lot further there than it would here. The items she'd already chosen were adding up too fast. She was afraid to even glance at the prices of the shoes.

Mason stepped up beside the cart and leaned down, reaching in to spread out the meager items within. "This doesn't seem like much."

It's not, but oh, is it going to drain my account anyway.

Tears stung her eyes, and her bottom lip trembled. "I can't afford the clothing here."

He turned his head to look at her. His brows were drawn low, his lips downturned. "You don't have to worry about that, Gabriela."

"I do, Mason. I know you're paying for everything today, but I only have so much to pay you back with right now."

His frown deepened. For a moment, he looked away, searching the clothing racks until his eyes settled on Ana, who was looking through some shirts nearby. Seemingly satisfied with that, he turned toward Gabriela fully. His long stride ate up the distance between them in a flash, and then he was right there. His scent, which she'd smelled faintly off and on through the store, washed over her.

Mason placed his palms on her elbows and guided her to face him. "Tell me what you are thinking, Gabriela."

She blinked and ducked her head, tears escaping to flow down her cheeks. She was glad for the high racks of clothing on either side of them to hide her breakdown from the other shoppers.

"I'm broke," she said in a quiet, strained voice. "I have seventy-two dollars in my bank account. That's all. I have to pay you back, I need to get a new copy of my license and all our documents, I need to buy food and clothes and hairbrushes, I need a car, a-a hotel room, and I have seventy-two—" Her words broke off in a sob. "Ana won't have any Christmas gifts. They burned up with everything else. Everything. I have nothing left, n-nothing t-to provide for my daughter. We're *homeless.*"

"No," Mason growled. "You have a place with me. Don't need a hotel."

"I just... I don't know what I'm going to do, Mason."

He lifted a hand, curled his finger under her chin, and brushed the pad of his thumb beneath her lip, making a shiver run through her. "You are going to get whatever you and Ana need."

"I won't be able to pay you back. Not for a long, long time."

"I don't want you to pay me back."

Her brows furrowed. "Mason, I...I can't let you do that. You've already done so much for us. We're basically strangers still, and—"

Mason pressed his thumb over her lips, silencing her. There was a warm light in his eyes—kindness and compassion, yes, but something more, too. Something that sparked heat low in Gabriela's belly. It was as though the rest of the world had fallen away, and there was only the two of them here in this moment.

"I will do everything I can for you, Gabriela," he said, his voice low and rumbly. "Everything."

Her watery eyes searched his as emotion tightened her throat and her lips quivered under his thumb. "Why?" she breathed as more tears spilled down her cheeks. "Why would you do this for us?"

He shifted his hand to brush away her tears with those big, surprisingly gentle fingers. "You have always been kind to me. You're the only one who treats me like...a person. And I have wanted you since the moment I first saw you."

Gabby's eyes flared and she drew in a small, sharp breath, stunned into silence. He...he had?

"I have watched over you and Ana since I moved into my house," he continued, "and I've done all I could to help you from afar, never knowing how to get close. But I know you are unclaimed. I want you to be mine, Gabriela. I want you for my mate, and I want Ana to be my kit. I want to care for you, to protect you, to be your male. You are so strong, but...you don't need to carry your burdens alone. Not anymore."

Mason again wiped the moisture from her cheeks, and when his thumb grazed her bottom lip, his eyes dipped to her mouth and remained there. That heat in his eyes intensified. "I crave you, female. And I will make you mine fully. In time."

His violet eyes met hers, and for a brief instant, she could have sworn they glowed.

He dropped his hands from her and stepped back. "Put *everything* you need and want in the cart, Gabriela. I will check on Ana."

Gabriela stood there, dumbfounded, as Mason turned and walked away from her. Her heart fluttered, and her breaths came short and quick. She could almost still feel his touch upon her face, could almost still feel those gentle, careful caresses of his fingers. It had been so, so long since she'd been touched by a man, but she'd never been touched like that. She'd never been treated as though she was the most precious, delicate thing in the world. She'd never been treated as though she were some-one's *everything*. But Mason looked at her as though she was.

I want you to be mine, Gabriela. I want you for my mate, and I want Ana to be my kit.

Mate? Kit? Female?

He had an unidentifiable accent, and sometimes his word choice was odd. Was he from another country originally? She barely knew anything about him. Shouldn't that have been a sign that they were moving too fast?

But hadn't she already wasted so many years alone? And when she was around Mason, she felt...safe. Despite virtually being strangers, she never felt threatened by him, and she trusted him around her daughter. Every time he looked at Ana, there was only patience and fatherly affection in his eyes. And when he looked at Gabriela...

She'd seen his desire. Even a year ago, when they'd first spoken, it had been there, but she'd been so oblivious to it then and every time after when they'd interacted, even though she'd felt no shortage of attraction to him. But she'd been focused on her duties as a mother, focused on her work, her schedule, on taking care of her daughter's needs. Gabriela had brushed aside her own needs and loneliness as though they weren't important.

Now...now her eyes were open.

She tilted her head as she watched Mason interact with her daughter. He asked Ana something, and she pointed at several items of clothing—each of which he lifted from the rack and draped over his arm. Ana's face broke out in delight and she jumped up and down excitedly.

Gabriela pressed her palm over her heart.

Mason wanted her to be his mate. He wanted Ana to be his...kit.

The corner of her mouth quirked.

What if this—if Mason—was too good to be true? It was all so much, and everything in her life seemed to be happening so quickly lately...

But part of her said she'd be a fool not to accept this. To accept *him*.

Maybe it was a leap of faith, the biggest she'd ever considered taking in her life, but she was tempted to do it.

Mason turned his head and met Gabriela's gaze. Her core clenched. He didn't hide the hunger that burned within the depths of his eyes.

I want him, too.

Then maybe it was time she allowed herself to reach out and take what *she* wanted.

TEN

After their trip to the grocery store, Mason took Gabriela and Ana to a couple other stores that had wider selections of clothes, shoes, and coats, telling them to get everything they needed. Gabby insisted it was all too much, that he *really* didn't need to do all this. Mason—as big and unmoving as a mountain in this—would hear no arguments.

Though most of the stock available in town was winter wear and the typical outdoorsy stuff, Gabriela and Ana had enough clothing by the time they left the last store to feel almost normal, at least as far as their wardrobes went—especially once they changed into their new clothes. There were even items Mason had added himself, usually when he'd seen Gabriela look at something, see the price tag, and hurriedly return it to the rack.

And even having paid for all that, Mason took them to the little café he'd mentioned a couple days before, where he bought them steaming mugs of hot chocolate with whipped cream piled high over the rims.

When Mason lowered his mug after his first drink of hot

cocoa, he had a thick whipped cream moustache left behind, complete with a few chocolate sprinkles that made Gabriela and Ana break out into giggles. He looked at them with narrowed eyes before attempting to lick away the whipped cream, contorting his face and wrinkling his nose to get at it all.

Gabriela and Ana laughed so hard it almost hurt, and for a little while, Gabby's cares were forgotten.

Despite her humor, she couldn't ignore just how long and dexterous his tongue was—and she couldn't stop herself from considering other uses it could be put to. That thought sent a rush of heat to her lower belly, making her core clench and ache with sudden need. She squeezed her thighs together beneath the table, but that didn't dull the sensation.

Thankfully, Ana provided enough of a distraction with her chatter to take Gabriela's mind off more...intimate matters.

She never would've thought it possible to enjoy a date the morning after losing everything, but she did. Mason was reserved, as he so often was, but he was also incredibly attentive and engaged, allowing Gabriela—and more often than not, Ana—to steer the conversation wherever they liked. Mason laughed and smiled as often as Gabby and Ana, and whenever he did so, his eyes lit up, becoming impossibly more violet.

Gabriela left the café feeling a little lighter, and that was more than she could ever have hoped for. They returned to Mason's house, and she didn't allow herself to look across the street at the ruins of her former home. She had to keep moving forward.

Mason, unsurprisingly, insisted on bringing everything inside himself. After a bit of pushback from Gabby, he accepted help—allowing Ana to take a few of the lighter bags. The little girl beamed at that and proceeded to shoo Gabriela inside as Mason looked on with a smirk.

"You need rest, Mom. Go on," Ana girl said.

"I slept in! That's more rest than the mother of a crazy nine-year-old can ask for," Gabriela replied as she stepped into the house.

"I'm nine and a *half*," Ana countered.

Gabby chuckled. She paused in the middle of the living room to look back at Mason as he entered. "Where...should we put our clothes?"

He halted just inside the doorway, holding at least twenty bags stuffed with clothing, groceries, and toiletries, and furrowed his brow. There was no question that those bags were heavy, but he showed no signs of strain. "We'll leave them in the bags for now and put them in the bedroom. I'll figure something out."

Mason and Gabriela put away the groceries as Ana hauled the bags of clothing to bedroom. When they were done, the fridge and freezer were full near to bursting, and the previously bare cupboards and pantry were well-stocked. Mason turned to Gabby, smiled, and told her to make herself at home before striding to the front door.

"Where are you going?" she asked.

He tugged open the door and looked at her over his shoulder. "Few more things to get. Be back in a couple hours."

As though he'd not done enough already, now he was giving them free reign of his home, trusting them while he was away? Where was this man ten years ago, when Gabriela's ex had abandoned her and her unborn child?

"Okay. You don't want us to come?" she asked.

Mason chuckled. "No. Settle in and relax. Treat this place like your own."

He stepped outside and started pulling the door shut, only to pause and ease it open a bit. He leaned across the threshold and said, "Lock the door."

And then he was gone.

Gabriela heard his truck start in the driveway. She walked to the front window just in time to see him backing out. He caught sight of her and lifted his hand in a small wave. Smiling, she returned the gesture before he drove off.

Gabby still hadn't quite shaken her shock from what he'd said in the grocery store. He was moving in on her hard and fast, and well...she wasn't put off by it in the least. And it wasn't simply because of her current situation. She would never, *ever* take advantage of Mason. She'd always been attracted to him, since the moment she saw him moving into this house.

There'd been many times when she'd stopped what she'd been doing—whether cleaning house, helping Ana with school-work, cooking, sorting through her bills—to catch a glimpse of him, usually shirtless, mowing his front lawn. To watch his muscles flex and bulge, to watch sweat drip down his skin, to stare at his jeans clinging to his shapely ass. He was a gorgeous man.

She'd just never dreamed he would want her in return, especially knowing she was a single mother—and that she therefore came as a package deal.

Though he sometimes spoke strangely, Mason was a good man, and he instilled her with...hope. Hope that she had a chance at a real relationship with a man who wanted her *and* her daughter. Hope that Ana could have the father she so longed for, and hope that they'd be...a family.

Jeez, we really are *moving fast.*

"Can I watch TV?" Ana asked.

Gabriela jumped back from the window, casting a guilty look at her daughter.

Ana grinned. "You *do* like him."

"Oh, shush you, and go ahead."

Ana laughed and plopped down on the sofa, dragging down one of the blankets folded across the back to cover herself. She turned on the TV, selected the YouTube app, and surfed through her favorite content creators.

She'd be entertained for hours watching them.

So what could Gabby do to occupy herself?

She glanced around. She...could get to know Mason a little more by exploring his home. Not that she'd was nosy or anything, but he *had* said to treat this place like home. Maybe she could even tidy things up a little. His house wasn't filthy, but there was a thin layer of dust gathered on the edges of the shelves and atop the carved bear in the corner. It could be Gabriela's way of paying him back, if only a little, for all he'd done for her and Ana.

After locking the front door, she walked into the kitchen and opened the cabinet under the sink. Sure enough, his cleaning supplies were inside, standing in a small plastic tub. It looked like he only had the basics, but that was good enough for her. She tucked the wood polish under her arm and grabbed the duster before conducting another search that resulted in her finding some rags in one of the kitchen drawers.

Armed and ready, she went to work.

Gabriela more or less blocked out the TV, letting it become background noise—though the occasional piercing scream from whatever YouTuber Ana was watching sometimes broke through. She dusted the shelves and the décor upon them, dusted the pictures on the walls, dusted around the TV and the TV itself.

Some of the things Mason owned didn't quite seem to fit him; they were old objects, bordering on antiques. The sorts of items she'd seen time and again in rental properties in and around McCall time and time again that were meant to give the places a taste of that rustic aesthetic.

Metal cowboy boots with spurs hanging from horseshoes, generic paintings of skies, mountain meadows, snowy woods, and reflective lakes—she'd seen their like a hundred times, and a few of Mason's things had that same feel.

But there were some items that seemed to reflect his personality. The chest-high carved bear in the living room corner, in particular, reminded her of him. Yeah, she'd seen such bears on people's porches and front yards pretty often, but it said something to her that his was inside. It was in the heart of the home. A big, gentle looking creature that was capable of immense strength and savagery when necessary in defense of its family.

The scene from last night—Mason lifting Mr. Jensen clear off the ground with one hand—came to mind. She knew it was probably wrong to smile, but she didn't stop herself.

He stood up for me.

That was already far more than she could ever have said of her ex. James had preferred to let things go, to brush aside her issues and avoid any sort of confrontation on her behalf, even if it meant ignoring slurs that had been thrown her way. Of course, his nonconfrontational nature seemed to vanish whenever he'd been mad at Gabriela.

When Gabby reached the bookshelf, which was filled with well used paperback books, she smiled. Were they Mason's, or had they, too, come with the house? Had he read them? She ran the duster along the shelf and over the tops of the books, reading the titles as she went.

There were nonfiction books on countless subjects. Astronomy, philosophy, various historical eras, even a couple science textbooks. She spotted a few self-help books interspersed here and there, and she smirked at one that was titled *How to Approach a Woman.*

The nonfiction books were outnumbered by fiction of seemingly every genre—mystery, horror, fantasy and science fiction, literary classics, westerns. But to Gabriela's surprise, the majority of those books were romances. There were historicals, contemporaries, fantasies, and paranormals, most of which were all uniform in size. But there were a few that stood taller and appeared newer than the rest, though they'd still clearly been well read.

She drew one off the shelf and turned the cover toward her. Upon it was a sexy, bare-chested man covered in stripes with a woman peering out from behind him, her hand poised precariously close to his groin. The title read, *Have Tail, Will Travel.*

Did that mean the man had a tail?

Gabby returned the book to the shelf, tucking the title away in her memory for later, and moved her hand to the thicker book next to it called *The Bridal Hunt.* The cover featured a gasping woman and a...a white-furred man behind her? Gabriela turned the book to read the back. Her brows nearly shot to her hairline. An abominable snow beastie? As the love interest?

"I will be coming back to *you* later," she said, intrigued, as she put the book back in its place.

Alien and monster romances? She hadn't known such things existed! Perhaps it was time for her to take up reading again.

There was another book sitting on the shelf, lying on its back with a bookmark sticking out of it. *Prisoner of My Desire.* Gabriela grinned.

My mountain man reads romance.

Something about that was utterly endearing, all the more so because it was something she'd discovered about the man who wanted to claim her.

Gabriela glanced at the clock. Only thirty minutes had passed since Mason left. Anxiousness fluttered in her stomach as she turned her face toward the front window, as though that could somehow make his truck appear in the driveway.

He said a couple hours, Gabby. He's not coming back yet.

Still...she wanted him here. She wanted to watch him interact with her daughter, wanted to talk with him, touch him, be touched *by* him.

"Slow down, Gabby..." she muttered, and set about dusting the rest of the living room.

Once that was done, and all the wood surfaces had been polished to a shine, she checked one of the closed doors off the short hallway and discovered a mostly empty bedroom. There were only a couple old pieces of furniture within, including a vintage end table—the kind that had a little raised section on the back. Four cardboard boxes were stacked in the corner, the flaps open on one of them. Gabriela peered inside to find more books.

Maybe Mason wouldn't accept money as repayment, but whenever she was able to afford it, Gabby guessed another bookcase or two would make a great gift for him.

She dusted the room—mainly the blinds—and, with little else to do in there, moved on to the master bedroom.

She cleaned the master bathroom first and was about to unpack the toiletries they'd purchased, but she decided it was better to hold off on that. There was a chance Mason would have Gabriela and Ana use the guest bathroom so he could have his own space again; she didn't want to presume anything in that regard.

Returning to the bedroom, she paused and surveyed her surroundings. Gabby hadn't really had a good look at the room last night. She'd been exhausted both physically and mentally and had registered little but Mason's kindness and thoughtfulness. Her eyes dipped to the foot of the bed, where he'd sat her down, removed her socks, and massaged warmth into her feet with those big, confident, clever hands of his.

Despite her weariness and the fact that Mason had

changed the bedding before he and Ana went to sleep, she swore she'd smelled hints of him beneath the scent of detergent when she had lain down.

You're in here for a reason, Gabriela, and it's not to get all hot and bothered.

Steeling herself, she set about her task, trying to think of this as she would a client's bedroom. She dusted, cleaned the headboard, picked up the few articles of clothing on the floor and tossed them into the hamper, and made the bed. Yet she couldn't help herself; she *had* to look at his things.

Not that there was much. Just like the rest of Mason's home, there was little in the bedroom that seemed to represent the man himself. There was a small piece of paper atop his dresser with a pencil that had been worn down to a two-inch-long stub. A list had been written on that paper in compact, slightly uneven letters, all caps. *BOOKS TO LOOK FOR.* Each title was written on its own line, accompanied by what must've been the last names of the authors.

But the bottom of the paper was separated by a firm pencil line, beneath which was printed one word—*TERMINATOR.* She leaned closer to the paper, narrowing her eyes slightly. There were still tiny flecks of graphite on the paper around the letters; they were recently written.

She smirked. Ana must've mentioned that movie to Mason this morning. God, she'd felt like such a terrible mother when she'd let Ana watch it a year ago and had found out the girl had told all her friends at school the next day. What had the other mothers thought of Gabby?

Fortunately, she'd quickly realized she didn't give a damn what the other mothers thought. If her daughter loved The Terminator, good for her. Sarah Connor was probably a better role model than some of the princesses in the movies they watched.

Gabriela cleared away the graphite dust and continued cleaning—though by now far more of her attention was turned toward studying Mason's room.

When she spotted the little bears on the nightstand, she probably shouldn't have thought much of them. They were the kinds of knickknacks that were popular in the region, especially in vacation homes and rentals, the kinds of things that tourists bought at the giftshops in town. And she knew she was probably reading into them too much, but...

There were three carved bears, black with brown snouts. A big bear, a little bear, and a medium bear. The two smaller figures were close to one another, but the big one was several inches away from the others—and it was turned very slightly toward them.

Frowning, Gabriela stared at those bears. She stared at them for much too long, but something about them—that bit of extra space, the way the big bear seemed to be looking at the others—nagged at her. What had Mason said earlier?

I have watched over you and Ana since I moved into my house.

Loneliness. Just as she'd realized in hindsight that Mason had always looked at her with desire, she realized now that he'd always carried a faint air of loneliness. He wasn't the mopey sort who made a show of it, didn't seem the kind of man who complained about it or grew angry because of it, but she knew he'd harbored it all along.

Gabby's heart ached for him. She could've easily taken his confession as a red flag, but she didn't see it that way. She recognized his loneliness for what it was—because she felt it too. And it wasn't like she hadn't been checking him out from afar at every opportunity.

Mason's words, combined with his actions, proved that he'd only been looking out for Gabriela and her daughter.

If it weren't for Mason, I would have lost Ana.

Her chest constricted further, making it a little harder to breath, and her eyes stung with the threat of tears. She placed her hand over her heart, willing it to ease as she took in several deep, calming breaths.

Ana is here. She is fine.

Gabriela slowly exhaled. Once she'd pulled herself together, she looked back down at those bears. Placing her hand behind the big bear, she slid it toward the smaller two, making their little family unit whole. She smiled.

After she'd finished cleaning, she grabbed the hamper and carried it out of the bedroom. She peeked in on her daughter, who'd lain down on her side and had the blanket drawn up to her chin. Ana giggled at something on the TV.

See, Gabby? Ana is totally fine.

It didn't take long for Gabriela to find the laundry room, which was located past the kitchen. Mason's laundry room was larger than the one she'd had. The cubby shelves lining one wall were filled with tools, extra lightbulbs, flashlights, extension cords, and other random items. There was even a red fire extinguisher, the sight of which produced a pang in Gabriela's chest.

She shoved aside that flare of emotion; by the time she'd realized what was happening in her home, it had been much too late for a fire extinguisher to have done any good.

Gabby hefted the hamper and started transferring clothing into the washer, picking out the whites to wash separately. When she pulled one of Mason's shirts out of the hamper, she paused. For a few moments, Gabriela worried her lower lip, struggling with a new urge she'd never anticipated.

She lost that struggle. Lifting Mason's shirt to her nose, she closed her eyes and breathed in his earth, pine, and spice scent.

"Oh, my God," she groaned softly, burying her face in the

fabric to muffle her voice. She inhaled Mason's scent again, deeper this time. How the hell did the man smell so damn *good*? Her pussy clenched. His scent was like an aphrodisiac, making her feel warm and aroused, fogging her mind with lust.

Ana's sudden laughter coming from the living room snapped Gabriela out of it. Feeling like a teenager who'd been caught doing something naughty, she quickly threw the shirt into the washer. Her face burned with mortification.

She'd never done anything like that before. Not even with James's clothing.

What I'm starting to feel for Mason is nothing like what I felt with James.

This was just so...powerful.

Before she could give in to the temptation to steal his shirt out of the washer again, Gabby turned back to the hamper and finished sorting the clothing, leaving all the whites for the next load. She added detergent to the washer and closed the lid a bit harder than she'd intended, startling herself with the metallic bang.

She stood with her hand on the washer's lid long enough to catch her breath, long enough for a little of the heat to fade from her cheeks. Then she started the washing machine and hurriedly retreated from the laundry room.

Gabriela busied herself by cleaning the kitchen, deciding a thorough deep-cleaning was in order—not because his kitchen was filthy, but because she needed the distraction. If she was getting all worked up just doing some laundry for him, how was she supposed to control herself when the man was actually standing in front of her, and his scent was coming directly from his skin? When his unique, intense eyes were staring down at her...

By the time she was done with the kitchen, only a little over an hour had passed since she'd begun cleaning the house. And it was too early yet to start preparing dinner. She'd give herself thirty minutes to relax, maybe to check her e-mail on his laptop and see if her parents had replied yet, and hopefully by then Mason would be on his way back.

Gabriela walked to the sofa, smiled at Ana, and crawled onto the cushions, maneuvering so she was behind her daughter. Ana scooted forward, allowing Gabriela more room to lie down behind her.

After drawing the blanket over the both of them, Gabby wrapped her arm around Ana and hugged her close. "I love you."

Ana settled her hand over hers. "Love you, too, Mom."

ELEVEN

As Broxen shut off the truck's engine, he lifted his eyes to glance across the road. It was a natural thing to do by now, a habit developed over the last year—any chance at a glimpse of Gabriela was worth taking.

But, of course, Gabriela wasn't over there. Broxen's gaze fell only upon the charred remains of her home, which were accompanied by the blackened car still in the driveway. Something about the fast-fading daylight made those ruins seem even lonelier and more sorrowful.

With a grunt, he opened the truck door and stepped out of the vehicle.

Though his circumstances had been quite different from what Gabriela and Ana were facing now, he knew well what it was like to suddenly lose a home, to look back on a place that was once safe and comfortable and see nowhere to go. To feel utterly, impossibly alone.

He didn't intend to let his females go through that.

Broxen walked around to the back of the truck and lowered the tailgate. As his eyes swept over the objects in the truck bed, his excitement brushed aside any lingering traces of sorrow. He hoped these things would bring smiles to his females' faces. He hoped this surprise would ease Gabriela and Ana's worries a little more, that it would help them settle in.

He hoped this would help his females understand that, though they'd lost their old home, they had a new one here with him.

Reaching forward, he lifted the headboard and footboard, standing them up on their feet, pressed together. He slid them out of the truck and leaned them against his leg. Then he dragged the bundle of wooden slats closer, pairing them with the two siderails. He took the boards in one hand and the rest under his other arm, carrying them to the front door.

He set down the boards briefly to unlock the door. Once it was open wide, he walked inside, and was hit by a wave of pleasantly warm air that was laden with even more pleasant smells. Gabriela's scent was in the mix, strong enough that it nearly made him groan, but there was something else even stronger.

There was chicken in that scent, he could tell that much, but there was so much more layered with it that he couldn't identify the rest. Whatever it was, it smelled amazing. His stomach growled in sudden hunger.

Stepping farther into the house, Broxen looked toward the kitchen.

A head popped up in the living room. Ana was seated on the floor at the coffee table, drawing on a piece of paper. Her face lit up with a big smile. "Mom! Mason's home!"

Gabriela, who was standing in front of the stove stirring something in a large pot, turned to look at him. "Dinner should be done soon." She gave him a shy smile. "I...hope you don't mind?"

Something inside Broxen softened at that, and the tip of his tail curled against his calf. He couldn't recall a single time that he'd come home to find freshly prepared food waiting for him. Not on Earth, obviously, but not back on Turata, either. This wasn't anything he'd asked for, wasn't anything he'd expected, but it only made him appreciate his female even more.

"No," he said. "Smells good."

That smile of hers widened, flashing her white teeth and making those dimples on her cheeks deepen before she dropped her gaze to the objects he was carrying. "What's that?"

"A bed."

"Oh." She tucked her hair behind her ear. "Sorry, didn't mean to hold you up. It looks heavy."

And you look beautiful, Gabriela.

"It's not that bad. Don't have to go far, either."

She nodded and turned back toward the stove.

Though he would've been happy to linger there, just watching her—or to walk up behind her, grasp her by the hips, and tug her ass back against his aching groin—there was more in the truck that needed to be brought inside, and he had work to do after that. Having smelled Gabriela's cooking, he had incentive to get everything done as quickly as possible. Broxen continued forward, carrying the disassembled bedframe into the spare bedroom.

He stood the boards against the wall and laid the slats on the floor next to the siderails. As he stood up, he drew in a deep breath and paused.

Broxen hadn't known what to do with this room when he moved into the house. He didn't have much in the way of belongings, didn't need an office or a game room or whatever other rooms humans often had. Until now, this had been slowly becoming a book storage room, and he'd considered installing bookshelves all around the walls and just turning it into a little library at some point. The boxes of books in the corner had been the main source of the smell in this room—that particular scent, the blend of paper and glue that had grown on him so much during his time here.

But there was a trace of Gabriela's scent in here now. Broxen took in a second deep, appreciative breath, and noticed another out of place smell.

It was...lemony. That artificial sort of lemon, though, the kind that could become overwhelming in greater concentration. It took him a few seconds to recall that he had cleaner under the kitchen sink with that scent—the wood polish.

With a deep, thoughtful hum, he stepped out of the room, only to pause again when he glanced through the open door of his bedroom. The bed had been neatly made, and the floor had been picked up. He moved into the doorway and glanced around. The hamper was missing, and the wood surfaces of the dresser, nightstand, and headboard gleamed in the light cast through the blinds by the setting sun.

None of that was as impactful as what most people would've considered the smallest change. Broxen's gaze fixed on the three bear figurines atop the nightstand, the largest of which had been shifted so it was right alongside the other two.

She'd probably just bumped that figurine while she was cleaning. It had probably been an accident.

But Broxen knew, somehow, that this had been no accident.

Ah, female...

He grinned and eased out of the room. Again, he found himself battling the desire to go to Gabriela, but this time, that desire was even more primal. It was almost animalistic. It was a pull he'd never felt toward another female in his lifetime.

He wanted to rut.

No, he didn't just want to rut Gabriela, he wanted to mark her with his scent, with his bite, wanted to lay his claim on her fully and forever.

Clenching his hands tight enough to feel the prick of his claws against his palms, he forced himself back outside.

Focus, Broxen. You don't want to scare her.

He hauled everything else into the house in a few quick trips—a tall white dresser with a few scratches and some old, colorful stickers on the upper drawers, a box spring and a brand-new full mattress, one of those wide-drawered plastic storage bins, a new pink bedding set, two pillows, and a plain cardboard box that contained a few things to hopefully help Ana feel more at home. After retrieving a few hand tools from the laundry room, he returned to the spare bedroom.

He had just finished attaching the siderails to the headboard and footboard when Gabriela stepped into the room and gently closed the door behind her. Broxen sat back on his heels as he looked up at her.

She swept her gaze over the bed he was assembling, wringing her hands nervously in front of her. "Is this room for me and Ana to stay in?"

"No. Just Ana."

"Oh. I can share the bed with her, that way you can have your room back so you're not—"

"You'll sleep in my bed. With me."

Her eyes widened. "With...you?"

Broxen nodded and turned back to his work, laying a slat in place and plucking up the screwdriver and a pair of screws. "Yes."

She stood there, silently watching him, and though that shouldn't have been a distraction, it was. *She* was.

He'd always prided himself on his ability to remain calm and collected. It had been a big part of his job. But her scent and nearness were driving him mad, making it difficult to focus. All he wanted to do was reach out, drag her beneath him, and tear off all her clothes to bare her luscious body to him. What did she look like beneath her clothing? Were her nipples pink or dark? Did she have hair between her thighs, or was she bare? Did she have any unique markings upon her flesh? He hadn't seen any on her limbs when she'd worn more revealing clothes in the summer, but that didn't mean there weren't any hidden elsewhere.

"Were you serious about what you said earlier?" Gabriela asked, her voice breaking through his imaginings.

He slid a screw into one of the predrilled holes and tightened it down. "About what?"

"About...wanting me."

Broxen froze. Did his female still question his intentions? He raised his head and met her gaze. Her dark, entrancing eyes were filled with uncertainty.

"I want you, female."

"If this..." She took in a deep breath, dropped her hands, and straightened her back. "If this is about sex, I can't do that. I can't do that to Ana. I...I won't sell my body for a bed or food or a roof. I'll find another way, just like I always have."

Broxen gritted his teeth, dropped the screwdriver and the screw, forgetting them the moment they were no longer in his hands, and stood up. He held Gabriela's gaze as he stalked toward her.

She sucked in a sharp breath and backed away from him until her back bumped the door, her eyes wide but steady.

Bracing his arms on the door to either side of her, Broxen bent forward, dipping his head until his lips were within a couple inches of her ear. Gabriela's soft, sweet scent struck him anew, stronger than ever. More arousing than ever.

"I long to rut you, female," he growled. "I won't lie about that. But I want all of you. Not just your body, but your heart, your mind, your everything. I want a *mate*."

She shivered, lips parting, and lowered her gaze.

Broxen caught her chin, tilting her face toward his. "You are not homeless, Gabriela. You have a home. Here, with me."

"A...mate?"

Without realizing what he was doing, he dropped his eyes to her mouth and grazed her bottom lip with his claw. He was so tempted to close the distance between them, to capture her mouth with his, to kiss her, to know her taste. He brushed her hair away from her neck with his other hand and stroked the backs of his fingers over the bared flesh there—where she would one day bear his mark. "I will be your mate. Your protector."

Gabriela's breath quickened, and her dark eyes smoldered with passionate embers. She tentatively reached up and pressed her palm against his chest. She swallowed thickly. "Dinner...is almost done."

The corner of Broxen's mouth quirked. His strong female was skittish, but he could feel the desire radiating from her. He could *smell* it.

Soon.

He caressed her chin before dropping his hands, settling one upon her lower back. That word, *soon*, was so short and simple, but it felt impossibly larger, felt like an eternity. He ached with want for this female; his cock was hard and throbbing against his thigh, held in check only by the denim of his jeans, and his tail was coiled around his leg so tightly that his foot was likely to go numb before long.

But he forced himself to step away from the bedroom door, guiding Gabriela along with him. Once she was clear, he reached forward and opened the door, leaving it wide.

"I'm almost done, too," he said. It was a struggle not to clench his teeth against his overwhelming needs, to maintain his composure despite the torture of holding himself back.

"Okay," she said a little breathlessly as she drew away from him. She bumped into the doorframe, which startled her, but then she laughed. "I...guess I should watch where I'm walking, huh?"

Broxen chuckled, and though he didn't allow his gaze to drop, he couldn't help but notice her shapely ass as she turned and slipped out of the room. His internal struggle only intensified. Following her would've been so damned easy.

But his work wasn't done—and he was hungry. He didn't plan on being late for the meal she'd been cooking.

He shifted all his focus to the bed, quickly installing the remaining slats before putting the box spring and mattress in place. Getting the fitted sheet on properly was a struggle; he had to take it off and redo it because he'd apparently misjudged which sides were shorter than the others. But once it was in place, it was easy to drape the top sheet and the matching pink comforter over the bed. He stuffed the pillows into the pillow-cases and placed them against the headboard.

Broxen took a step back to survey his work. Gabriela had already demonstrated that she could make a bed far more neatly than he could, but what was that human saying?

It's the thought that counts?

"Not done," he muttered, grabbing the end table that had been sitting in here, unused, for months. He placed it beside the bed. The table's dark wood and styling wasn't quite a match for the bed, but that didn't matter. If he'd made the right choice, Ana would only care about what was *on* the table, not the table itself.

Opening the box he'd brought back from the thrift store, he removed the item that had very likely been the best find of the day—a lamp with a shimmery, pearlescent white lamp shade and a glittery pink unicorn as its base.

Ana had mentioned her love of unicorns several times in the year that he'd known her—including during their conversation this morning. When he'd seen this lamp at the thrift store, he'd known that he had to get it for her.

He placed it on the little table next to the bed and bent down to plug it in.

"Mason?"

He looked back to see Ana lean into the open doorway.

"Mom said—" She gasped, her eyes rounding as she looked at the bed and the lamp. "Is that for me?"

Following her gaze with his own, Broxen straightened. "All yours."

Silence reigned for a few heartbeats. Then a cry escaped Ana, and her eyes, filling with tears, met Broxen's. She made a high-pitched whine; as alarming as her tears were, that sound set Broxen on alert.

He turned toward her. "Ana?"

Her features crumpled, and she darted into the room, rounding the bed to slam her little body against him. She hugged him around his waist and cried.

All Broxen could do was stand there in stunned silence, staring down at the little kit without a clue as to what was happening. When he finally broke his stupor, he took hold of her wrists and gently pried her arms apart so he could drop down to a knee, bringing himself closer to her eye level.

"Ana, what's wrong? Did I...did I do this wrong?"

She looked at him, lashes spiked, cheeks wet with tears, and her shoulders and chest heaving with ragged, hiccupping breaths. "N-no, you d-didn't."

Gabriela appeared in the doorway, a hand braced on the frame. Her brows were creased in worry. "Ana?"

Ana looked at her mom then back to Broxen. He was growing quite concerned; her breathing wasn't normal, and she looked like she'd spilled enough tears to dehydrate herself.

The kit tugged her hands free and wrapped her arms

around his neck in another embrace. She sniffled. "Thank y-you."

Gratitude? Ana's hysterical crying had been in...gratitude?

He didn't understand these humans at all.

Or...perhaps he did.

She lost everything. And I...I've given her something back.

Broxen wrapped his arms around Ana, returning the hug. Her grip on him only strengthened.

"I wish you were my dad," she whispered.

His brow knitted, and something tightened in his chest. He shifted a hand up to cup the back of her head. As much as her tears had alarmed him, there was a warm feeling inside him, a *good* feeling. He couldn't change what had happened in his females' lives. He couldn't change their pasts any more than he could his own, couldn't protect them from the hurts they'd already suffered.

But he could do everything possible to protect them now—and forever after.

Broxen glanced at Gabriela. She remained in the doorway, her hands covering her mouth, tears brimming in her eyes.

"You like it?" Broxen asked, combing his claws gently through Ana's hair, hoping to soothe her.

"I love it," Ana said.

"Good. Then no more tears."

She laughed. "Okay."

"Now what was it you came to tell me?"

Ana finally loosened her arms and drew back. There was a smile on her face. "Mom said dinner was ready."

"Perfect timing," he replied, smiling back at her. He flicked his gaze to Gabriela again, and his smile widened further. "Been hard not to go into the kitchen and steal a taste. I'm starving."

Gabriela laughed softly and wiped her cheeks with the

backs of her hands. "Wash your hands. Both of you. I'll get the table set."

She left them, and Ana took hold of his hand, leading him out of the room and into the bathroom. Ana stood patiently as he removed the adhesive bandages from her palm, revealing only healthy skin beneath. They shared a grin. When Ana was done washing her hands, Broxen sent her off to see if Gabriela needed help before stepping to the sink himself. As he scrubbed his hands clean, he couldn't help but wonder at what he was feeling.

Contentment? Completion? Wasn't it too soon to feel that way? Gabriela and Ana had been here for a day, and nothing was certain.

I'm certain. They are mine. My family.

Yet there was a shadow hanging over those good feelings, one he'd thought about but hadn't yet decided how to handle. This secret of his—the secret that had kept him alive to this point, the secret that had allowed him a chance at making a new life, a chance at having Gabriela.

He turned off the water and stared at himself in the mirror as he dried his hands. In his mind's eye, he could see himself as he actually appeared. Red skin, black horns, a long tail. Claws and fangs, purple irises in pools of black. But the face in the mirror was a stranger. A human—or, worse, an impostor. Was this...was it a betrayal? Was he betraying Gabriela by hiding the truth?

Soon. I'll tell her...show her...soon. She doesn't need any more surprises now. I'll wait until the time is right.

All he could do was hope that he wasn't helping his females establish a new normal only to shatter it again when he revealed himself. All he could do was hope that Gabriela came to trust him and care for him enough to accept what he was.

He exited the bathroom and joined them at the dining

table, where Ana and Gabriela were already seated. There were three plates of steaming food set out—one each in front of the females, and another in front of an empty chair. The food's aroma was even stronger now than when he'd come home, and his stomach growled as he breathed it in.

The females smiled at him as he took his seat. Their food was untouched, and their forks still lay beside their plates. He glanced down. Chicken thighs and potatoes in some sort of golden sauce with little bits of green cilantro sprinkled in it, accompanied by white rice and wedges of avocado.

Broxen met Gabriela's gaze. "What is this?"

"*Sudado de pollo*," she replied, her smile taking on a wistfulness he'd not seen before. "My *abuelita* used to cook it for my mom when she was a girl, and my mother taught me to make it. It's like...Colombian chicken stew."

"It's *good*," Ana chimed in. "Can we eat now?"

Gabriela chuckled. "Yes, we can eat now."

They all dug in eagerly. Broxen sat back and groaned as he chewed his first bite. It had been a long while since he'd had a home-cooked meal—if he could really consider the simple foods he'd prepared for himself in the past *meals*—and this put everything else to shame. It was unlike anything he'd tasted yet, a blend of spices and flavors he'd never encountered, and it was delicious.

Of course, it was even more enjoyable considering Gabriela had made it for him.

Her *sudado de pollo* was so good that Broxen didn't even realize how fast he was shoveling it into his mouth until his plate was almost clean except for the bones—and he knew it couldn't have been more than a couple minutes since he'd started eating.

Gabriela grinned. "I take it you liked it?"

He paused with the final bite in his mouth, shifted the food aside, and asked, "Is there more?"

"Don't talk with food in your mouth," Ana chided.

Broxen snapped his mouth shut, eyebrows rising as he glanced at the kit.

"Mom says it's rude." She looked at her mother. "Right?"

Gabriela was covering her mouth with a hand as she laughed. "Yes. And yes, there's more."

Swallowing his food, Broxen offered a quick sorry before standing up and bringing his plate to the kitchen for another helping.

"It's also rude to scold our host, Ana Sofia Romero," Gabriela said.

Broxen glanced back at them to see Ana duck her head and smile sheepishly.

"Oops." Ana looked at him. "Sorry, Mason."

"No problem," he said as he carried his freshly loaded plate back to the table. "I, uh...didn't have a mother to teach me that stuff. So it's good I have you to tell me now."

"Did your mom leave you like my dad left us?" Ana asked.

Broxen eased onto his chair, unsure of how he felt. His childhood had been a long time ago, and the situation had simply been what it had been. He'd done what he had to in order to overcome it. He never really thought about it much, just like he never really thought about family, or the familial bonds that could be forged between people. Just like he never thought much about the love and support some families provided.

But he couldn't help thinking about those things lately.

"My parents didn't really care what happened to me," he said. "Learned to get by on my own, and one day...I left. And it was hard, for a long, long time. Wish I had a mom like yours."

"My mom's the best." Ana grinned mischievously. "I can share her with you."

Gabriela made a choking sound as she drank her water. She quickly set the glass down and turned her head, coughing.

Broxen glanced between the two females, smirking. "Not exactly looking for a mother right now."

"How about a wi—"

"Ana," Gabriela intoned, her cheeks flushed. "Eat your dinner before it gets cold."

Broxen chuckled, but when he shifted his gaze to Gabriela, his amusement faded. He knew exactly what Ana had been saying, and he was sure the clever kit knew exactly what she was doing.

I wish you were my dad.

He did, too.

This right here, this dinner...somehow, it was one of the best moments of his life. This simple gathering, sharing a meal and conversation, this outshone almost everything else he'd ever experienced. He didn't care if it was greedy; he wanted more of this.

He wanted this forever—with Gabriela and Ana.

TWELVE

"You brushed your teeth?" Gabriela asked as Ana hopped onto her new bed.

Gabby still couldn't quite believe what she'd seen when she'd stepped in this room a few hours ago. She'd watched Mason bring the bedframe inside, but she'd returned her attention to dinner as he hauled in everything else. To say he'd gone above and beyond was an understatement.

The pink bedding, the dresser with its cartoon stickers, the unicorn lamp, the decorations he'd hung on the walls after dinner—all of it had been to help Ana feel more at home. To give her something when she had nothing left. And each of those items made the rest seem even more thoughtful, even more meaningful, especially considering that he didn't have to do anything at all. He had no obligation to Gabriela and her daughter.

What he'd done...it was stunning, and it was heartwarming, and amazing.

But what had really floored Gabriela was Ana's gut-wrenching sobs as the girl embraced Mason—and her whispered words to him.

I wish you were my dad.

Those words had repeated in Gabby's mind over and over since she'd heard them, and every time she looked at Mason, all she could see was how wonderful a father and husband he'd be. He was thoughtful, kind, and compassionate, and he genuinely cared about Ana. Gabriela had seen it in his every small act over the last year.

She'd be stupid to let him slip through her fingers.

I long to rut you, female. I won't lie about that. But I want all of you. Not just your body, but your heart, your mind, your everything. I want a mate.

Her stomach was still in knots from what he'd said to her. And tonight...

"Moooooom," Ana whined.

Gabriela jerked, turning her face toward her daughter, who was now lying down. "Sorry. Did you say you brushed your teeth?"

"Yep. See?" She drew her lips back and bared her teeth.

Gabriela leaned closer to inspect them. "Hmm... I think I see something."

"What?"

"I see...a tickle monster!"

Ana squealed with laughter, wiggling and squirming as Gabby tickled her sides.

"Stop! Stop! No more!" Ana cried. "I'm going to pee!"

Gabriela stopped immediately. She arched her brow at her panting daughter. "Did you go to the bathroom before bed?"

"Yes, I did."

"Then you won't pee." Gabriela resumed her tickling.

"Mason, help! Mom's going to kill me!"

"Sorry," he called from the kitchen, "don't think I'm supposed to get between a mother and her kit."

"Noooooo! Mooooom!"

Gabriela laughed. "Okay, okay. I'm not supposed to rile you up before bed anyway."

Ana turned her head, closed her eyes, and dangled her tongue out the side of her mouth.

"Oh, no!" Gabriela cupped Ana's cheeks. "I guess I'll have to give her mouth-to-mouth."

Ana's eyes snapped open and she pulled away. "Ew! No way."

Gabby smiled. "I do want a goodnight kiss, though."

"*That's* okay." Ana spread her arms open, and Gabriela leaned in, pressing a kiss to her forehead.

"Love you, baby."

"Love you, too."

Gabriela reached across the bed and turned off the unicorn lamp, leaving the room dark but for the light shining in from the hallway.

"Have a good night," she said as she stood up.

"Goodnight, Mom." Ana drew in a deep breath. "Good night, Mason!"

Mason leaned in through the bedroom doorway. He was wearing a pair of gray sweatpants and a tank top that stretched across his broad chest, showing off his bare, muscular arms, and his long black hair hung loose around his shoulders. "Night, Ana."

Ana grinned up at him.

Gabriela met Mason's gaze. Her heart quickened, and her belly fluttered. They were going to sleep together. It had been years since Gabriela had slept with anyone other than Ana. And to be lying next to Mason, lying together in the dark...

And based on the heat in his eyes, she knew he was thinking the same things.

The house was cleaned up, the laundry was done, they had already showered, put on their pajamas, and brushed their teeth. There was nothing else to do. There'd be no more delaying the inevitable.

They were going to bed together.

"Come, Gabriela," he commanded softly, holding his hand out.

She raised her hand, hesitated for a moment, then placed it within his. He closed his fingers around hers and tugged her toward him. Gabby followed, closing Ana's door on her way out.

He closed the door once they were inside his bedroom and drew her close. She flattened her palms on his chest, feeling the brush of his pelvis against her belly. His erection was unmistakable.

Capturing her face between his hands, Mason bent down and locked his violet eyes with hers as he stroked her cheeks with his thumbs. His hands were so big—*he* was so big—that she felt tiny in comparison. There was no denying the strength in his fingers or the roughness of his palms, yet his touch remained gentle, remained soothing, as he searched her gaze.

"You don't need to be frightened of me, Gabriela."

"I'm not scared of you, Mason. It's just..." She took in a deep, fortifying breath, and slowly released it. "I...I haven't been with a man since I was pregnant with Ana."

His nostrils flared, his body tensed, and his fingers flexed, making his fingernails—which felt oddly long and sharp—dig lightly into her skin. That heat in his eyes took on a new sheen, becoming tantalizingly possessive. He closed his eyes and leaned his head down slowly, inhaling deeply through his nose. His chest rumbled; the sound was a cross between a purr and a growl, and its vibrations went straight to Gabby's core, making her pussy clench and her clit pulse.

Mason opened his eyes and tucked her hair behind her ear, which he traced with a finger. "Nothing will happen, Gabriela. We're just going to sleep. I want you to feel comfortable with me. To feel safe."

"I *do* feel safe with you. I just thought... After what you said earlier, about wanting me as your...mate..."

"I want you, female. Even now, smelling you, touching you, it's hard to restrain myself. But in this, it will be when you decide."

So much of the tension in Gabriela's body vanished in an instant. Mason was giving her the choice. He wasn't pushing her, forcing her, coercing her. He was letting her choose when she was ready to be with him.

How many times had James guilted her into sex? How many times had he made her feel like refusing meant she didn't care for him, or that she somehow owed it to him, that she was being a shitty girlfriend if she denied his desires?

Gabriela could fall in love with Mason so easily. Hell, she might have been falling for him already. Every time she watched him interact with Ana, every time she saw how great a dad he could be, her panties melted. And hadn't she waited long enough for someone like him to come into her life? Why wait longer? Why fight it, especially when he'd stated his intentions so boldly and clearly? This wasn't the time to deny an opportunity.

Yet as much as her body craved him—as much as she craved him—she didn't need to rush this. She could see where it would lead, and if the time came, if it felt right...she wouldn't resist it.

And she had a feeling that the right time would come sooner than expected.

She smiled and reached up, meaning to sweep Mason's hair

back from his face, but he gently caught her hand before it could go higher.

He brought her hand to his mouth, and, without breaking eye contact, brushed his lips over her palm. Gabby's breath hitched as a thrill rushed through her, making skin pebble and her nipples taut. Heat flooded her between her legs.

"Get in bed, Gabriela," he said, his voice rough and husky, before releasing her hand and stepping aside.

She caught her lower lip between her teeth. Her eyes lingered on him as she stepped forward, somehow keeping steady despite the overwhelming anticipation fluttering in her stomach. She walked around to the other side of the bed, drew down the covers, and climbed on.

Gabriela lifted her gaze to Mason again just as he flicked off the lights. The room was plunged into darkness—but for an instant, she swore she could see two faintly glowing violet orbs where his eyes had been. When she blinked, those orbs were gone.

Her eyes were slow to adjust to the dark, but she heard Mason make his way to the other side of the bed, and she heard a swish of cloth that sounded like clothing being removed. The bed creaked softly as he settled onto it; she felt his movement through the mattress.

After a few seconds, he seemed to settle. Able to discern little more than deeper shadows amidst the darkness, Gabriela turned to lie on her side, facing a wall she could not see. The bed seemed far larger than it had last night—and, though he was so close, far emptier. It couldn't have been more than a couple feet separating her from Mason, but it felt like an immense rift had been torn open between them, and she longed for it to be closed.

As though reading her thoughts, Mason shifted closer to

her. Something tightened low in her belly, pouring a fresh wave of heat into her core.

With a growl, Mason wrapped an arm around her, his hand covering her stomach, and drew her back against his chest—his now very *naked* chest. She felt his face against her hair, felt his breath against her scalp. His body was big and hard and warm, and she fit so perfectly spooned against him, felt so immediately...comfortable and safe, just like he said he'd wanted.

But safety and comfort weren't all he was making her feel. Her backside was tucked against his pelvis, and even through their pants, she couldn't mistake the long, thick hardness of his cock pressed firmly along the crease of her ass and lower back.

The ache between her legs intensified, and his hand was so close to the source of her discomfort.

No rushing? Ha! Patience be damned.

She willed him to slide his palm farther down, willed him to dip his fingers under the waistband of her pajamas, to slip those long, powerful, confident fingers into her pussy and soothe that tormenting ache.

Gabriela pulled her lips into her mouth and squeezed her eyes shut. She slipped an arm under her pillow, grasping it in her fist, while she clenched the blanket with her other hand.

She needed a distraction.

"Mason?"

"Hmm?"

Once more, his voice rumbled in his chest, vibrating against her back, making her nipples harden and throb.

That is so *not helping.*

"Could you tell me about yourself?" she asked.

Perfect! Safe subject, and she could learn more about the man who she was thinking about having a relationship with.

Who she was *most definitely* going to be in a relationship with.

Or was she already in one with him now?

They'd gone on a date, she was staying at his place—sleeping in his bed—and her daughter had her own room here. Things were certainly moving fast, and the circumstances were anything but typical, yet it all felt...right.

And Gabby really, really, *really* wanted to have sex with him.

She was absolutely with Mason.

"What do you want to know?" he murmured.

"Anything. I'd...like to get to know you. I'd like to know what your favorite food is, your favorite ice cream, if you prefer chocolate or vanilla Oreos—and just saying, vanilla is the best—what your favorite season is? Your past, where you're from, what you do for a living, and maybe what made you move here?" Realizing she was possibly delving into things he might not have wanted to talk about, she hurried to say, "You don't have to tell me. And...and I won't judge. Lord knows I've made some dumb choices in my life."

Mason grunted; the sound was oddly thoughtful. He drew her a little more firmly against him, curling his hand around her side to take a snugger hold. "That's...a lot."

"I know," she said softly. "I don't want you to feel pressured or anything."

"No, it's all right. Haven't had anyone to talk to about... anything for a long time. Maybe feels like longer than it's really been, but..." His chest swelled with a deep breath, which he released in a slow, heavy exhalation. "I want to talk to you. Want to share with you."

Gabriela smiled. "I'm listening."

"All right. Uh, well... Like I said, I left my parents. Guess I wasn't too much older than Ana. Grew up in a rough neighborhood, so had to mature fast. For too many years, I did what I had to do to survive. Not proud of any of it, but there's nothing I can do about it now."

"I'm sorry you had that kind of start in life," she said.

"Yeah. But it brought me to you eventually, right?"

His words kindled a warmth in Gabriela's chest that quickly spread up to her cheeks.

She didn't even want to think about Ana having been forced to grow up like Mason had, and even though she still knew so little about him, her heart grieved for him. How terribly alone he must have felt.

But for him to brush aside all that pain he must've carried, to act like it was worth it because it had led him to her... Wasn't that the kind of thing you only saw in movies?

"I was always big, and I was good at fighting. Wound up as a bodyguard eventually. And that was...my calling, I guess. Wasn't always protecting the best of people, but the last one became a friend. Only one I'd ever really had. We were different, more different than I can describe, but I... What is that saying? I loved him like a brother. He challenged me. Showed me there were other ways to do things. Ways I never would've come up with on my own."

He was speaking slowly, his unplaceable accent thicker and more pronounced, and he seemed to be pausing often to consider his choice of words. Gabriela knew that he hadn't lied—he had no one to talk to, and he wasn't used to speaking about these things. But he was trying, and that only endeared him to her even more.

She knew also that he was purposely omitting the details. With the way he'd so effortlessly and without any hesitation grabbed Allen Jensen and lifted him into the air, she'd guessed there'd been violence or danger in his past, and his story was only confirming that.

Yet she couldn't ignore the sorrow underlying his voice. It

was subtle, and he didn't betray much of it, but he didn't have to.

"What happened?" she asked gently.

Mason's fingers curled against her middle, and she once again felt the strange, sharp prick of his nails. "He was from a very powerful family, and he wanted to change the way they conducted their business. When he took over, there were people who didn't like it. Didn't like him. And I...I failed to do my job."

Mason didn't have to say what had happened. Gabriela knew he'd lost the only person he'd called a friend, that he likely still carried guilt over it. Her heart hurt for him. How long? How long ago had this been?

She slipped her arm beneath the covers and rested her hand over his. "I'm sorry, Mason."

He raised his thumb, brushing it along the side of her hand. "Don't be. I couldn't do it anymore once everything was over. Couldn't continue that life. I was...well compensated from my work, had more money than I knew what to do with, so I just left, went as far away as I could. Moved around a few times. Didn't feel right anywhere. And eventually I...I found myself here. Never lived anywhere like this, and I didn't know if it'd work out, but I saw you and...I knew that I'd find a way. That I had to."

Gabriela turned her head toward him, catching sight of a flicker of violet in the darkness, but that light vanished in an instant. "I'm glad you did. And that you finally got the courage to ask me out."

"Me too."

She laid her head down on the pillow but kept her eyes open. "There's just one thing bothering me, Mason..."

"What's that?"

God, she loved how his voice rumbled into her when they were lying together like this.

"You never told me. Chocolate or vanilla Oreos?"

He laughed. "Prefer the peanut butter ones."

Gabriela chuckled. "Okay. That's acceptable."

"You asked about my favorite food, too?"

She closed her eyes, simply taking comfort in his embrace, in his voice, in the rhythmic beating of his heart against her back. "Mmhmm."

"As of today, *sudado de pollo*."

Gabriela couldn't hold back a grin. "Guess some of your relationship advice books have helped, huh?"

Mason grunted. "You saw those?"

"Mmm... And the romance books."

"Ah, female"—his hand finally slid down, and his finger brushed along the waistband of her pants—"now those have taught me some things that will make you *very* happy."

Her breath hitched as that ache reignited within her core.

So much for the distraction.

"Sleep well, Gabriela," he purred; she could hear the smirk in his voice. He knew exactly what he was doing to her.

Her one consolation was that he wasn't unaffected. He'd be suffering right along with her if that giant rod throbbing against her backside was any indication. She gave her ass a little wiggle, making him groan.

"Good night, Mason."

THIRTEEN

Awareness slowly returned to Broxen as the fog of sleep dissipated. He was first caressed by a sense of contentment like he'd never felt, a sense of fullness that hummed in his chest and coursed through his languid limbs. Next, he felt the mattress under his back, cradling him with just the right blend of softness and support, and the blanket draped over his body to cocoon him in warmth.

But there was another source of warmth here that was far more satisfying—the female tucked against his side. One of his arms was curled around Gabriela, keeping her firmly in place against him, and one of hers lay on his chest. Her head was resting upon his shoulder, her breath was fanning across his skin, and she had one leg hiked up atop his.

Broxen inhaled, filling his lungs with air perfumed by Gabriela's sweet scent, and groaned. His tail, still stuck in his pants, twisted against his leg. He loved her scent, loved the feel of her, loved having her here, with him. This was where she belonged.

My mate.

For all the good, there was one source of discomfort that couldn't be ignored—his cock. It had been erect and aching when he'd climbed into bed with Gabriela last night, and its status hadn't changed. Clenching his jaw, he grasped the bedding in his free hand, squeezing tight as he struggled to resist the urge to take hold of his shaft.

Gabriela stirred, emitting a soft moan that made his cock twitch, and somehow, harden further. Seed seeped from its tip. Broxen groaned again.

She sighed and stretched, straightening her leg along his, pressing her soft breasts against his side, and smoothing her palm down his chest and over the muscles of his abdomen. Broxen's breath hitched, and his whole body tensed.

Tilting her head back, she looked up at him with sleepy, half-lidded eyes, and her lips stretched into a smile. "Good morning."

"Morning," he rasped through his teeth. He longed for her hand to trek lower, to find the source of his need and tend to it.

But that hand stilled low on his belly just as her fingers grazed the waistband of his sweatpants.

Gabriela gasped and jerked away from him, putting a distance between their bodies that might as well have been a canyon and leaving his side cold. "I'm so sorry!"

Growling, Broxen rolled over, hooked a hand around her hip, and dragged her beneath him. He shifted his body upon her, curling his fingers around the backs of her thighs and drawing her knees up on either side of him. He bent low so his face was inches from hers. His long hair fell around them.

"*Never* apologize for touching me, female."

She stared up at him with wide, dark eyes. Her hands lay on the mattress beside her head, fingers slightly bent, and her chest rose and fell with her rapid breaths. Broxen's gaze settled on her breasts, where her budded nipples were visible through the thin fabric of her shirt, teasing him, tempting him.

Only then did he realize the position they were in—and that his cock was pressed along her slit.

He was poised as though to rut her.

Broxen looked down at where they their most intimate parts were in contact and gritted his teeth. Thin layers of cloth, each a mere fraction of a centimeter thick, were all that separated their bodies. The restraint it took to keep from bucking his hips was immense.

"Mason..."

He took in a deep breath—one that was fragranced with her desire—and dragged his eyes back up to meet hers. There was still surprise in Gabriela's gaze, but there was fire in it, too. There was yearning.

His jaw tightened further as a new instinct flared within him. He bent down, lowering his face to where her neck and shoulder met, and drew in her scent again. The tip of his nose brushed her soft skin, and she shivered. Broxen's gums ached, and his fangs itched at their bases, threatening to elongate.

He needed to bite her. He needed to mark her, to make his claim known to all. It was a primal drive, unfamiliar but powerful, something ancient.

Gabriela slid her hands around his sides and undulated her hips, causing herself and Broxen to draw in sharp breaths. She did it again, and again, rocking against his cock.

Pleasure jolted through him, as delightful as it was maddening, building that pressure in him. Though it was almost too much too bear, he couldn't get enough. He felt her heat, felt her essence dampening the fabric separating their skin, and he craved more. He longed to tear the clothes from their bodies and feel her slick flesh, to plunge into the hot depths beckoning him.

Broxen dropped one of his hands onto the bed beside her head and curled his claws into the mattress. Unable to remain still any longer, he thrust against her, grunting at the pleasure that was spearing his core and racing up his spine. Much more of it, and he'd unravel. Coming undone had never seemed so appealing as it was right now.

Gabriela moaned and arched up against him, her blunt nails digging into his sides. The air grew thick and heady with her scent, clouding his mind with a haze of lust, driving him harder, faster. He used his grip on her to pull her against his every thrust.

Soft gasps escaped Gabriela. She caught her bottom lip to silence herself, but her silence didn't last long.

"Mason," she rasped, reaching up to cup his jaw.

Their eyes met for a fiery instant before she lifted her face and pressed her mouth to his.

Broxen stilled utterly. His breath caught in his throat, his heart ceased beating, and his mind was suddenly empty. Given everything else—her scent, her warmth, the friction of her body against his—that simple press of lips should barely have been noticeable. He'd seen people kiss back on Turata, had seen humans do it in person and countless times in their entertainment, but he'd never experienced it, and had never imagined it would feel like this.

Gabriela's plump lips were soft, smooth, pliable, and yet so confident. And she tasted even sweeter than she smelled.

He cupped the back of her head with one hand, closed his eyes, and leaned into that kiss, deepening the contact between them and his taste of her.

Her mouth opened, and she caressed his upper lip, flicking it with her tongue. Broxen groaned low and swept his tongue out along hers, and she coaxed it into a dance that he swiftly took control of. Needing more, he slammed his mouth upon hers, devouring her.

Wrapping her legs around his waist, Gabriela ground her sex hard against his cock. He swallowed her moan of pleasure and hissed his own.

"Don't stop. Please don't," she pleaded against his lips. "It's been so long. I need—"

The bedroom door swung open, bumping into the doorstopper.

Broxen snapped his head up and turned his face toward the doorway just as Ana stepped into the room.

"Mom, I'm—" She came to an abrupt stop. Her eyes rounded, and her jaw dropped.

Gabriela shrieked. Planting both her palms against Broxen's chest, she heaved him off her. Taken completely by surprise for the second time in a minute, he offered no resistance, and he didn't realize until it was too late that she'd shoved him away from the side of the bed where he'd slept.

His side came down on the very edge of the bed, and he bounced before tumbling onto the floor, landing heavily on his back with a thud that must've shaken the whole house. And of course, the way his tail was tucked away meant it absorbed a significant portion of the impact.

He barely held in a growl of pain, baring his teeth and sucking in a sharp breath instead.

Least it wasn't my cock.

"I'm sorry," Ana said. The door slammed shut a moment. Her muffled voice came from the other side when she said, "Just wanted to tell you I'm hungry!"

Gabriela scrambled up into a sitting position, entering Broxen's field of view. Her hair was mussed, her cheeks were flushed, and there was a panicked look in her eyes.

"Oh, my God. She... We were... She saw—" She pressed

her hands to her face and groaned. "I've scarred her for life." Dropping her hands, she peered at Broxen over the edge of the bed and winced. "I'm sorry."

Broxen chuckled despite the twinge in his tail—and in his still-throbbing cock. "Guess she knows to knock next time."

Though she pressed her lips together tight, a laugh burst from her mouth. "Not funny!"

Grabbing a pillow, she threw it at him, hitting him in the chest. He only laughed harder as he caught it.

My lusty, feisty female.

FOURTEEN

"Where are we going?" Ana asked from the back seat of Mason's truck.

"Can't tell you," Mason replied, glancing at her in the rearview mirror.

"Why?"

"It's a surprise."

Gabriela, who was sitting in the passenger seat, turned her head to look at her daughter. Ana was staring at the back of Mason's head with a skeptical frown that was completely at odds with the excitement sparkling in her eyes.

"Can you give me a hint?" the little girl asked.

The corner of Mason's mouth quirked up ever so slightly. "No."

Ana groaned and crumpled with a theatrical flair, falling into a slouch with her arms limp beside her and her head lolling back. "Why not?"

"You're too good at guessing."

"Well, how would you know that?"

Mason shrugged; it was amazing how nonchalant the

gesture looked despite the breadth of his powerful shoulders. "Just a guess."

Gabriela shook her head and laughed at Ana's exaggerated *ugh*. She knew Ana wasn't truly upset about this, she was just overly excited and antsy—like most kids were in the days leading up to Christmas.

Only four more days to go. It hurt that Gabby didn't have anything to give her daughter for Christmas, that there were no presents for the girl to open, but Ana had already demonstrated maturity beyond her years when it came to this situation.

It hurt Gabriela's heart even more to know Ana would swallow her own disappointment and sadness and soldier on for her mother's sake.

Next year, Ana. Next year, you're going to have so many presents on Christmas morning that you won't know where to start.

But Gabriela did have *some* money in her account. Perhaps Mason would let her borrow his truck for a bit so she could at least get stocking stuffers and a gift or two for her daughter. He'd insisted on buying everything else for them, but Gabby had to do at least that much.

"Mom, will you tell me?"

"Sorry, Ana. I don't know either."

"Come on, I know he told you."

Gabby glanced at Mason just as his eyes flicked toward her. For a moment, they held each other's gazes, sharing a smile.

"He didn't tell me anything," Gabriela said as she turned her attention to the window. "That's why it's such a surprise."

They were currently driving through downtown McCall on their way to wherever it was Mason was taking them. The streets were lined with piled snow, and the light posts along the sidewalk were adorned with garland and lights and big snowflakes that would shine after dark. Even if this town got a little crazy when it was full of tourists, especially during the Winter Carnival every January, and even if this part of it was designed to cater to those tourists, there'd always been a charm to it.

"Can you at least turn down the heat?" Ana asked. "It's hot."

"You can take off your coat," Mason said. "Going to be driving for a bit."

Ana didn't waste any time in tearing off her heavy winter coat, filling the cab with those swishy sounds for several seconds as the material rubbed against itself.

It wasn't long before they turned off Third Street and left downtown behind them. Gabriela tried to take in the scenery as they drove—though she'd lived in the area for her entire life, it seemed there was new construction she hadn't known about everywhere she looked—but her eyes kept creeping back to Mason. He was just as sexy in profile as he was head-on, especially with that gleam in his eye.

She really didn't know where he was taking them. He'd told them to bring their big coats, snow boots, gloves, hats, and scarves, so she knew they'd be outdoors, but that was it. And though she wasn't necessarily the biggest fan of the cold, she was glad to get out of the house after that awkward breakfast—during which Gabriela had been unable to look at Ana without nearly dying of embarrassment, whereas every time she'd so much as glanced at Mason, memories of what they'd done in his bed had sparked that flame in her core anew.

But she was an adult and didn't feel shame for what she and Mason had shared. She was allowed to...enjoy herself, to have sexual relations with a man, to feel pleasure, to feel like a *woman* again.

To be more than just a mother.

Though she could have done without her daughter

popping in and interrupting them. Gabby had been so close. *So close.*

Looks like I'm going to have to have The Talk *with Ana sooner than I expected.*

As they drove on, the homes and cabins on the sides of the road became sparser, and the pine trees that dominated the region filled in the gaps. That was always one of the things Gabriela had loved about living up here—drive five or ten minutes in almost any direction, and you'd find yourself surrounded by nature.

They passed a sign declaring that they'd entered the Payette National Forest not long afterward. Gabriela's gaze wandered a little more easily out here. She'd always loved the way the forest looked in the winter, with the ground blanketed in white and clumps of glistening snow clinging the boughs. When the sun hit the snow just right, it set all the ice crystals aglow like they were countless glittering diamonds. She'd never seen anything quite like winter in these mountains.

Mason turned onto a side road, and the truck jostled as it left the pavement and rolled onto packed snow. Ana grasped the two front seats and pulled herself forward to look out the front.

Shimmering white dust fell from branches overhead, melting as it hit the windshield. Snow crunched under the tires, as loud as it would've been had the truck been driving over loose gravel.

"So what are we doing out here?" Ana asked.

Gabby chuckled, though she was quite curious herself. "It's a surpriiiiiiise."

Her daughter rolled her eyes.

"We'll stop soon," Mason said, glancing at Gabriela and Ana for a moment. "Snow will be too deep if we go too much farther."

Gabriela twisted to look out the back window. The narrow road they were driving on was flanked by trees on both sides, and they'd already driven far enough that the main road was out of sight.

"That's it. We're lost," Ana announced.

"Not lost," Mason corrected, another faint smirk lifting his lips, "but we could wind up stranded."

Gabriela stared at him.

His brows rose, and he chuckled. "We'll be fine. If the truck gets stuck, I can push it out."

Now Ana was staring at him, too.

Shaking his head, he shifted on his seat, reached down, and tugged his phone out of his pocket. "Also have this."

A minute or two later, the road opened into a small clearing.

"Hold on to something," Mason said.

Gabriela arched a brow at him as she reached up for the *oh shit* handle on the doorframe. "Sit back, *nena.*"

As soon as Ana had leaned back, the engine rumbled, and the truck put on a burst of speed.

"Oh my God, what are you doing?" Gabriela breathed, tensing and slamming a hand onto the dashboard. She was almost certain that had all come out of her mouth as a single, prolonged word.

Of course, Ana was giggling in the back seat.

Mason turned the wheel, guiding the truck into a turn that whipped its back end around. Snow sprayed in the air all around the vehicle, and Gabriela could feel the tires sliding, and though that adult, maternal side of her said she should panic...she couldn't deny the thrill.

She hadn't done anything like this in years—not since she was a teenager, when everyone would mess around in the snow trying to drift around turns and make their pickups fishtail.

The truck came to a smooth stop, rocked very slightly on its shocks, and was still. It was now facing the road they'd just come down.

"Again, again!" Ana cheered.

Mason turned his face toward Gabriela, grinning. "You all right?"

Gabby's heart was pounding, and her stomach still felt like it was down by her feet, but she grinned back at him. "Yeah."

For an instant, his grin took on a wicked slant, and heat danced in his eyes. Then he turned his attention forward, shifted the truck into park, and killed the engine. "We're here. Coat on, Ana."

"Yay!" Ana threw off her seat belt and grabbed her coat, jamming her arms through the sleeves.

Gabriela unbuckled her own seatbelt and picked up her coat, which was bundled on the wide armrest between her and Mason.

"And what are we doing here?" she asked as she pulled her coat on.

Ana bounced on her seat. "Are we going to build snowmen?"

Mason tugged on his own coat and zipped it closed. "I guess if you show me how."

She gaped at him. "You've *never* built a snowman? Mom, we gotta teach him."

Gabriela chuckled. "I think we do. But we'll do that at the house."

"Awwww, but Mooooom."

"How can we make a snowman without a carrot for a nose?"

"Okay, fine." Ana placed her hands—now bundled in gloves—on the front seats and leaned forward again. "So, what are we really doing?"

"It's Christmas in four days," Mason said. "We need a tree, right?"

Ana's face lit up. "We're getting a tree?"

"Here?" Gabriela asked.

"Tree lots in town packed up already." Mason shrugged. "Figured there are plenty of trees out here."

"Don't you need a permit to chop a tree down?"

Mason's brow furrowed, and he tilted his head. "A permit? What do you mean?"

"You know, like a piece of paper from the government or whatever that says you have permission to cut down a tree. I'm pretty sure they sell Christmas tree permits from the forest service that have certain parameters for what you're allowed to cut down and all that."

The crease between his brows deepened, and his lips fell into a frown. He swept his gaze over their surroundings, over all the trees at the edges of the clearing, before looking back at her. "There are millions of trees here. Why do I need a piece of paper to say I can cut one down?"

Gabriela tilted her head. Mason was genuinely perplexed by this. It was no different than a fishing or hunting license, which most people who lived in this area had. How did he not know what a permit was?

"Because...it's the...law?" she said, wondering if *she* was the crazy one.

"Is there someone who will come count the trees and notice one missing?"

She laughed. "No, but someone could see us."

"Then we better not get caught!" Ana said, poking her head up between the adults.

Gabriela gaped at her. "I thought I taught you better than that, young lady."

Ana shrugged. "It's the rebel in me."

That response stunned Gabriela into silence for a moment, but once that moment had passed, she couldn't hold in her laughter. Mason and Ana joined her, filling the truck with laughter.

Mason ruffled Ana's hair. "Better rein that rebel in after we steal this tree, kit, or we'll both be in trouble."

Gabriela, still grinning, shook her head as she met Mason's eyes. "Come on. Let's go commit grand theft conifer."

They opened their doors, and Gabriela hopped down from the cab, boots sinking up to mid-shin in the snow. The cold nipped at her face. She shivered, already missing the warmth and coziness she'd enjoyed in the truck.

She closed her door and walked to Ana, crouching and helping the girl zip her coat; she couldn't manage it on her own thanks to the gloves. Ana's pink hat was jutting from her coat pocket. Gabby plucked it out and pulled it into place on her daughter's head, making sure to get it down over her ears.

"Thanks, Mom" Ana said.

Gabriela smiled and pressed a kiss to Ana's forehead before rising.

The driver's side door slammed shut. Snow crunched under Mason's boots as he walked alongside the truck bed, pausing to reach inside and lift an axe from within. He proceeded around the back of the truck until he was standing just ahead of Ana and Gabby. "Ready?"

Ana grinned up at him. "Yes!"

Gabriela pulled her gloves out of her pocket and tugged them on as she walked toward Mason. "Lead the way, oh faithful leader, and we shall follow."

They trudged into the forest single file—or at least Gabby and Ana trudged. The snow that slowed them down seemed to offer little hindrance to Mason, either because he was so big, because he was so strong, or a combination of both. But he glanced over his shoulder regularly to check on them, often adjusting his pace so they could keep up.

And Gabriela was grateful that, if nothing else, he was breaking a path for them that made it easier to walk. She could only imagine how difficult it would be for her and her daughter to traverse this snow on their own. When they did hit deeper patches—some of which almost came to Gabriela's waist—Mason helped them through, lifting Gabriela as easily as he did Ana.

Thankfully, those times were few and far between.

Reaching down, Gabby gathered some snow and formed it into a ball. She glanced at Ana, grinned, and brought a finger to her lips. Ana grinned in return and nodded.

Gabriela turned toward Mason, drew her arm back, and launch the snowball at his back. It struck with a dull *thump* and exploded, splattering snow across his coat.

Mason halted mid-stride, shoulders slightly hunched.

Ana erupted into a fit of giggles. Gabriela laughed, and was already forming another snowball when he turned around.

That crease was back between his eyebrows, and his mouth was downturned in a frown that seemed more confused than anything else. He met Gabby's gaze. "Did you throw sn—"

She threw her next snowball, hitting him square in the chest with another *thump*.

He blinked and flinched his head aside as bits of snow sprayed up into his face.

Ana was giggling so hard that she lost her balance and fell onto her knees, but she used it to her advantage, gathering a big handful of snow.

"Come on," Gabriela said, "you *have* had a snowball fight before, haven't you?"

"Snowball fight!" Ana threw her snowball at Mason. It flew a little too far to the right, only clipping his thigh.

He glanced down at the bit of snow left behind on his pants, tilted his head, and looked up at Gabriela again. His lips spread into a wide, wolfish grin.

Gabriela's heart sped. Mason's expression was sinful and just a little frightening, and it made her warmer than the truck's heater ever could.

But it also meant they were in trouble.

"Ana, run," she said, and darted toward a nearby tree. Just before she was behind its cover, she saw Mason crouch, standing the axe straight up beside him, and scooped up some snow.

Ana laughed and ran in the opposite direction.

Gabriela bent and made a couple haphazard snowballs before peeking around the tree. She barely had time to widen her eyes before Mason launched a snowball at her. It hit the tree trunk and burst apart, spraying her face with snow. She started, retreating into cover, where she shook her head and wiped the snow out of her face.

"Mason, you can't get me," Ana taunted.

He growled, and Gabriela eased around the trunk just enough to see him give chase to Ana. Gabby grinned and followed. It wasn't easy maneuvering between trees and the deep snow when her legs were so much shorter than his, but she was patient. And her patience—along with the fact that he wasn't moving anywhere near as fast as she knew he could— allowed her to catch up just as Mason was throwing a snowball at Ana. Her daughter ducked to avoid it with a giggle.

Gabby launched her own snowball. It struck exactly where she'd intended—Mason's ass.

Mason spun to face her, and only then did she notice that he still had snow in one hand. That wicked grin returned to his face, accompanied by a heated gleam in his eyes, and for a second it was hard to tell whether he meant to throw the snow-ball at her or lay her down right here and have his way with her.

He raised the snowball.

"I'll save you, Mom!" Ana plunged both her arms into the snow and swung them up, sending a geyser of powder into the air—and all over Mason.

He tensed, momentarily obscured by that cloud of snow, and was left covered in white—his hair, his coat, his pants. He looked like he'd just awoken from a nap in a snowdrift. "Ah, that went down my back," he grumbled.

Ana threw her hands in the air. "We did it! We—"

Gabriela's next snowball struck her daughter in the chest.

Ana turned shocked eyes toward her mother. "We're supposed to be on a team!"

Gabby stuck her tongue out. "I never said that."

Laughing, Mason bent down, scooped up some snow, and rose to charge at Gabriela. She screeched and ran, though she wasn't sure whether she truly wanted to escape him.

They played for some time, their laughter filling the forest, until they were exhausted and covered in snow. Even though Gabriela knew they'd all be freezing pretty soon, she felt good. She didn't feel like she'd just lost everything—she felt like she'd found the piece of her life that had been missing all this time.

Both she and Ana dropped back into the snow, panting, and stared up at the trees for several seconds. Gabby's cheeks, nose, and chin were so cold they were partially numb, and her legs burned with exertion, but she didn't care.

Ana swept her arms and legs in wide arcs over the snow, making a snow angel. How the girl still had the energy to do that, Gabriela did not know.

With a gentle smile on his face, Mason leaned back against the trunk of a tall tree, his eyes shifting back and forth between

Ana and Gabriela. If he was tired, he wasn't showing it, even though he'd run around just as much as Ana had.

Gabby met his gaze and smiled. "I guess we should find our tree before we all freeze."

His eyes darkened, and his expression grew serious. "I'll warm you, female." His eyes roved over her. "All night long."

He warmed her all right. That seductive look, combined with his words, sent a burst of heat straight to Gabriela's core, and her skin flushed.

"Gross," Ana said, putting her gloved hands over her ears. "There's a kid here!"

Yup, The Talk *is coming.*

Mason laughed, pushing away from the tree, and strode over to Gabriela. He held his hands out to her. He didn't need to say anything for her to know what he was thinking—and she had a pretty good idea that he knew her thoughts were similar.

Gabby placed her hands within his, and he helped her rise, lifting her easily out of the snow and keeping an arm around her until she gained her balance. She looked up at him and smiled. His tousled hair hung all about his face. She reached up, intending to tuck his hair back, but he caught her wrist and gently halted her arm.

They stared at one another, and the world around Gabriela was so peaceful and quiet that it fell away from her perception. She didn't know why he'd stopped her from touching his hair. He'd done so once before, and she couldn't help but wonder at his reasons. His action seemed so at odds with the way he was looking at her, with the desire in his eyes.

Perhaps, given a few more seconds, she might've brought herself to ask him about it. Perhaps she might've regained her wits enough to do so. But before that could happen, Mason bent down and pressed his mouth to hers.

His lips were hot, firm, and commanding, and they washed

away any questions she might have had. A soft sound escaped her, and she leaned into him, pressing her body against his.

She tilted her head back as far as it could go, just so he'd kiss her deeper. And he did. Mason slanted his mouth overs hers, and she opened to him, letting in his tongue—his incredibly *long* tongue—to twine with hers. She brushed her tongue over his teeth, tracing one of his canines, which felt oddly—but thrillingly—longer and sharper than it looked.

Mason's arms wrapped around her, and one of his hands settled on her ass as he clutched her to him. His cock, hard and hidden beneath his coat, pressed against her belly, but there was too much padding separating them. His growl shot straight to her clit, causing it to pulse.

Gabby's mind was immediately transported back to this morning. Back to the feel of his long, thick, and strangely ridged shaft nestled against her pussy, rubbing back and forth, stroking her clit again and again, sending the most delicious pleasure through her. She wanted more of that—needed more of that.

No, she craved everything. All of him. Naked, with no barriers between them. She wanted to feel him *inside* her.

Ana's exaggerated gagging sounds broke through the haze of passion that had overtaken Gabriela's mind.

She tore her mouth from Mason's, though he seemed reluctant to release her, keeping his arms and hands firmly in place. Cold winter air swept in to replace the warmth his lips had left upon hers. She looked at her daughter.

Ana had stood up while Mason and Gabriela were kissing, and she was looking at them now with disgust on her face. "You were sucking each other's tongues!"

"You wanted him to be my boyfriend, right?"

"Well...yeah."

Gabriela smirked. "Well, get used to it. This is what boyfriends and girlfriends do."

Frowning, Ana turned away and trudged onward. "I'm staying single forever. That's just gross."

Gabby laughed. "Sounds fine by me!"

When she turned her attention back to Mason, she found him still staring down at her, his eyebrows low. "Boyfriend?"

"Ah, well..." Her cheeks warmed, and she ducked her head, lowering her gaze to his chest. "That's what you are now, right? That is...if you want to be?"

He hooked a finger beneath her chin and lifted it, forcing her eyes back up to his. He wrinkled his nose, and his lip curled. "I am no *boy*, female, and we are far more than friends." He stroked his thumb over her bottom lip, which was tender from their kiss. "I am yours, Gabriela—your mate. And you are *mine*."

"I...like the sound of that," she said, a little breathlessly. She really, really did. Who cared if no one else she'd ever known talked like that? It was sexy as hell. It was like he was staking his claim on her, and allowing her to claim him right back.

Mason's lips spread into that sensual smile she loved so much. "Mmm... Good." His gaze moved to her lips, and he dipped his head.

"Hey! I found our tree!" Ana called. "It's short and fat with a skinny stick on top. It's perfect!"

"That's great, baby," Gabby replied before easing closer to Mason, lashes fluttering shut in anticipation of the coming kiss.

"M-mom?" Ana's voice trembled with fear and uncertainty, piercing straight through Gabriela and replacing the heat she'd felt a moment before with bone-deep cold.

Gabby swung her gaze to her daughter, and her heart stopped.

Ana was standing deathly still with her back toward Gabriela, clumps of snow clinging to her clothing from head to toe. Directly ahead of Ana was the largest mountain lion

Gabriela had ever seen. Its shoulders were hunched, its ears back, and its eyes were locked on her little girl.

Mason snarled something in a language Gabriela didn't recognize and released his hold on her. Gabriela staggered in the snow, unable to take in a breath, unable to think, unable to act. There was far too little distance between her baby girl and that beast.

The mountain lion's lips peeled back as it made a low, rolling growl.

Ana took a small, unsteady step backward.

That growl rose into a yowling roar, the sort of call that had always prompted Gabriela's father to load his shotgun when she was a child, and the mountain lion charged across the snow.

With a scream, Ana stumbled back. Her boot caught in the snow, and she fell onto her backside.

"Ana!" Gabriela cried, trying to run forward, but the damned snow made it feel like she was moving in slow motion.

There was another growl, this one much more powerful and from much closer—from Mason. He darted forward, barreling through the snow like a charging rhino, moving faster than anyone as large as him had any right to. His long legs ate up the ground between him and Ana.

The mountain lion leapt into the air with its big paws splayed and its claws extended.

Mason bounded over Ana. But what landed in the snow in front of the little girl looked nothing like the man Gabby knew —he wasn't even human. He looked like a demon. A red-skinned, horned demon.

The mountain lion collided with him, its front half coming down on his shoulder and its paws slamming down on his back. The animal twisted its head, opening its fanged mouth wide, and lifted its hind legs as though to claw at the demon's stomach.

But the demon—*Mason*—seemed unfazed. He lifted his hands quickly, bracing them against the big cat's midsection, and heaved it off with a mighty shove. The mountain lion's claws shredded his coat, but it could not keep hold. The beast yowled and flipped head-over-tail before crashing into the snow a good fifteen feet away from Mason.

The cat scrambled onto its feet, huffing and shaking its head. Growling, agitated, and wary, it prowled to the side as though it meant to get behind Mason.

Gabriela stumbled and dropped down into the snow beside her daughter, who was staring up at the huge man standing between her and the aggressive cat. Gabby pulled Ana against her, watching the scene in wide-eyed shock.

Mason held his arms out to either side and stepped forward with one foot. The roar he released was unlike anything Gabby had ever heard; there was a hint of his voice in it, but it was primal, gravelly, bestial, a sound that put the mountain lion's calls to shame. That roar echoed across the winter sky, strong enough to make loose snow fall from the nearby trees.

The mountain lion's ears folded back, and it retreated several steps. A moment later, it turned and ran, disappearing into the woods.

Mason stared after the beast for a time with his back to Ana and Gabby. His coat was torn open along his back, but as far as Gabriela could see, there was no blood.

Finally, he turned around to face Ana and Gabriela, his broad chest heaving.

Gabriela's breath hitched, and she clutched her daughter closer.

The eyes looking down at them glowed a vibrant purple, a sharp contrast to the black sclera surrounding them. Mason's features were sharp, sharper than they'd been when he looked human, and long, pointed ears stuck out of his dark hair. Even longer black horns protruded from his hair above his temples, curving toward the back of his skull. And his long, powerful fingers were tipped with black claws.

"Are you okay?" he asked, revealing his sharp fangs.

That was what she'd felt with her tongue when they'd kissed—not a canine, but a *fang*.

The air fled Gabriela's lungs, coming out in a cloud, as she ran her eyes over him. "M-Mason?"

His expression tightened, and he glanced down at his hands, balling them into loose fists. "Ah, *gur'osh brakhan*."

"Are you the devil?" Ana asked, sounding a bit out of breath but startlingly unconcerned.

"Am I—what?" Mason shook his head. "No. I'm... My real name is Broxen kor'Stygos."

"What...are you?" Gabby asked quietly.

"The same male you've known, Gabriela." His gaze roamed over her and Ana, and his frown deepened. He released a soft huff through his nostrils. "I'll tell you everything later. When you're both warm, safe, and indoors."

Something flickered over his red skin; it was there only long enough for Gabby to glimpse some sort of hexagonal pattern, like a grid projected onto his flesh. Then it vanished, and he was...Mason again. No horns or fangs, no black-and-purple eyes, no claws, no red skin. All of it was gone as though it had never existed.

But now that'd she'd seen the real him, she couldn't pretend those parts didn't exist. She couldn't pretend he was...human.

Mason—*Broxen*—sank into a crouch, holding out one hand to Gabriela and the other Ana.

Ana leapt out of Gabriela's arms and threw herself at him. He caught her with one arm, holding her close as she clung to him. He looked back at Gabby.

Gabriela hesitated. Hurt flashed in his eyes, and though they were not his true eyes, the emotion was real.

"Everything I said is still true, Gabriela," he said, his voice low and raw. "I would *never* hurt you or Ana."

"I know," she said.

And she *did* know it. He'd saved her daughter—twice. What...what did it matter that he looked like a demon? He'd offered them his home, clothed them, protected them, *cared* for them. Nothing had changed...nothing except that they now knew the truth.

Tears flooded Gabby's eyes, and she reached out, placing her hand in his. "I know."

The smile that settled on his lips was subtle, but it brimmed with relief. He closed his fingers around her hand with all the gentleness he'd always shown her and lifted her up to her feet. She immediately stepped into the shelter of his body and wrapped her arms around him and Ana, pressing her face to his chest. Broxen banded his arm around Gabriela, clutching her against him.

"Are you hurt?" she asked.

He rested his cheek atop her hair. "No."

Ana tilted her head back. "Can we get the tree now? Before that cat comes back?"

Broxen chuckled. "Yes, we can get the tree. But I don't think the beast will come back."

"Good. I probably taste bad, anyway."

Gabriela, still feeling as though her heart was in her throat after nearly seeing her daughter attacked by a mountain lion, couldn't help but laugh at Ana's lightheartedness.

Gabby definitely hadn't fully processed the fact that her new boyfriend—her new *mate*—wasn't human, but she knew, somehow, that everything was going to be okay.

Better than okay.

FIFTEEN

THE RIDE HOME began with Ana asking Broxen a rapid string of questions, but after a firm shake of Gabby's head, the girl quieted. He'd said he'd talk to Gabriela when they returned to the house, and she could tell by the look on his face that he was deep in thought as he drove. She already knew he wasn't comfortable talking about himself or anything personal. It wasn't such a stretch to imagine that this situation would be even harder for him to explain.

Without conversation to occupy her, Ana's exhaustion caught up to her, and she nodded off and dozed the rest of the way home. But Gabriela couldn't stop glancing in Broxen's direction.

It was so strange using another name for him. For a year, she'd known him as Mason Lee. She'd thought he was human. Now all that had changed.

When they were nearly home, Gabriela reached into the backseat and gently shook Ana. The girl raised her head a little unsteadily, looking disoriented.

"We're home, baby," Gabriela said softly. "Time to wake up."

"Okay," Ana mumbled, rubbing one of her eyes.

Broxen turned into the driveway and shut off the truck. He handed the keys to Gabriela. "You two can head inside. I'll get the tree."

Ana opened her door. "I'm hungry."

"I'll make you some lunch in a bit," Gabby said as she climbed out of the cab and closed the door. "Come on."

When they reached the front door of the house, Gabriela unlocked it and pushed it open for Ana to enter ahead of her. She glanced back to see Broxen reach into the truck bed from the side and take hold of the tree.

"Do...you have a tree stand?" she asked.

He looked at her and tilted his head. "A tree stand?"

She nodded. "To stand the tree up with and keep it watered."

His brow knitted, and he scowled down at the tree. "Oh. No. Didn't know about that."

Of course he wouldn't have known. Just like he didn't know what a permit was, or what a snowball fight was, or how to build a snowman.

"It's okay," she said, offering him a small smile. "I'll find something."

Gabriela stepped into the house.

Ana had plopped onto the couch. She sat limply, browsing through the content from the channels her YouTube subscriptions. Her coat, hat, boots, and gloves were all strewn about the floor.

Some things never change.

Gabriela picked up the articles of clothing and the boots, hanging the coats in the closet and placing the footwear on the floor below. She toed off her own boots and placed them beside her daughter's.

Making her way to Ana, Gabby crouched down in front of her and placed a hand on her daughter's knee.

"You okay, Ana?" Gabriela asked.

Ana smiled. "Yeah. I'm good. Just tired."

"Yeah, I know. Too tired to hang up your coat and put away your boots, right?"

Her daughter grinned. "Yep."

Gabby rolled her eyes. Taking a deep breath, she fixed Ana with a serious look. "Really though, *mija*. Are you okay? After the mountain lion, and...and..."

"After finding out Mason's a demon? Yep, all good."

"His name is Broxen, and he's not a demon..." *I think.* Gabriela's brow furrowed, and she frowned. "You're taking all this really well."

Ana shrugged. "He said he'd always look out for us, that he'd keep us safe."

Gabriela's frown eased. "He told you that?"

Her daughter nodded. "I don't think he's scary. I still want him for my dad." She grinned and leaned closer to Gabriela. "I'll be the only kid in school with a *demon* dad."

Gabriela laughed; her little girl was hopeless. "He's not a demon. And not your dad."

Yet.

She caught her bottom lip with her teeth. Broxen wasn't Ana's father yet, but...Gabriela wanted him to be. Even with today's revelation. It hadn't changed what she felt for him.

I want you for my mate, and I want Ana to be my kit.

Though it wasn't loud, a rustling sound at the front door made Gabriela start. She looked that way to see the top of the tree jutting in through the doorway. Broxen ducked and stepped across the threshold, carrying the tree in fully. His footfalls were heavy on the floor.

He was tall enough that he had to duck through most doorways, but now Gabby recognized what she'd seen but never questioned—he always dipped his head quite a bit lower than seemed necessary. She had simply assumed it was one of those better safe than sorry situations, that he'd hit his head a few too many times to want to chance it anymore, but now she knew it was because he had *horns.*

You were supposed to get something to stand the tree in.

"Oh. Sorry, Broxen." Gabriela gave her daughter's knee a gentle squeeze and pushed herself to her feet. She hurried into the kitchen to search the cabinets for a large, sturdy bowl, though she wasn't sure if that would work. While she was kneeling to check under the kitchen sink, she recalled the bucket she'd seen in the laundry room.

"One sec!" Gabriela closed the cabinet, stood up, and jogged the short distance into the laundry room. She retrieved the plastic bucket from the corner, filled it partially in the deep sink, and hefted it out into the living room.

Broxen was standing just inside the front door, holding the five-foot-tall tree nonchalantly.

Even if it didn't seem to be a burden to him, Gabriela felt bad making him stand and wait. But that made her wonder... how strong was he? He'd flung that mountain lion away like it had been a rag doll, and that thing had to have been over a hundred pounds, and every time he'd lifted her he'd done so like she was weightless.

"Where do we want it?" she asked, shifting the bucket to her front to grasp the handle with both hands.

Broxen turned his head, running his gaze across the living room and dining room, but before he could offer a response,

Ana hopped down from the sofa and ran to the carved bear in the corner.

"Here," she said. "Next to the bear."

"Fine with me," Broxen said, meeting Gabriela's gaze.

Gabby swallowed thickly. She quickly looked away and carried the bucket to the spot Ana had indicated. "I'll get your lunch ready. How's a peanut butter, banana, and honey sandwich sound?"

"Good. Can I have chocolate milk, too?" Ana asked.

"Yep."

She cast a glance back at Broxen before she made her way into the kitchen. As she took out all the items needed to put the sandwich together, she listened to the soft rustling of the tree as Ana and Broxen discussed how best to stand it.

"This side is fuller," Ana said. "Turn it this way."

"Like this?" Broxen asked.

"Well...now it's leaning."

"It's going to lean. It's standing in a bucket."

"But that makes it look tired."

"It's had a rough day."

"You're right. Mom, is there like...a spa day for trees or something?"

Gabriela's shoulders shook as she tried to hold in her laughter. "Maybe. We'll...give it an aspirin."

"Do trees get headaches?" Broxen asked, clearly confused.

"It's supposed to help with the...water flow?" Gabriela's brow furrowed as she spread peanut butter on a slice of bread. "You know, I'm not really sure, but they always tell you to do it when you go to tree lots."

"Are we going to make ornaments?" Ana asked. "I think it'd be happier if it wasn't naked."

"It's not naked," Broxen said. "It has all these prickly things. Needles."

"It's supposed to be a *Christmas* tree. We have to dress it up. You wouldn't go out to dinner in your underwear, right?"

Broxen huffed. "What does that have to do with anything?"

"Just trust me, okay?"

"Why don't you draw and color some ornaments, and we'll cut them out to hang on the tree?" Gabby suggested as she placed banana slices atop the peanut-buttered bread.

"Okay!"

Gabriela squeezed some honey onto the banana and peanut butter and put the two pieces of bread together. She cut the sandwich in half down the middle—because Ana was particular about which way her sandwiches were cut—and mixed a cup of chocolate milk. Picking up the plate and cup, she made her way into the living room.

Ana was already sitting at the coffee table with a stack of paper and her box of canyons, TV turned on to a kids' arts and crafts video. Gabriela set the plate and cup down on the table.

Ana looked up from her drawing and smiled. "Thanks, Mom."

Gabriela returned the smile. "You're welcome."

When she straightened, she turned her attention to Broxen. He'd removed his coat and boots, and was standing by the tree, watching Gabby and Ana. When he met her gaze, there was something in his eyes—a hesitance, a longing, a hint of sadness.

She was putting distance between them, and he felt it.

He didn't take his eyes off Gabriela as she walked over to him. Reaching out, she slipped her hand into his and stepped back, giving his arm a tug.

Broxen didn't resist. Gabriela led him into the bedroom, where she guided him to move in front of her so she could close the door. For a couple seconds, she stood facing the door, steeling herself. She had no idea what she was about to learn.

No idea how she'd managed to remain calm through the drive home, no idea how she was calm now.

But when she turned toward Broxen and looked up at him, she saw the same man who'd moved into this house a year before. The same man who'd always been so kind, who'd always helped when he could, who'd always been there when they needed him.

The same man who'd said he wanted her as his own.

"Can you...remove it?" she asked.

Vague as that request had been, he understood. That strange, hex pattern coursed over him again, fading rapidly hex-by-hex to reveal the true Broxen, to reveal his red skin and his beautiful, glowing, inhuman eyes. This time, she felt no fear, no uncertainty, no confusion. Only curiosity. Only...fascination.

Gabriela ran her eyes over him, taking him in. He had been a gorgeous man in his human form, but strangely, she was finding this new look...more appealing. If anything, she found this Broxen sexier.

"Were you ever going to tell us?" she asked. "Were you going to tell *me* before...before we..." Heat flooded her cheeks as she once again thought back to that morning, to him lying atop her, grinding against her pussy.

He lifted a hand to rub the back of his neck, briefly offering her a glimpse of his claws. "Yes. Eventually. After what you've been through, I didn't want to scare you."

"This is kind of something I deserved to know. Especially if we had gone any further."

Though she could just imagine her shock if he were to have dropped his disguise while they'd been *in the moment*. To have looked up and suddenly find a demon-like man over her...

I would've shrieked loud enough to make the walls collapse.

"I didn't like hiding it from you," he said, closing the

distance between them. He reached up and lightly brushed the backs of his claws over her cheek. "Does it change anything?"

Gabriela stared up into his eyes, searching them. They were so strange, so unearthly, so beautiful. His body was tense, his expression tight, and his apparent uncertainty and vulnerability was wholly human, even if he was not.

"No," she finally said.

The tension fled him as he released a soft breath. His shoulders relaxed, and his lips parted slightly, giving her a glimpse of his fangs.

"Can I...touch you?" she asked.

He dipped his chin in a nod.

Gabriela started with his hand, taking it in hers and trailing her fingers along his, all the way to the tips of his long, sharp, black claws. She'd felt their points on numerous occasions, but it had never registered as anything abnormal. She thought he'd simply had long fingernails, not...claws. But now that she was seeing them, she couldn't help remembering when she'd felt them this morning when he'd clutched her thigh as he thrust against her.

She looked up at him, released his hand, and reached for his face. He bent down into her touch, letting her cup his jaw. Slowly, she moved her palms up and traced his long, pointed ears with her fingertips. Broxen closed his eyes and let out a quiet groan.

"Is this why you never let me touch you here before?" she asked. "Why you always drew my hands away?"

"Yes. Even if you couldn't see them, they were always there."

Gabby moved her hands up. Her fingers delved into his hair until she grasped the bases of his horns. He shuddered, and his hands settled on her hips. His fingers flexed slightly, and again she felt the pricks of those claws through her clothing. It sent a thrill through her, making her core ache and her nipples bud.

"I take it that felt good?" she asked with a knowing smile.

"Mmm." Broxen's eyelids rose, and he looked down at her with gleaming, half-lidded eyes.

She explored the roots of his horns, stroking the skin around the hard, dark bone that protruded from above his temples. His lips drew back in a hiss, baring those sexy fangs.

"Gabriela..." he growled low. "Do not tease me."

She chuckled. "Okay, okay. I'll stop." Her features grew more serious as she smoothed her palms over his horns. "That night, during the fire, with the window... You broke it with these, didn't you?"

"I did. It was...instinct. But I would've thrown myself through that glass if that was what I had to do to get to her."

Tears stung Gabby's eyes. She still felt the fear and desperation of that night, like echoes of a nightmare. She knew, in time, it would fade, but it was still too new, too raw. "You saved her."

Broxen cradled the back of her head with his hand, slipping his fingers into her hair. "Thought I was going to lose both of you that night."

"But you didn't, and here we are." Gabriela smiled and dropped her palms to his chest. "Is...there anything else I'm not seeing?" Her cheeks flushed, but she didn't look away from him. "Is your...um..."

He withdrew his hands from her, moving them both to his waist to unbuckle his belt.

Gabriela's wide eyes fixed upon them. "I...I didn't mean... You don't..." Except she couldn't deny her anticipation of what he was going to show her. What *did* it look like?

"I see that hunger in your eyes," he said with a bit of gravel in his voice. He unbuttoned the top of his jeans, but didn't lower the zipper; instead, he reached around behind himself... and pulled out a *tail*.

She gasped, her gaze flicking between that long, red appendage and his eyes. "You...have a tail? All this time? Stuck in there?"

"Yes. Haven't had much of a chance to stretch it out lately. As for the other thing..." He grinned and chuckled, briefly catching his bottom lip with a fang as his eyes roved over her slowly, ravenously. "It...looks a bit different but works the same way. You'll find out for yourself soon enough."

Gabby found that she *really* couldn't wait for that. Her curiosity was positively eating at her, and desire blazed through her veins. She squeezed her thighs together as her pussy clenched.

Broxen caught her chin and tilted her face up. "I will please you, my mate. When you're ready, I'll learn every way to make you scream with pleasure. With my fingers, my tongue, my cock, and my tail." He punctuated that last bit by winding his tail around her leg, sliding its tip down her calf.

The air fled her lungs in a rush.

I'm not going to survive him.

To go from no sex to sexed-to-death?

What a way to die.

But this wasn't all she'd pulled him into the room for. She wanted answers. Well, *more* answers.

"Hold up a minute," Gabriela said, her voice thick. She cleared her throat, but it was impossible to ignore his tail, still wrapped around her leg.

A freaking tail!

Oh, my God, the possibilities...

Gabby! Head in the game!

She patted his chest. Such big...solid...muscles... "Okay, question time. What are you?"

"An omnyrian. My kind originally came from a planet called Ketarn, I think, but I was born on a world called Turata."

"Oh. Wow. So aliens *do* exist."

Not a demon but an alien.

Wait until Ana finds out...

I hope she knows how to keep a secret.

"Are there others like you here?" Gabriela asked.

"Other nonhumans, yes. Don't know about other omnyrians. Earth is supposed to be off limits. I think most are like me, and came here to disappear."

She frowned. "Why did you need to come here to disappear?"

Broxen smoothed his hand down her hair. "Everything I told you before is true. I left out details, but I didn't lie to you. My friend, Astius...he was assassinated by members of his own family. They tried to implicate me for his death, and I...I avenged him. It was all I knew how to do. Another family member took power in the aftermath. They were grateful for what I had done, but there was still a faction of traitors left behind who had insulated themselves within a rival organization. They put a bounty on my head.

"So, the new leadership helped me escape. Set me up to go somewhere else. Astius always talked about a different kind of life, an honest life, without all the illicit activity and whatever. Thought about that a lot after he was gone. Was still thinking about it when I found my way here."

Broxen combed his claws through her hair and stroked the back of his finger along her jaw. "And when I saw you...for the first time, a different life really seemed possible."

Gabriela's fingers curled slightly into his shirt. His touch was so soothing, so calming, but it didn't quell her spark of unease. "But you're safe now, right? No one will come here looking for you to get the bounty? No one will find...us?"

Find Ana.

He shifted his hand and brushed the pad of his thumb over her cheek. "No one will find us. You and Ana are safe with me, Gabriela. I will never hurt either of you, and I'll tear apart anyone or anything that tries to harm you."

"I believe you." Gabby reached up and cupped his jaw, grinning. "I really shouldn't be turned on by that, but I am."

The corner of his mouth tilted up; the expression was all the more devilish given his true appearance. His tail coiled just a little tighter, and its tip slipped under the hem of her pant leg to stroke her bare skin. "And how about the tail?"

A shiver coursed through her. "There are *so* many naughty things going through my head right now."

His grin stretched wide as he chuckled. He slid his hands down to grasp her ass. "My bloodthirsty, lusty mate."

Gabriela's clit pulsed. "Oh, just kiss me."

With a growl, Broxen pulled her against him and slanted his mouth down over hers, claiming her lips in a ravenous kiss that stole her breath and made her toes curl.

SIXTEEN

Nakonin, the city on Turata in which Broxen had spent his whole life before coming to Earth, was an urban sprawl of towering, oppressive buildings and dark streets that served as a home to tens of millions of people. It was the kind of place where there'd been activity at all times of day and night, where hundreds of species and cultures slammed together into something that was sometimes amazing and often violent.

Boise was barely a city in comparison. It had the sprawl, as there'd been plenty of room for the humans to expand outward, but it lacked the *urban*. Even by Earth standards, it was a small, lightly populated city. Not even half a million people lived here as far as he knew.

But right now, two days before Christmas, it felt like the most crowded place in the entire damned universe.

The drive from McCall had been quiet, and Highway Fifty-five, which wound down along the Payette River for much of its course, had been thankfully clear of ice and snow. It had allowed him time to think. Though he hadn't wanted to reveal the truth of who and what he was to Gabriela and Ana like that, he didn't regret instinctually dropping the holoshroud's illusions. He'd done it to save them.

Things could have gone differently in so many ways, could have gone terribly, but they hadn't...and both his females had accepted the truth with an ease he could never have predicted. That left him feeling better than he ever had in his life. They saw him for what he was, and they weren't afraid. They weren't put off.

More than ever, he felt like they were a real family.

He had trouble believing he'd only taken Ana and Gabriela into his home four days ago; he felt like they'd been there forever, like they belonged there.

But that quiet, simple drive changed as he'd neared the tiny town of Horseshoe Bend, where there were suddenly more cars on the road. The traffic had only worsened from there, hitting its peak as he entered Boise.

The stoplight ahead—where he needed to turn into the mall parking lot—had gone through two full cycles since he'd taken his place in the line of vehicles. It seemed to allow dozens of cars to cross the intersection from every other direction, yet when it was time for Broxen's lane to go, only four or five cars could proceed before the light changed again.

The six or so hours he'd estimated to travel to and from Boise was already far too long a time to be away from his females. A couple hours of shopping in between those trips was all he could've brought himself to bear, but at this rate, he was likely to be stuck in Boise for half the day.

It's for them. For Gabriela and Ana.

He had a feeling he'd be reminding himself of that often today.

When he was finally able to turn into the parking lot, he

was greeted by a sea of parked vehicles, hundreds and hundreds of them gleaming in the late morning sun. The two-lane road circling the outside of the parking lot was almost as busy as the city streets beyond it, and there were streams of people walking in and out of the mall.

Broxen clenched his jaw and—after another damned wait in a turn lane—turned down one of the rows of parking places. For what felt like an eternity, he wove up and down those lanes, seeking out an empty spot. Every time someone pulled out of a parking place, there was another vehicle ahead of him to claim it, or he'd already passed the spot and someone behind him swooped in to fill it.

He'd rather shovel snow from the driveway all winter—and risk attacks from hungry mountain lions—than deal with this regularly.

"Never realized how much I hate living in cities until I left Nakonin," he muttered.

That thought only solidified what he'd already known— that house up in the mountains, surrounded by pine trees and fresh air and quiet spaces, that house where Gabriela and Ana were waiting for him...that was home. Not just *a* home, but *his* home. More than Nakonin or Turata had ever been.

When he finally found a place to park, it seemed as though he were miles from the mall building. He strode across the asphalt, passing other pedestrians and maneuvering around slow-moving cars whose drivers were seeking parking spots of their own, until finally he reached the mall entrance.

He hadn't seen so many humans crammed into one place since he'd left New York City. They were walking alone, in pairs, in groups, adults and children, young and old, and every one of them had their own pace and seemed oblivious to everyone but their companions. Even with his height advantage

—allowing him to see over the heads of most of the humans—it was difficult to navigate the crowd, especially considering just how many of those humans seemed to think it was okay to stop in the middle of walkways.

But Broxen held back his growing frustrations, once again reminding himself that this was for his females.

He waded through the crowd as gently as he could, mindful that his size and strength could lead to injuries were he to simply plow through these people. They were all likely here for the same reason he was—last-minute Christmas shopping. He couldn't be irritated at them for that.

Broxen worked his way into a store that was packed with children and adults alike—a place that sold video games. He knew little about such things apart from them being popular. Fortunately, a couple of overheard conversations reassured him that he wasn't the only adult in the store who knew nothing about the products it sold.

He wasn't sure if Ana enjoyed video games, wasn't sure if she'd ever even played them, but he was operating with only a vague sense of her interests—fueled by an immense drive to ensure her Christmas would be the best it could be.

Over the last few days, he'd done research. He'd read up on Christmas, its meaning, its purpose, on the associated traditions. Ana seemed the sort of child who'd be happy no matter what she woke up to on Christmas morning. She was grounded, grateful, and tougher than many of the big, brawny criminal thugs Broxen had associated himself with long ago. But he didn't want her to walk out of her room in two days and find nothing but their squat, leaning tree.

She deserved better than that, much better. So did Gabriela.

The store's employees were quite knowledgeable, and they

recommended products that might appeal to nine-year-old girl —something called a *Switch* and a few games. They'd asked him whether he wanted to preorder one video game or another or sign up for some sort of membership at least half a dozen times before he'd finally paid for his purchases and exited the busy store. He figured the four games he'd picked up would be enough for a start.

A few minutes later, he found himself in front of a directory, staring at the map and the list of stores upon it. The names meant little to him. When he pulled out his phone to check what the stores sold, nothing would load. The internet signal was terrible here. Likely a result of too many humans with their handheld devices crammed into one place at a time.

Humans milled about him ceaselessly, occasionally brushing against his back and arms as they passed. He curled his hands into fists and gritted his teeth, his tail—which was stiff after the long drive—twisting around his leg.

It had been hard to leave home this morning. Gabriela had slept with him again last night, and there'd been no hesitation this time; she slid right into his arms after they'd climbed into bed, curling up against him as though it were the most natural thing in the world. But perhaps the most heartening part of it was that she'd asked him to deactivate his disguise before they'd gone to sleep.

She'd wanted him in his true form.

If she could accept an alien as her mate, B'roxen could brave crowds of Christmas shoppers. He wanted nothing more than to see Gabriela and Ana smile. He wanted nothing more than to make them happy. If that meant he had to walk the entirety of this mall while it was this busy, if it meant he had to check every damned store along the way, he would do so.

Twisting the bag from the video game store a little more

snugly around his hand, he plunged back into the mass of people.

Broxen hadn't gone far before a patch of bright pink, exactly the shade Ana loved, caught his eye. He found himself looking into one of the stores ahead. Though storefront and the walls and ceiling inside were dark, the place had warm lighting, and there were those splotches of pink to contrast the black. The name of the store, like so many others, held no meaning to him. But that shade of pink...perhaps he could find more gifts for Ana there?

He returned his attention to the people around him as he walked toward the store. His course carried him through several streams of moving humans, each of which was meandering in its own direction, at its own pace. Though Broxen towered over most of them, they were largely oblivious to him. He avoided several collisions only because of his own reflexes and alertness.

By the time he finally reached his destination, his jaw muscles were ticking, and he was barely holding back a growl. He tilted his head sharply to the side, popping his neck, and finally lifted his gaze to look at the store he'd just entered.

Broxen's eyebrows shot up, and that growl escaped him. "Not for Ana."

The store was filled with female undergarments in more colors, fabrics, patterns, and cuts than he'd ever thought possible. Nearly everyone inside was female, including the employees, and the couple other males present had looks of uncertainty on their faces.

Broxen stepped over to a nearby table that had rows of lacy panties laid out atop it. He plucked up a pair to study the tiny floral designs in the lacing. In his imagination, he pictured what it might look like on Gabriela, pictured her wearing this in place of the bikini bottoms she'd worn during the summer.

His cock twitched, and another growl threatened to emerge from deep within his chest. He gritted his teeth and swallowed the sound.

Laying the underwear on the table, he swept his gaze around the store. There were dozens of things he'd love to see Gabriela wearing, dozens of things that would flatter her body—not that she needed anything to look sexy as hell. The clothing choices in McCall's stores had been limited, especially due to the season. She looked good in anything she wore, but he thought she'd like things like this—pretty clothing for a beautiful woman.

His eyes settled on a set of displays deeper in the store, where mannequins without arms, legs, or heads were dressed in clothes that looked like mixes between undergarments and sleepwear, most of which were quite revealing.

Broxen pictured Gabriela wearing those items as he walked toward them, but he knew his imagination would never do her justice—and that, if he did this for too long, he wouldn't be able to hide the evidence of his lustful thoughts.

Kruk, this place could be my undoing.

He knew enough about humans to understand that such a display wouldn't be looked upon kindly.

Lifting one of the garments off the nearby rack, he frowned at the sizing tag. It had taken him long enough to figure out men's sizes for clothing and shoes; puzzling out the sizes on these items would be like deciphering an alphanumeric code in comparison. And he'd never been good at that sort of thing.

Holding the hanger by the hook, he lowered the garment until it was roughly around the height it'd be if Gabriela were wearing it. She was so tiny—but most humans seemed small to him, and it was hard to tell if the hem of this garment would reach her mid-thigh or down to her knees. His frown deepened as he adjusted the height of it again.

"Can I help you, sir?" asked a female from nearby.

Broxen turned his head to see one of the store's employees standing nearby, her smile friendly but her brow slightly furrowed.

"I want to buy some of these for my mate," he replied, turning his attention back to the garment.

"Great. I can totally help you with that." The female moved closer to him, smile softening. "Do you happen to know her size?"

Flattening a hand, Broxen held it up to the middle of his chest.

"Um..." The female tilted her head.

"She is this tall," Broxen said.

"Oh!" The employee laughed nervously. "I meant her clothing size and her bra size, but I guess that helps a bit."

He only realized then that all the clothing Gabriela and Ana had selected when he'd taken them shopping had tags displaying their sizes. He should've saved himself the trouble and checked before he left.

What *was* Gabriela's bra size?

Returning the garment to the rack, he cupped his hands in front of his chest, imagining the soft flesh of Gabriela's breasts in his hands. "About this big."

The female's eyes widened, and she nodded. "Okay. Well, the good news is that we have a ninety-day return policy if stuff doesn't fit, so...let's work with what we have."

He exited the store sometime later with a large paper bag stuffed nearly full, wondering why the females at the cash register had been giving him such surprised looks. Had he bought more than seemed normal?

Broxen didn't dwell long on the matter, however, as his gaze fell upon a jewelry store across the way, where the lighting made everything sparkle and glitter. *Surprise her this*

Christmas, said one of the signs on the counter, bearing a picture of a gold necklace with shining diamonds on its pendant.

But his thoughts were not upon that necklace as he approached the jewelry store. No, his mind had turned to something else, to something new—the rings lined up in the display cases.

He knew the human custom, what they called a *proposal*. He knew, at least in vague terms, the way they went about becoming mates. He'd seen it in their shows and movies, had read it in several books.

And it always started with a ring. Even if he didn't understand why the gifting of a ring was important to human mating, it *was* important.

I could claim her in my way, and in the way of her kind...

But would she be ready for that? Would she be prepared for that sort of commitment? He knew he was moving fast, that he was being too bold, but he also knew what he wanted.

Gabriela.

He released a harsh breath through his nostrils, turned, and walked away from the jewelry store. Making his full claim on Gabriela—and her accepting it with equal fullness—was inevitable. It would happen. He didn't need to rush anything, and yet...

Broxen glanced over his shoulder, glimpsing the jewelry store's bright lights and gleaming displays from the corner of his eye. His lips fell into a frown. He'd have to revisit this matter after giving it some thought—and he doubted that he would be able to do that while he was here.

Forcing his face forward, he continued onward.

His frustration and annoyance flared often as he worked his way around the mall, navigating between clusters of shoppers and vendors offering him free samples of who knew what.

There was a word that seemed to fit the people here, one that had stuck with him for some reason ever since he'd first seen it in a book—*masochist*. He'd known a few people on Turata who'd fit the definition of it. He couldn't imagine anyone *wanting* to be in this mall right now who didn't enjoy a little suffering.

Every store had lines at the registers. Every cashier seemed slower than the last. But every time he thought he had enough, that he'd seen all there was to see, he'd spot something in another display window that would make him think of Ana or Gabriela, and he'd find himself heading into a new store.

There were also a few other jewelry stores, taunting him with their glinting displays as he passed them.

The number of bags in his hands grew as he went from store to store, and as it did, it became more of a challenge to avoid bumping anyone. The little kits walking with their parents were particularly difficult to look out for, and more than once Broxen had to swing his arms up high to avoid knocking over a tiny human.

With his hands full, he couldn't check his phone, but he felt the minutes burning away. He felt every mile between himself and his females.

It is for them.

Broxen's irritation was nearing its peak when he entered a store with signs that said it specialized in *pop culture memorabilia*; he wasn't sure what that meant, but it had many items with cartoon characters upon them, and he had a feeling Ana would have loved to look around inside.

Unfortunately, the store space was crammed with display racks and shelving, and some of the walkways were so narrow that he could barely fit through without turning sideways and lifting his bags over his head. It was exactly the sort of place he would have strongly recommended Astius avoid back when

Broxen was still a bodyguard—a security nightmare where the escape routes were effectively blocked no matter where you were because it was so crowded.

He found himself forced to stop in a narrow aisle where a small, frail looking female—an elder of advanced years, by the looks of her—was staring up at an item on a high shelf.

"Sorry to bother you, young man," the woman said in a quavering voice that was barely audible over the store's loud music as she looked up at Broxen through the thick lenses of her glasses, "but could you help an old gal out?"

She smiled at him with a genuine warmth he hadn't encountered since entering the mall. There was a piece of paper in one of her hands with words written on it in neat, flowing cursive, some sort of list.

"What do you need?" Broxen asked.

The elder grinned and turned her head so her ear was toward him. "Eh? Hard to hear you from all the way down here."

The corner of his mouth tilted up as he bent down so he was closer to the woman. "How can I help?"

She lifted the hand with the list in it and pointed at an item on the top shelf. Her arm trembled slightly. "Could you get one of those down for me? I've been trying to get help, but this place is so loud."

Broxen set down the bags he was holding in one hand, straightened, and grabbed one of the boxed items off the high shelf. There was a strange, blocky toy inside, a green thing with a big cube head and black squares that made up its eyes and oddly sad mouth.

The elder's face lit up as he handed it to her. "Oh, thank you. It's for my great grandson. From some game he loves. *I want Minecraft stuff for Christmas, Nana*, he said, and of course he waited until a few days before."

Minecraft. That was one of the games he'd bought earlier, and he was fairly certain he'd overheard the word a few times when Ana had been watching TV. While his hand was still free, he took down one of the boxes for himself.

"I don't understand it," the elder said with a chuckle, "but it makes the kids happy, so who am I to criticize? Lucas showed me a mansion he made in the game once, and I couldn't believe that he'd come up with all that on his own! Maybe he'll be an architect one day."

Though he wasn't sure what to say to all that, Broxen was moved by the woman's adoration and enthusiasm. "Maybe."

"Do you have a child interested in it, too?" the elder asked, dipping her chin toward the boxed toy in Broxen's hand.

"I...think so." He pressed his lips together for a moment. "My ma—uh, girlfriend's daughter. Don't know much about this stuff yet, but I'm trying."

"Well, you're a keeper, aren't you?" she said, offering him a playful grin and swatting his arm lightly with her hand. "Always loved that about my Jerry. He didn't always know, but he always showed interest in what me and the kids enjoyed. When our oldest was still a little girl, she got a pink bicycle that had dangly ribbons on the handles. Some of the neighborhood boys made fun of her, so Jerry painted his bicycle pink and hung even longer ribbons from the handles. He rode up and down the street with her for weeks, and she never cared what those boys had to say again."

Broxen smiled, feeling that tightness and warmth in his chest—he couldn't help but think of Ana and the sort of father-daughter relationship he hoped to build with her. "Sounds like a good man."

"He was the best. Fifty-four years married."

"That's a long time." Was it too much to hope for that long with Gabriela? "You must love each other very much."

"Oh, my Jerry passed a few years ago." The light in the elder's eyes was sorrowful and joyous at the same time. "But I still love him. Everyone thought he was crazy because he proposed when we'd only known each other for a month, but I knew just from looking in his eyes that he was the one."

"I...know what you mean." That was how Broxen had felt since the first time he'd seen Gabriela. He'd lacked the confidence to approach her, had lacked the insight to understand what he'd felt, but it had been there all the same.

In that moment, Broxen wanted more than anything to go back to his females, to hold them in his arms, to see them laugh and smile. But he wasn't done yet. He hadn't finished what he'd set out to do.

"You happen to know somewhere that might have decorations? Christmas decorations?" he asked. "Haven't seen anything in the mall."

"You might check the Target just across Milwaukee Street. But I don't think anywhere will have much left by now." She grinned. "Should've done your shopping sooner, but you can probably find good deals now."

"Hopefully." Broxen tucked the boxed toy under his arm and crouched to collect the bags he'd set down. "Thank you."

"No, thank you. And Merry Christmas."

He smiled and nodded. "You, too."

Broxen maneuvered through the crowded store—grabbing a couple more items for Ana on the way—to get in line for the register, barely stopping himself from fidgeting with impatience. He wanted to get back home, but there was still so much to do. He needed to check this Target for decorations; he'd told Gabriela that was the reason he was making the trip down into the Treasure Valley today, and even if it hadn't been the *only* reason, it wasn't a lie.

But there was one more stop he had to make in the mall before he left, perhaps the most important one of them all.

Whether it was instinct or something more, whenever he looked into Gabriela's eyes, he knew she was the one.

He knew she was his.

And he couldn't wait to claim her.

SEVENTEEN

G̲abriela sat cuddled beneath the blanket with Ana on the couch, watching Beauty and the Beast. She couldn't help but smile at how the movie had taken on a new relevance to her.

Of course, the details were different; Broxen had saved them from a mountain lion instead of a pack of wolves, and though he was often reserved and had a tendency to be terse, he wasn't grumpy and coarse like the Beast. Then there was the matter of him being a demon-like alien masquerading as a man rather than a man cursed to live as a beast.

And haven't I always been disappointed, even as a child, over the fact that the Beast changed at the end of the movie?

Now Gabby had her very own beast who meant to take her as his mate.

But where was he?

Not for the first time, she glanced toward the front door. Broxen had left early this morning, right after breakfast, saying he was going to Boise in search of Christmas decorations. Over eight hours had passed since then, and he still wasn't home.

Snow was lightly falling outside, and the highways could be dangerous even in clear weather. Worry gnawed at her.

I don't even have a phone to call him.

Broxen had ordered her a new cellphone, but it wouldn't arrive until after Christmas.

Ana's giggles drew Gabby's attention away from the door. The movie was at the scene where the furniture had come to life to defend the castle. Gabriela smiled and smoothed her hand over her daughter's hair.

Broxen is fine.

But no matter how many times she told herself that, she couldn't stop fretting over all the things that could go wrong during his trip. So much had happened recently, and the thought of losing him...

Gabriela's stomach knotted and cramped.

Nothing is going to happen to him. Nothing.

"Are we going to make cookies for Santa?" Ana asked, turning her head to look up at Gabriela.

"We'll bake some chocolate chip cookies for him tomorrow so they're fresh."

"The best kind. Especially when the chocolate is all warm and gooey."

"Mmm. I agree."

"Are there carrots for the reindeer?" Ana turned her face back toward the TV.

"Yep. You know I wouldn't forget them."

The front door swung open, startling Gabby and Ana. Large, clumped snowflakes blew in on a gust of wind. Gabriela turned her head, and her heart leapt when she saw Broxen's big, broad-shouldered, muscular body filling the doorway. Ducking his head, he stepped inside, carrying multiple shopping bags with red Target logos. He kicked the door shut behind him.

"Broxen!" Ana threw off the blanket, jumped off the couch, and raced toward him. He had to hurriedly shift the bags out of the way as she threw her arms around his waist and hugged him tight.

Gabriela's relief was immense and immediate. She stood and followed her daughter's suit, wrapping her arms around Broxen's chest and pressing her face against his coat. The melting snow on his coat wet her cheek, but she didn't care. He was safe. He was home. She breathed in his spicy pine scent, which was currently mixed with the crisp smell of winter, and sighed contentedly.

He chuckled, producing a rumble in his chest. "I missed both of you."

"I missed you, too," Gabriela said, rubbing her cheek against his chest.

"Me, three. Now what'd you get?" Ana asked, pulling away with a bright smile. She was nearly vibrating with excitement.

"Everything they had left," he replied with a smirk.

Gabriela drew back, glancing at the bags hanging from his arms. She held her hands out. "Let me help with those."

Broxen met Gabriela's gaze, and that lustful gleam sparked in his eyes as he looked her over. "I'm fine, female."

Gabriela's breath hitched, and heat flooded her core. She never would have imagined being called *female* would be so sexy, but spoken in his rough, rumbling voice, that word was enough to wet her panties and make her weak in the knees.

"Are the blinds closed?" He didn't look away from her. There was so much wicked promise within his eyes.

"I'll get them," Ana said, running to the front window.

As soon as the blinds were closed, that hex pattern shimmered over Broxen's skin, and Gabriela's prince became the beast again. It was still hard to believe that such alien technology—that *aliens*—really existed. It was a shock to see the changes overcome him so swiftly, but she was growing more and more accustomed to it. And she had no doubts now; he was more attractive in his natural form.

She was turned on by a beast with horns, claws, fangs, and a tail.

Broxen set the bags on the living room floor.

Ana plopped down and started pulling things out of the bags. There were giant and tiny red velvet bows, ribbon in a variety of colors, fake wreaths, garland, a golden tinsel star tree topper, ornaments of all kinds—colored bulbs, sculpted food, balls and players from different sports, cartoony people, animals, and more. One bag was filled with packages of tinsel, and two more were stuffed with boxes of Christmas lights, almost all of which were the warm white kind no one seemed to buy.

There were also metal reindeer that looked like polished gold, stuffed snowmen and Santas, some that sang and danced when Ana pressed their buttons, a white tree skirt with multi-colored polka dots and pom-poms around the edge, and three stockings—one in the traditional red and white, one with green stripes and the letter Z on the front, and a knitted Star Wars R2-D2 stocking.

Almost none of it matched. It was the kind of stuff you usually saw on the shelves after Christmas, the stuff that always ended up on clearance.

"Wow. There really is a little bit of everything," Gabriela said with a laugh.

"Can we decorate now?" Ana asked, clutching a pickle ornament as she looked up at Gabby and Broxen.

"Yes," Broxen said, removing his coat, "but only if you're lead decorator."

"You got it." Ana rose to her feet. "This is going to be the most beautiful tree *ever*."

Gabby grinned. Maybe not the most beautiful, but it would be the best tree they'd ever decorated.

"We should put the lights up first." Ana plucked up two of the boxes of Christmas lights and held them out to Broxen and Gabriela.

As she accepted the lights, Gabriela exchanged a glance with Broxen, and he gave her one of those disarming, fanged smiles before he took the other box from Ana and stepped toward the tree.

Gabriela stared after him, and her affection for him only grew during that moment, becoming so vast and deep that she knew *affection* was no longer the right word. Her feelings for him were so much more than that.

This...this was love.

She didn't know how it had happened so fast, but it was real. People always talked about love at first sight, sometimes with enthusiasm, but more often in ridicule. They'd call it lust. Gabriela wouldn't deny the lust was there, burning like fire in her veins, but what she felt was so much deeper. And *no one* had the right to judge her for it or tell her it wasn't real.

I...love Broxen.

Gabriela's heart fluttered, and she smiled wider.

With Ana's direction and assistance, they decorated the tree. They laughed and smiled throughout, especially at some of the ornaments Broxen had bought—particularly the one that was just a cat's hindquarters with a raised tail and a tiny pink butthole. They wrapped the tree in strands of lights, tied on one of the big red bows, and hung all the ornaments they could fit on the branches, including all the ones Ana had made herself.

Trash from the packages built up around the coffee table, pieces of plastic and cardboard tossed aside to be cleaned up later. Gabby couldn't deny the joy of this. The decorations themselves didn't matter, their lack of coherence made no difference. The only important thing was that she was doing this with Ana. That she was doing it with Broxen.

They were doing this as a family.

The little director of decorations allowed her assistants great freedom of expression when it came to the items that didn't go on the tree, though she offered a few suggestions. Before long, they had wreaths, garland, and bows hung up all over the living room, dining room, and kitchen, and little Santas, snowmen, and reindeer scattered all over.

Ana hurried to the tree to put on the tree skirt, fastening it around the trunk just above the rim of the bucket. The polka-dotted fabric hung down like an actual skirt—or maybe a little more like a circus tent—with the rainbow pom-poms dangling against the side of the bucket, the bottom few inches of which remained exposed.

When Ana returned to the dwindled stockpile of decorations, her eyes widened. "Ooo, tinsel!"

As she tore open one of the tinsel bags, Broxen picked up another, studying the contents with a more thoughtful and serious look than any tinsel had likely received since it was first invented.

"What do we do with it?" He opened the package and slid out the piece of cardboard that held the silvery strands in place, brushing a finger through them.

"We throw it all over the tree," Ana said with a big grin, "and maybe a few other places, too."

Gabriela picked up another bag of tinsel, smiling down at it. She and her parents always put tinsel on their tree when she was young. Ever since then, a Christmas tree without it had never seemed quite right, but still... "This stuff makes a big mess, Broxen. We don't have to put it up if you don't want to."

Broxen held up the cardboard, letting the strands of tinsel dangle down from it. "How big a mess?"

"Like we'll still be finding pieces of it scattered around the house this time next year."

He laughed and lifted hand, sweeping his hair back between those curved horns. "That's all right. Whenever we find a piece, we'll think of today, right?"

The way he looked at her as he said that, the way he smiled... There was that fire in his eyes, yes, but there was something deeper, too. Caring. Affection.

Love? I know he wants me, but...does he love me?

Gabriela stepped closer to him, close enough to feel the heat radiating from his body. She tilted her head back and smiled up at him. "Right."

Broxen leaned down and nuzzled her hair, drawing in a deep breath. He groaned softly. "I truly did miss you, Gabriela."

"I missed you, too," she whispered, closing her eyes. "And I was worried."

He cupped the back of her head with one of his big hands and brushed his lips over her forehead. "It'll take a lot more than holiday shoppers and some snow to keep me from you, my mate."

My mate.

She shivered. God, she loved hearing that.

She sighed and brought up a hand, pressing her palm to his chest, over his heart. "I'll hold you to that."

"You better not be sucking tongues again," Ana said.

"Not yet." Broxen's chest vibrated with those low, rumbly words.

Gabriela opened her eyes and laughed as she glanced at her daughter. Ana was staring at them with skepticism.

"I was just...making Broxen look a little more festive." She reached into the bag of tinsel, drew out several strands, and hung them over the root of one of his horns. The silvery strands mixed with his hair and sparkled from the light hitting them.

Ana laughed.

Broxen lowered his hand from Gabby's head and straightened, looking down at her with a smirk. "So, is this like a snowball fight now?"

Gabriela arched a brow. "Not unless you *really* want a mess. There shall be no throwing of the tinsel unless it's onto the tree."

He raised the dangling tinsel in his hand and glanced at it from the corner of his eye. "Hmm."

"I don't like the sound of that."

"But I like the sound of you draped in this...and nothing else."

"Hello! Kid right here," Ana said. "Let's get this stuff on the tree *before* you two start kissing."

Both Gabriela and Broxen laughed.

When they were finally done decorating, and Broxen had hung the stockings—with care—at the fireplace, they stood back and looked at what they'd accomplished.

Gabriela tilted her head. "You know...it really is a beautiful tree."

"Told you!" Ana said, flashing a grin.

The tree was still leaning to the side, causing many of the ornaments and the tinsel to hang at an angle, the plastic bucket was still clearly visible under the bottom of the tree skirt, and none of the decorations matched, but it was bright, and sparkling, and Gabriela loved it.

Broxen wrapped his arm around Gabriela and pulled her into the shelter of his body. She leaned against him and hugged Ana.

It wasn't a perfect tree, but it was *their* tree.

EIGHTEEN

Christmas Eve had always been a day of frantic, last-minute preparations, a day of stressing about whether the gifts were what Ana really wanted or if Christmas morning would be special enough. But it had also always been a day of excitement. Perhaps, were it not for Ana, the Christmas magic would've worn off for Gabriela years ago. Ana's joy, the light in her eyes, had ensured Christmas held its charm.

There were so many reasons for this Christmas Eve to be the worst Gabriela could remember, and those reasons had already been tumbling through her head when she'd woken up alone in Broxen's bed this morning. Losing a home was a devastating experience any time of the year, but to go through it right before Christmas...that was especially crushing.

Gabby had borrowed the truck the other day and, after shifting the driver's seat *way* forward, had gone into to town to buy stocking stuffers and a gift for Ana just so the girl would have something to open on Christmas. Still, it hurt Gabriela's heart that she couldn't provide more.

Yet her excitement was by far stronger than any negative emotions as she got out of bed.

Despite what they'd lost, there was *so* much to be grateful for. They'd escaped tragedy with their lives and their health. They'd found a new home, and they were forming a new family with Broxen. Maybe there'd be little in the way of presents tomorrow, but Gabby and Ana had received so much more than they could ever have hoped for.

It was the little things; the memories they were making, the love they were sharing. It was the way Broxen encouraged Ana to try new things, the way he kept her involved, the way he talked to her with respect and encouragement. It was the way he held Gabby, the way he looked at her, or how he seemed to always be making little adjustments around the house to make things more comfortable for her. It was the way he'd offer to help her in the kitchen even when he clearly had no idea what he was doing—or how he simply stood near and talked to her when she didn't need help.

It was the thoughtfulness of leaving an extra light on for a little girl who'd had to move into a new place unexpectedly, the simplicity of scrambled eggs and jellied toast, the kindness of the fluffiest towel in the house always being ready when Gabby took a shower.

When Gabby emerged from the bedroom, she was hit immediately by the mouthwatering aroma of fresh pancakes. Her eyes rounded as she found Ana and Broxen in the kitchen.

The place was a mess. Flour was scattered everywhere, including on the two chefs. It stood out especially on the red skin of Broxen's arms and hands. There were tiny globs of pancake batter splattered across the countertop, along with several folded and wadded paper towels smeared with more batter—and with blue and red stains, undoubtedly from the blueberries and sliced strawberries in two nearby bowls. A third bowl held sliced bananas.

Broxen was at the stove, tending a skillet in which a big pancake was cooking. His tail was free, swishing lazily in the air behind him, and he'd pulled his long, dark hair back into a messy manbun. For being a huge, muscular, horned alien, he sure looked good performing such a mundane task.

He'd look sexy doing any *task.*

Ana was beside him, holding one of those microwave lids over a plate piled with pancakes, its clear plastic all steamed up. There were three empty plates stacked beside that one, and a few items that would've triggered the mom alarms had Gabriela seen them in front of her child any other time.

Three bottles of syrup—maple, chocolate, and strawberry—and a can of whipped cream. Sugar, sugar, and more sugar.

"Ready," Broxen said.

Ana lifted the plastic lid, bouncing in place. Broxen picked up the skillet, slid the spatula beneath the pancake, and flopped it atop the stack on the plate. Ana covered the food again as soon as the spatula was clear.

Seeing the two of them working together like that was bittersweet. She wished that Ana hadn't had to go nine years of her life with no father, that she'd had to wait so long for moments like this.

She wished that they both hadn't had to wait this long for Broxen.

"You two have been busy," Gabriela said with a smile.

Ana turned her face toward Gabriela, lips spreading into a huge grin that made her missing canines seem more prominent and adorable. She had a smudge of flour on her nose. "Morning Mom. We're making you breakfast. Well, there's some for us, too, but mostly it's for you."

Broxen chuckled, glancing at Gabby briefly as he poured

more batter into the skillet. He had some flour smeared across his cheek and one of his horns, and several loose strands of hair dangled in front of his face; his smile was somehow sexier than ever in that moment. "Morning, Gabriela. We're almost done."

Gabriela placed her hand on his back, leaned forward, and drew in a deep breath. "Mmm. Smells good. I can't wait."

Broxen dipped closer to her, brushing the tip of his nose over her hair, and inhaled. His tail stroked her calf. "You smell better, female."

She caught her bottom lip with her teeth and looked up at him.

"*Please* don't ruin my appetite," Ana said.

Laughing, Broxen straightened and returned his attention to the skillet—though his heated gaze lingered on Gabriela for a fraction of a second longer before he did so.

Ana lifted the plastic lid and transferred one of the large pancakes onto an empty plate. "What do you want on yours, Mom?"

"Blueberries, strawberries, bananas, and whipped creamed."

"What syrup?"

"I don't need any." Gabriela pinched Ana's cheek. "You're too sweet for me already."

Ana giggled and wriggled out of her mother's clutches. "*Mooooom.*"

They all sat at the table to eat after Broxen was done cooking, Gabby and Ana laughing at the massive stack of pancakes Broxen had served himself, which was overflowing with every topping—including all three kinds of syrup.

Though he didn't ask Gabriela to help clean up afterward, Broxen didn't turn her away, either; they cleaned the kitchen together, and she was unable but to shake her head at the mess they'd managed to make.

Once everyone was dressed and had brushed teeth and hair —and Broxen had reactivated his human disguise—they bundled up and ventured outside to hang the remaining Christmas lights on the house.

That led into Ana finally getting to make her snowman. She made a small one on her own, first, to show Broxen how. Then Ana and Gabriela had worked together to make a bigger snowman—one about the same height as Ana herself—while Broxen began one of his own.

Just the base snowball he rolled was as tall as Ana. When he was finally done, the snowman he'd built—more like a snow behemoth—was even taller than Broxen himself.

It was also more crooked than their little Christmas tree, and its head was nearly the same size as its middle.

After they used rocks for eyes, mouths, and buttons, carrots for noses, and sticks for arms, their snowmen were complete.

"Not bad for a first timer," Ana said, one hand on her hip as she inspected Broxen's creation, "but you need to work on your basics."

"I think it's good," Broxen replied with a frown. He crouched down, scooped up a handful of snow, and tossed it at Ana. It struck her coat with a soft *piff*.

She gasped, her expression one of pure shock and insult. "I *can't* believe you did that."

Gabriela grinned, packed her own snowball, and threw it at her daughter, striking her in the shoulder. "Maybe you should be a little nicer."

"It's on!" Ana declared.

Unlike the forest battlefield where they'd had their first snowball fight with Broxen, there was little cover in his front yard, and the three of them were coated in snow in short order. Broxen finally retreated to take shelter behind his snowman, the only thing big enough to shield him.

"No fair," Gabriela called.

Broxen leaned to the side to look at her. "How?"

The snowball she threw—a soft, powdery one—hit him in the face, bursting into a cloud that left him looking like he'd dunked his head in a bag of flour.

"*That's* not fair," he said, shaking his head to shed excess snow. "You're playing—"

A snowball from Ana zipped past his ear, prompting him to duck behind the snowman again. He muttered something. Though Gabby couldn't be sure what it was, it sounded an awful lot like *devious females*.

"You can't hide forever," Ana shouted.

"My snowman will protect me," Broxen replied. As he shifted his position, one of his legs jutted out from behind the snowman.

Gabriela hit the toe of his boot with another snowball, and he yanked it back into cover. They'd reached a point that so many snowball fights often came down to—the stalemate. But she refused to accept it. There was only one way to end this properly.

She looked at her daughter. "Ana."

Ana turned her head toward her.

"Dogpile," Gabby said.

Ana grinned. "Yes!"

"What's that?" Broxen asked.

"Charge," Ana cried, racing toward the big snowman.

Smiling so wide her cheeks hurt, Gabriela ran alongside her daughter. They split apart when they reached Broxen's snowman, rounding it on opposite sides. Broxen, who'd been kneeling atop the snow, darted his gaze from Ana to Gabriela just before they leapt atop him.

His eyes widened in surprise a split second before he fell backward and threw his arms around them with a playful growl, sinking into the snow beneath him. That growl quickly gave way to laughter.

"Your attack failed," he declared, "and now I've captured you both." He pressed his cold face against Gabby's neck and snarled.

Gabriela giggled at the vibrations it caused—and at the bolt of desire it sent through her. She shrieked when his tongue flicked her skin an instant before he stroked his lips over the spot. "Broxen!"

"Mmm," he purred and loosened his hold on Gabriela.

For a minute or two, they lay on the snow, catching their breath. That as all it took for the cold to truly settle in. Ana was the first to start shivering, but Gabriela wasn't far behind. With a grunt, Broxen said it was time to head in. They disentangled from one another, stood up, and wiped snow from each other's clothes before hurrying into the house.

They all quickly changed into dry clothes, Broxen lit the fire, and Gabriela headed into the kitchen to make some hot chocolate. With steaming mugs in hand, all three of them sat on the couch. Ana selected a movie to watch—Elf.

Though Gabriela could tell some of the jokes went clear over Broxen's head, he laughed and smiled throughout most of the movie—though his hardest laughter came when Ana, in a totally serious voice, asked if they could have spaghetti with maple syrup, marshmallows, toaster pastries, and chocolate for dinner.

Gabriela gave her daughter that *are you for real* look, barely suppressing a shudder. Her teeth ached just thinking about eating something like that. "Heck no, girl."

But she couldn't hold in her own laughter when Broxen, suddenly just as serious as Ana had been in her initial request, looked at Gabby and asked, "Why not? Looks good."

She wrinkled her nose. "I am seriously starting to question your tastes."

"Maybe in food," he said, smirking, "but my taste in females is perfect."

Gabriela grinned. "Damn right, it is."

They soon finished their hot chocolate, set the mugs on the coffee table, and snuggled together under a big blanket, though Broxen's legs totally stuck out. He put one arm around Gabby's shoulders as she leaned against his side, and the other around Ana as she snuggled against his opposite side.

They watched another movie after Elf, lounging and relaxing until well into the afternoon, when Gabriela declared it was finally time to make cookies. Ana came to serve as her assistant, and Broxen leaned on the counter, chatting with them as they worked. Ana insisted he have the first taste of the chocolate chip cookies when the first batch came out of the oven.

The cookie was soft, nearly falling apart as he picked it up, and the chocolate chips were gooey. He popped it into his mouth and groaned as he chewed. "Delicious."

He reached for another one, but Gabriela gave his hand a little swat, making him pull it back in surprise.

"No more," she said, smirking. "Everyone gets one now, then we make sure Santa gets his share tonight. We can eat whatever's left *after* dinner."

Broxen tilted his chin down and growled. His violet eyes took on a new glow as he held her gaze. "You'll pay for that later, female."

Gabriela's cheeks warmed, and that now familiar desire coiled tight in her lower belly at the dark promise in his voice. She pressed her thighs together, but it did nothing to alleviate that needy ache.

Down, girl. Soon.

Once all the cookies were baked and set out to cool,

Gabriela got to work on dinner, preparing *arroz con pollo*; chicken and rice. A quick and easy meal after a long, tiring, fulfilling day.

It'd been a *wonderful* day.

It was quiet as they ate dinner, but not because of any awkwardness or solemnity. Broxen and Ana both were scarfing down their food. He finished his third plate before he finally sat back in his chair and let out a satisfied sigh, and Ana had seconds—something Gabby couldn't recalling having ever happened except with pizza, mac and cheese, or chicken nuggets. Though the girl did pick out all the green beans.

Broxen insisted on cleaning up after dinner since she'd done all the cooking. It was almost instinctual for Gabriela to brush that off and help anyway, but she decided to take the opportunity and get her shower done, instructing Ana to do the same.

She made the water as hot as she could bear and relished it long after she was done shaving and washing, for once allowing herself to feel no shame for indulging. The troubles that had begun the week seemed so distant, seemed like they'd occurred so long ago, and the future... Well, Gabby didn't know what the future held, but she was thrilled by the possibilities in a way she hadn't been since her teenage years, back when it seemed like the whole world was open to her.

Gabriela loved her daughter with all her heart, but she hadn't realized just how alone she'd felt all these years. She hadn't realized how big that missing piece of her life had become—not until Broxen had swooped in to fill it.

It was like she'd been waiting for him for all that time.

The fire was still crackling when she stepped out into the living room, and the Christmas tree was as bright as ever—even brighter, maybe, now that it was fully dark outside. Broxen and Ana—who must have taken the world's fastest shower—were sitting across from each other at the dining table with the oldest game of Battleship Gabby had ever seen set up between them. Ana had a red case folded open in front of her, Broxen the blue.

He was hunched low over his game board, a deep frown on his lips, occasionally glancing over to Ana, who was idly swinging her legs as she waited.

"B-four," Broxen said.

"Miss," Ana replied sweetly.

With a huff, Broxen reached into the compartment full of tiny white pegs, and, after fumbling for a couple seconds, plucked out one of the pegs with the tips of his claws to add to the tracker board.

"B-four," Ana said.

Broxen's expression darkened. "Don't copy me."

"Well?"

He growled. "Hit."

Ana offered him a toothy grin and marked her board with another red peg.

There were a lot more hit markers on Broxen's ships than on Ana's.

Pressing her lips together to hold in her threatening laughter, Gabriela pulled out a chair and sat down to watch them.

"We're almost done, Mom," Ana told her.

"It's not done," Broxen insisted, but he didn't seem very convinced.

He was right—at least technically. The game continued for three more turns, when Ana placed her hand on the top of her case and folded it partially down. "F-two."

"*Zorak akai*," Broxen muttered. "You destroyed my battleboat."

"*Sunk* your battle*ship*," Ana corrected.

"Doesn't matter. It's gone now."

Gabby laughed. "All right, kiddo, how about we let Broxen reflect upon his defeat and start the preparations?"

Ana's face lit up. "For Santa?"

"Yup. And for bed."

The little girl crumpled dramatically. "Aww, Mom. I won't be able to sleep, I'm too excited."

"You're going to have to try. The faster you get to sleep, the faster tomorrow will come. But let's get everything set up first, okay?"

They set out two plates on the mantle—one with the chocolate chip cookies for Santa, the other with carrots for the reindeer—along with a glass of milk and a bowl of water. The latter, Ana explained to Broxen, was in case the reindeer were thirsty.

Once those were placed, Ana wrote out a note for Santa, folded it up, and leaned it against the milk. "Santa's going to love your cookies, Mom. And I think he'll really like your snowman, Broxen."

Gabby couldn't avoid that pang in her chest. God, she didn't want Ana to be disappointed tomorrow. The girl deserved better than that. She was so sweet and kind. "Really excited for Santa this year, huh?"

"Of course! It doesn't matter what Lindsey Ruttle says."

"Who's Lindsey Ruttle?" Broxen asked, arching a brow.

"She's a girl at my school. Same grade, but not in my class." Ana rolled her eyes. "She says Santa Claus is fake and that it's just parents who do all the stuff, but what does she know? Aliens are real. Santa must be real too, right?"

Gabriela was close to rolling her eyes, too. Why did other kids have to spoil the fun?

"Maybe he's an alien," Broxen offered.

"Hmm...maybe."

"We'll never know," Gabby said. "Did you brush your teeth?"

"Yep."

"All right, let's get to bed, *mija*."

Ana walked to Broxen, who sank into a crouch. She wrapped her arms around his neck and gave him a hug. "You did good for your first time playing the game, Broxen. Maybe next time you'll do better."

He chuckled and returned the embrace, rubbing her back gently with his big hand. "Maybe. I am a quick learner. Better watch out for your battleboat next time."

Ana giggled. "Battleship."

His grin made it clear that he'd known that already. "Whatever it's called, it's going down."

"We'll see." Ana pressed a kiss to his cheek. "Goodnight, Broxen. Merry Christmas Eve."

"Night, Ana. Merry Christmas Eve." He released her and looked up at Gabriela. "I'm going to take a shower."

Gabby nodded. "Okay."

That would give her a little time to get ready after she filled Ana's stocking.

Ana hurried into her room, and Gabriela followed behind her. The little girl went straight to her dresser. She opened the top drawer and reached inside, shuffling around her clothing for a few moments before taking out a folded piece of paper. She brought it to Gabriela, holding it out.

Gabriela took the paper, lifting it closer to inspect it. The front had a drawing of a Christmas tree with bright colors on it, and *MERRY CHRISTMAS* written on the top in Ana's big, bubbly handwriting.

"Oh, *nena*." Gabriela looked at her daughter.

"Since my present to you burned up, I wanted to make you something else. It's not as cool, but I hope you like it."

Returning her attention to the card, Gabby opened it. There was another drawing inside—three people cuddled together in Ana's super cute, cartoony style. A man, a woman, and a child. The man was much larger than his companions, and just happened to have red skin, a tail, and horns. The lines of the latter two clipped through his hair; Gabby smiled, tracing a fingertip over them.

"I made the card before we found out about Broxen," Ana said sheepishly. "I wanted to make sure it was right."

"It's perfect," Gabriela said.

There was a note opposite the drawing.

Dear Mom,

I know this Christmas is hard, but any Christmas I get to spend with you is the BEST EVER.

I love You!

Ana

Gabriela pressed her lips together as tears stung her eyes. She raised the card away to avoid crying on it, reached out blindly, and put her arm around Ana, drawing her into a hug.

"*Mija*, this is the best card ever. The perfect card. I love you so, so much. Thank you."

Ana squeezed Gabby just as tight. "Love you too, Mom."

Once Gabriela had composed herself and dried her eyes, Ana hopped onto the bed, bouncing on her knees.

"I can't wait for tomorrow." She flopped down on her back, head landing on her pillow. "But I already got my Christmas wish."

"Oh yeah?" Gabriela asked, picking up the comforter and draping it over her daughter. "What was it?"

"To have a dad."

Gabriela's brows shot up. "You're so sure, huh?"

Ana smirked. "You guys are basically kissing and sucking tongues *all* the time."

"It's not *all* the time," Gabriela laughed.

"Do you love him?"

Gabriela's smiled softened as she looked down at her daughter. She brushed aside a stray strand of hair from Ana's forehead. "Yeah. Yeah, I do. What about you?"

"I do. I'm going to tell him tomorrow for Christmas...and ask if I can call him dad."

Ana's words wrapped around Gabriela's heart and squeezed it, so sweet and warm that they made it hard to breathe, that they made it impossible to say anything in response. She already knew Broxen wanted them without a single doubt, so there was no reason to tell Ana that it was too soon, that they needed to wait or give it some time. He'd told her that it was their choice.

And I'm done waiting.

NINETEEN

Gabriela stood at the foot of Broxen's bed, listening to the shower running in the bathroom while nervously fidgeting with the end of the red velvet ribbon from the giant bow tied around her chest. She stared at the bathroom door.

Despite insisting she was too excited to sleep, Ana had conked out within minutes of lying down. Gabriela had tucked Ana's gift under the tree, filled her stocking, and made sure Santa and the reindeer had eaten their treats. Now...it was time to give Broxen his gift.

Her.

She was wearing nothing but the bow, white panties, and a bra. Though her undergarments had a little lace on them, they were nothing like the beautiful, sexy lingerie she wished she could've worn for him tonight. But something told her that he wouldn't care what she had on.

And it wasn't like lingerie stayed on for long when a man was desperate to have what was beneath it.

The shower turned off.

Gabby's stomach fluttered, and she caught her bottom lip with her teeth.

It'd been so long since she'd had to look sexy for anyone, since she'd *wanted* to look sexy for anyone, so long since she'd been intimate. Her body had never been the same after having Ana, and it had matured since she'd been nineteen; she was softer, her hips wider, her breasts fuller, and she had a little loose skin on her belly that had never gone away after having a baby. There were also the stretch marks on her belly, hips, and thighs.

What would Broxen think when he saw her?

She raised her hands to fluff her hair, then lowered them to her bow, readjusting it to make sure it was centered on her breasts.

Stop it, Gabby. Everything will be fine.

Gabriela dropped her hands, curled them at her sides, and took a series of deep, calming breaths.

The bathroom door opened.

She gasped as Broxen, wearing only a towel around his waist, stepped into the doorway with all that delicious red skin on display and his tail slowly swishing behind him. His long, damp hair was slicked back with a few stray strands defying his horns to hang down the sides of his face.

Those beautiful, glowing violet eyes locked on Gabriela. Broxen froze, tail stiffening, and the large bulge between his legs twitched and swelled under the towel.

She'd known he was large after having felt him against her through their clothes, but seeing it like this, unrestricted by his pants, painted a whole new picture. And she hadn't even *seen*-seen it yet.

Her pussy clenched, and heat flooded her core as anticipation and arousal thrummed through her. She wanted—*needed*—to feel his cock inside her.

"Gabriela?" Broxen's voice was thick and gravelly.

Gabby pulled her gaze away from the growing bulge of his erection to meet his eyes. Fire burned within their depths. She walked toward him, slowly, making sure to put a little sway in her hips. Broxen's eyes dipped to take in her body once more. His jaw ticked, and his muscles flexed, but he did not move—except for his tail, which flicked erratically behind him. Lust was etched on every bit of his body.

His nostrils flared when she stopped in front of him.

"I wanted to give you your Christmas present," she said.

"What is it?"

She reached out and took one of his hands, guiding it to the velvety bow. "Open it and find out."

For a moment, his eyes searched hers as though in disbelief, but that quickly passed. Releasing a heavy breath that was underlaid by a low growl, he grasped the ribbon and, keeping his gaze locked with hers, slowly unraveled the knot.

"I want you, Broxen," she said as the loosening bow slipped to her waist. "And if you want me, I'm yours."

"You are." There was no question in his voice, no uncertainty in his expression. "Ah, female, you've always been *mine*."

Tearing the ribbon away, he closed the distance between them, captured her face between his hands, and claimed her mouth with his. He kissed her savagely, with a possessiveness that laid claim to her very soul; his lips branded her forever with his heat and passion. Gabriela closed her eyes and gave in, returning the kiss with her reckless abandon. His mouth was an inferno, and his tongue stoked that firestorm as it twined and danced with hers, building the flames higher and higher.

She thrust her hands into his hair, sliding them up until she grasped the roots of his horns.

Broxen shuddered and growled, dropping his hands to her ass and squeezing it. She felt the prick of his claws against her skin, and the sensation only made her wetter. He lifted Gabby, clutching her against him, and she instinctively wrapped her legs around his waist.

He strode forward and laid her on the bed, coming down over her. She welcomed his weight, craved it, and moaned when she felt the length of his cock against her pussy. Broxen snarled and tore his mouth from hers, leaving her lips burning in the aftermath of his fiery kiss.

His mouth seared a path down her neck and shoulder, where she felt the light scrape of his fangs. She shivered.

"I claim you tonight, my mate," he said, his breath hot against her flesh. "You will be filled with my seed, you will bear my scent, my mark."

"Yes," she whispered, tilting her head back as he trailed more of those searing kisses along her collarbone. "Make me yours, Broxen."

His mouth dipped to her chest, and his lips brushed between her breasts as he slid his hands under her. Gabriela arched her back, and his fingers made quick work of her bra clasps. Broxen caught the front of her bra between his teeth and tugged on it. She shifted, letting the straps slide off her shoulders so she could withdraw her arms.

He snapped his head to the side, flinging the bra away, before turning his heated gaze back to her.

"I've dreamed of these," he said, cupping her breasts with his big hands. "My imagination did them no justice."

Broxen stroked his thumbs over her nipples, and Gabby gasped. Her nipples budded beneath his touch. He circled and stroked them as he squeezed and kneaded her breasts. The ache within them, within her core, intensified, making her breathless.

"You are beautiful, female."

He dropped his head and captured one of her nipples

between his lips. Gabriela whimpered at the heat of his mouth, her hands flying to head. He sucked her nipple deep, his tongue grazing it and twirling around it over and over.

"Mmm." She closed her eyes.

His fangs pressed against the tender flesh of her breasts, bringing the faintest whispers of pleasure-pain. Instead of making her afraid, that sensation thrilled her, awaking a craving she never knew she'd had.

She brushed her thumbs over the bases of his horns, caressing them, making him shudder and groan as her pelvis moved of its own accord to rock against his abs. But it wasn't enough. Her clit, throbbing in need, remained untouched, and that space within her remained hollow.

Broxen caressed her breasts and lavished her nipples with his tongue until they were tender, and she was writhing. The insistent throb between her legs became too much.

"Broxen...please," she begged.

He released her nipple, placing a gentle kiss upon it as he looked up at her. "Is my female in need?"

"Yes. Yes, she needs *very* much."

His lips stretched into a rakish grin.

"And what does she need?" He lowered his head and trailed kisses down her belly, sliding his body lower as he did so.

Gabriela's breath quickened as she watched his mouth move farther down her body. When that long tongue of his swirled around her belly button, she grasped the bedding beside her and said, "I...I need your cock."

Broxen's mouth was about to touch the waistband of her panties when he paused. He lifted his head slightly, closed his eyes, and inhaled through his nostrils. His lips peeled back, baring those fangs. "Think you need my tongue first."

Gabby could've come just from those words alone.

Oh God, yes.

Broxen rose onto his knees and hooked his fingers beneath the waistband of her panties at either hip. She lifted her bottom without hesitation, allowing him to slide her underwear off.

"So wet." He rubbed his thumb over the damp spot in her panties. Bringing them to his face, he inhaled and released a low growl that made her pussy clench. "You smell delicious, Gabriela."

Heat flooded her. She didn't understand it, but seeing him smelling her panties, taking in her most intimate fragrance, was such a turn on.

He tossed her underwear aside and grasped her thighs, spreading them wide. His gaze locked on her sex. The fire in his eyes blazed impossibly brighter, and his tongue slipped out to lick his lips. He dropped one of his hands, running the back of his finger over the small patch of dark hair and along her pussy before pressing another finger into place and parting her labia. "You *look* delicious."

Faster than Gabriela could utter another plea, Broxen dropped his head between her thighs and pressed his mouth to her core. She gasped, grasping his horns and arching her back at the sudden burst of pleasure. He lapped at her from bottom to top, teasingly flicking her clit with the tip of his tongue, seemingly determined to lick up every drop of her arousal and coax out more.

He groaned and slipped his arms around her legs, dragging her closer. "I will never get enough of this—of you—my mate."

Then he slipped that long tongue inside her, plunging it deep.

"Broxen," she rasped, squeezing her eyes shut. It had been so long, *so* long, that even this was stretching her. But it felt *good*. She undulated upon his thick tongue as it curled and twisted and thrust within her, hitting *that* spot. Pleasure coiled in her belly.

Spanning his hands over her pelvis, Broxen withdrew his tongue and latched onto her clit.

Gabriela cried out at the sharp, sudden rapture that bolted through her as he sucked and lashed the sensitive nub. At first, she tried to escape the assault, but he pressed her down firmly on the bed, forcing her to take to it all, to feel it all. Wild gasps spilled from her lips as she writhed. Squeezing his horns, she ground her cleft against his mouth, not only taking everything he had to give her but demanding more.

Were Gabriela able to look upon this scene as a spectator, she wouldn't have recognized herself—and she wouldn't have cared. This was all that mattered, this feeling, this moment.

Broxen.

He made her feel wanted, needed. He made her feel *alive*.

Yielding to the searing ecstasy roiling inside her, yielding to him, Gabby shattered.

Pleasure swept through her, consuming her in a scorching blaze of sweet agony. Her body tensed as tremors overwhelmed her, and her breath came in sharp, surrendering moans. Liquid heat flooded her.

Broxen growled, the vibrations pushing her to new heights while his tongue continued its ruthless movements. It was a delicious torment she never wanted to end. She whispered his name, she thrashed and twisted atop the bedding, she fought his hold and pulled him closer, begging for more.

And he gave it to her, again and again, until she was left breathless and trembling.

Just when she could take no more, Broxen released her. He gave her one long, final lick, and raised his head.

Panting, Gabriela dropped her hands from his horns and

met his gaze with a half-lidded stare. His features were bestial, his eyes hungry. He ran his long tongue over his lips, which still glistened with her essence.

The towel around his waist had come undone. Broxen tossed it away and drew himself over her, planting his hands on either side of her head. Gabriela looked down between their bodies. Her breath caught in her throat.

His cock was a deep, dark red, its long, thick shaft ending with a pronounced head and a tapered tip. There were multiple stacked ridges along its top, and she knew exactly where those would stroke inside her—but she could only guess at the immense pleasure they would give her.

Broxen lifted his hips and poised the head of his shaft at the entrance of her pussy. Her eyes met his.

"You're mine, female."

"Yours," she said, sliding her palms down his arms.

With her sex still quivering, Broxen thrust his hips forward, plunging into her heat.

Gabriela gasped. Even only partway in, his cock stretched her. She raised her knees and spread her legs wider. Broxen growled, baring his teeth as he drew back. The ridges on his shaft dragged along her channel and clit, coaxing moans from her. When he drove back in, he pushed deeper than the first time, and deeper still with each subsequent thrust.

And all Gabby could do was cling to him, eager for what was to come, eager for him to fulfill his word and make her wholly his.

Broxen shuddered. The feel of his mate's tight, hot, slick sex as it cinched around his cock was impossible to put into words. It was everything for which he'd yearned and so, so much more;

it was torturous and rapturous and a thousand other human terms he couldn't recall in the face of such overwhelming pleasure.

The pressure that had been building within him over the last year—more so by far in the last several days than ever before—was too immense to withstand. It threatened to tear him apart, it threatened to crush him. But he didn't want it to end, not yet.

He needed more. Forever more.

He slipped a hand between their bodies to grasp Gabriela's soft breast, caressing it and pinching her nipple, and watched her eyelashes flutter and her features contort in pleasure. He smoothed that palm up to cup her cheek, forcing her eyes to meet his.

"My beautiful mate," he said, thrusting deeper into her sex. "So beautiful."

Lips parted and softly panting, she smiled and framed his face with her hands. Her eyes were bright with desire and affection. "I love you, Broxen."

He knew the meaning of that word, *love*, but until a few days ago he'd never really understood it. He'd never understood the depth of what he truly wanted with Gabriela, couldn't have even imagined it. Love seemed too simple a word for what he felt for her, but it was the right word.

His chest swelled, flooding with heat separate from that of his lust, and his jaw clenched. It was fullness, happiness, it was...just *everything*.

Something else flared within him in that moment, something he'd felt with her before—a primal, deep-rooted instinct, a bestial drive that was closer to raw emotion than it ever would be to rational thought. His gums ached, and his fangs lengthened; he needed to mark her.

Gabriela is mine.

He swept his tail to the side, wound it around her calf, and hitched her leg high over his hip. Hooking his thumb beneath her chin, he turned her face aside to expose her neck. His eyes fell to that spot wherever her neck and shoulder met, the spot he'd nuzzled before.

Broxen dropped his head, sinking his fangs into Gabriela's soft, tender flesh even as he buried his shaft inside her to its base.

She gasped and stiffened beneath him. Broxen squeezed his eyes shut and shifted his free hand to her ass to hold her in place as he pumped his hips hard and fast. The sweetness of her skin, the saltiness of her sweat, and the metallic tang of her blood were overwhelming, making his head spin.

"Broxen," Gabriela rasped. Her hands dropped to his arms, and her fingers bent, scraping his skin. The little trails of pain left by her nails were thrilling.

Pleasure blossomed low in his belly, racing up along his spine and sparking outward. It was in direct opposition to that impossibly building pressure at his core, which felt like a star was collapsing inside him.

Beneath him, his female tensed. Her sex quivered and constricted around his shaft, heightening both his pleasure and his torture, and a fresh wave of heat flooded her as her moans escalated into cries.

Broxen snarled against her skin and rutted harder still, his own breath ragged. His rhythm faltered abruptly. For an instant, the pressure was so immense, so unbearable, that his mind went blank and his heart stuttered.

He pulled his mouth away from her and reared back, climaxing with a growl that would've been a wall-shaking roar had he not locked his jaw to suppress it. Ecstasy blinded him, but his hands found her hips regardless, slamming her against is pelvis and locking her there as his seed burst from him. Stream after stream filled her.

Awareness was slow to return. Broxen floated on a wave of bliss unlike anything he'd ever felt. He pumped his hips shallowly, groaning at the slick heat that was his mate's sex.

My mate.

Shoulders heaving with heavy breaths, Broxen opened his eyes and looked down at Gabriela. Her head was turned, her hair was fanned over the bedding around her, and her eyes were closed. One of her hands rested on her cheek, the other on the bed. Her breasts, nipples still peaked, rose and fell as she panted. Her skin glistened with sweat.

But it was his bite—his mark—that his eyes focused on.

He brushed her hair away from her neck, leaned down, and licked the small wounds. When he pulled back, pride blossomed within his chest.

A small smear of blood remained on her skin, but her wounds were already sealed. Even had he not learned it through his own research, he knew instinctually that omnyrian saliva could cause such rapid healing—while ensuring a visible mark would remain behind. *His* mark.

Broxen's chest rumbled with a possessive growl.

Gabriela's lashes lifted, and she tiredly peeked up at him. "You bit me."

"Can bite me next time if you want."

She grinned, and a wicked light danced in her eyes. "I just might."

His cock, still buried within her, twitched in anticipation. Broxen's arousal didn't ease when Gabriela chuckled, sending faint but unignorable vibrations through his shaft and sparking new pulses of pleasure.

"Looking forward to it, female."

Her eyelids fluttered shut and she took in a deep breath. "Ready for round two? Bet you could go all night, couldn't you?"

"Easily." He brushed the backs of his fingers across her cheek. "I'll never have enough."

"Mmm." Her features eased. "Don't think I will...either..."

Gabriela's breathing slowed, and her body relaxed. Broxen tilted his head. Had she just...fallen asleep?

His lips curled into a soft smile, and his heart felt like it had expanded to fill his whole chest. It would have been sheer bliss to simply lie down and sleep while their bodies were still connected like this, to enjoy this closeness through the night, but he knew if he were to do that, he wouldn't be able to accomplish everything he needed to get done tonight.

He also knew just enough about Christmas to understand what was likely to happen in the morning. The last thing they needed was for Ana to burst into the room in excitement only to find Broxen and Gabriela naked and entangled.

Moving as slowly as he could, Broxen withdrew from Gabriela, barely stopping himself from shuddering at the slide of her sex around his cock. She didn't even stir. When he finally pulled free, a trickle of his seed dripped from her entrance. Seeing it triggered that primal possessiveness within him; fire roared in his gut, and he captured his lip between his teeth and bit down to prevent himself from rutting her again.

The sting of pain was just enough to hold him back. That urge to fill her with his seed again, to ensure her womb was overflowing, was not one he needed to succumb to right now.

This had been the first time. There would be many, many more to come.

Pushing himself off the bed, he walked into the bathroom to clean himself up. He emerged a couple minutes later with a warm washcloth in hand. With as much delicacy as he could manage, he cleaned Gabriela, wiping their mingled essences from her skin. She moaned and shifted her thighs but did not wake. When he was done, he collected his discarded towel and Gabriela's undergarments, tossing them into the hamper along with the washcloth.

Broxen retrieved a pair of boxers, some sweatpants, and a t-shirt from the dresser, tugging them on before returning to the bed. He eased himself down to sit beside Gabriela. For a time, he simply stared at her.

Zorak akai, she was so damned beautiful.

And she's mine.

He ran his eyes over her, drinking in every little detail of her body, adoring every inch of her, right down to the faint, shimmery marks on her belly and the bit of loose skin there. Though he didn't know for sure, he guessed she'd earned those marks by carrying Ana in her womb. He gently ran the tips of his fingers over some of them, tracing their paths. Her belly quivered beneath his touch.

Stilling his hand, he snapped his gaze to her face. She simply nuzzled the bedding, releasing a heavy breath before settling again.

Broxen swung his eyes back to her abdomen. Now he settled his hand over it, marveling at the feel of her soft skin beneath his palm. It didn't matter if his seed took root or not. It didn't matter if she bore his young, didn't matter if she even could. He had everything he wanted right here and in the room across the hall—he had his mate, his kit, his family.

He yearned to lie beside her now, to take her in his arms and fall into the most contented sleep of his life. Longed to drift into slumber with her scent—with the scent of their mating— filling his nostrils. But tomorrow was Christmas, and Broxen had a long night ahead.

He stood up, turned, and carefully slipped the blanket out from beneath Gabriela. Once it was free, he gently draped it over her, covering her body. That done, he bent down and placed a tender, lingering kiss upon her lips.

"And I love you, my Gabriela," he whispered.

TWENTY

GABRIELA WOKE with a sense of contentment she hadn't felt in years—if ever. She was warm, cuddled against her man with her head on his shoulder, listening to his soft growls as he slept, and her body felt...languid.

It was also sore, especially her nipples and between her legs.

I had sex. Amazing, wild, mind-blowing, sex.

With an alien.

She grinned, running her fingers lightly over his chest, following the contours of his muscles.

I had the best sex of my life, with an alien, and then fell asleep before he even pulled out.

Her grin faltered.

No way. Wasn't it usually the man who fell asleep right after sex?

Gabby raised her head and looked at Broxen. His face was turned forward her, features relaxed in sleep. He lay on his back, one arm bent above his head, the other resting on his chest.

What had he thought of her?

She almost snorted. He'd likely patted himself on the back for sexing her to exhaustion.

But...she could make it up to him. Besides, it was Christmas, the season of giving. So why not gift him with something pleasurable to wake up to?

Slowly, she extracted herself from his side, rising onto her knees. She started when she felt something seep from her sex and wet her inner thighs.

Okay, so maybe a quick bathroom trip first.

She eased off the bed, taking great care not to jostle the mattress as she stepped down onto the floor, and hurried to the bathroom, emptying her bladder and making sure to clean herself up good—though she wasn't nearly as sticky as she remembered feeling right before drifting off.

"How does any man have so much cum?" she muttered, then snickered to herself. "At least it's not a weird color."

She didn't know what she'd expected—he was an alien, after all. She was just thankful it wasn't red. *That* would have been a mood killer.

After washing her hands, she looked up at herself in the mirror and paused. There, where her neck and shoulder met, was the bitemark he'd left.

She'd forgotten about it, had forgotten that moment of pain that had been swiftly overtaken by pleasure. Gabriela touched the marks. They weren't red or inflamed, there were no scabs, and they didn't even hurt. It was as though they they'd always been there.

Once finished, she peeked back into the bedroom. It was still early enough that the sun hadn't made its full appearance yet, leaving the room mostly dark. Hopefully that also meant it was early enough that Ana would sleep a while longer.

On that thought, Gabby stepped over to the bedroom door

and locked it. The last thing she needed was for her daughter to burst in and get another X-rated surprise.

She padded back to the bed and crawled onto the mattress, settling herself on her knees at Broxen's hip. Reaching out, she pinched the edge of the blanket and slowly drew it down his body, revealing him inch by sexy inch until his hard, thick cock sprang free.

She caught her bottom lip between her teeth. She'd only had a brief glimpse of his cock last night, but now she had to chance to inspect it closer. He'd told her that it didn't look like a human's, and he was right. Its skin was a darker red than the rest of him. Overlapping ridges ran along the top of the shaft, and there were defined bulges on the underside—as though even his shaft had muscles. All that led to the pronounced head with its tapered tip.

Gabriela had felt that tip, those ridges, those bulges, had felt *everything* inside her with his every thrust.

She couldn't wait to feel it inside her again.

Looking up at Broxen, she reached out, wrapped her fingers around the root of his cock, and lowered her head, taking him into her mouth.

He stirred; his shaft twitched, his fingers flexed upon his chest, and his brow furrowed. But he didn't wake. Not yet.

She moved her mouth up and down, her lips gliding over his bulges and ridges, and watched him all the while. Heat pooled in her core as her arousal grew. She nearly moaned when seed seeped from his tip. It was sweet with a hint of salt, tasting almost like the icing on a cinnamon roll. Pulling up, she locked her lips around the head and sucked, eager for more.

Broxen growled and raised his hips for a moment, his other hand curling to squeeze the bedding. He lifted his head to look down at her, his sleepy eyes—still glowing vibrant purple—locking with hers. "Ah, female..."

She loved it when he called her that. His voice caressed the endearment while at the same time instilling it with possessiveness. Saying it like she was his.

And she *was* his.

She twirled her tongue around the head of his cock and sucked his shaft deeper into her mouth. He was so thick that it was difficult to take much of him, so she used one hand to pump along his length, keeping it in time with the motions of her mouth, while fondling his heavy sack with the other. This time, when she tasted his seed, she didn't stop herself from moaning.

Broxen's eyelids fluttered, and he drew his lips back, baring his fangs.

His responses, his expressions, this very act in itself, made her pussy clench with need. She was so tender and aroused that a few strokes of her clit might have been enough to get her off.

Gabriela parted her thighs, withdrawing her hand from his sack and slipping it between her legs as she continued to suck his cock. She slowly circled her clit with the tip of her finger.

His nostrils flared with a deep inhalation, and he grinned. He reached up and brushed a finger over her sensitive nipple. "Does my mate seek relief?"

Before he'd even given her time to respond, she felt something brush her thighs. An instant later, his tail probed her sex, pushing into her.

Gabriela gasped. Though the tip of his tail wasn't as thick as his cock, it was more than enough to make her shudder with pleasure. He pumped it in and out of her, and she knew it wouldn't be long before she peaked. She already felt like she was right on the verge.

"So wet for her male," Broxen said huskily.

Breath quickening, she lifted her head, pulling her lips

away from his shaft. "Broxen... This...this was supposed to be for you."

"It is," he rasped, driving his tail deeper still. "*You* are for me. And I need more."

He sat up, abs flexing, and reached forward to hook his hands under her arms. As he lay back down, he dragged her up his body, creating delicious friction between her nipples and his skin, and withdrew his tail, leaving behind an aching emptiness.

Straddling Broxen, Gabriela flattened her hands on his shoulders and looked down at him, her hair falling loose around her face.

Broxen reached up and brushed his thumb over her lower lip. "As much as I love your mouth"—he dropped his hands to her hips and lifted her—"I need to be inside you, Gabriela."

That emptiness he'd left behind was swiftly filled as he slammed her down onto his cock. Her lips parted in a silent cry, and her pussy clamped around him as pleasure-pain tore through her. Teeth bared, Broxen grunted, lifted her, and yanked her back down again, forcing her to meet the upthrust of his hips until she'd taken him fully inside her.

In this position, he felt bigger, felt thicker, and every sensation was impossibly stronger.

As he allowed her time to grow accustomed to him, his hands explored her body, smoothing over her waist, her back, her shoulders and belly until, finally, he cupped her breasts. He was gentle as he stroked her nipples with his thumbs. Even that simple touch sent a bolt of pleasure through her, seeming to strike her clit directly.

"Broxen," she breathed, lashes fluttering, but she kept her eyes open and upon him.

He shifted a hand up to sweep her hair aside and bare the mark on her shoulder to his heated gaze. The growl that rumbled in his chest vibrated through her. Her fingers curled against his skin as she rocked upon him, needing more, needing him deeper.

She could feel his throbbing pulse through his shaft, could feel its every tiny twitch as surely as she felt those ridges glide over her G-spot with every motion of their hips. Warmth flooded her. She spread her thighs wider, reveling in the feel of him.

Gabriela kept her eyes locked with his as the pleasure sharpened in her core. Broxen's gaze communicated just how desperately he needed her, burning with a fervent intensity. His jaw was clenched, and his hands squeezed her thighs. She knew he was holding back, knew he was worried he'd get too rough, or worse, hurt her. But she knew he wouldn't. She trusted him completely.

"Take me, Broxen," she begged. "No holding back."

As though in response to her words, his cock swelled. She barely held herself up on her trembling arms as Broxen snarled and grabbed her ass with both hands. The tips of his claws pricked her skin as he pounded into her with fierce snaps of his hips.

Gabriela released a choked cry and clung to him. He was creating a maelstrom of sensation within her. Her breath came out in short and shallow pants, her thighs were wet with her essence, her breasts were bouncing, and the heat in her core intensified.

Then she felt something else nudge her—the tip of his tail. It slipped between them, dragging along her pussy, where their bodies were connected, coating itself with her essence.

A possessive, but devilish light gleamed in Broxen's eyes.

"You're mine, Gabriela," he grunted without slowing his pace. His grip on her ass cheeks shifted, and he spread them. "*All* of you."

His tail trailed up from her pussy, and its tip pressed against the tight ring of her backside.

Gabriela gasped, her eyes flaring wide. She'd never, ever had anyone touch her there before. It was foreign, it was taboo, it was...thrilling.

He slowly pushed his tail against her ass, slipping the tip inside. She whimpered. It stung, and the stretch burned, but those discomforts were quickly swept away by the pleasure of his pounding cock. He eased his tail back slightly and pushed it in again, a little deeper this time.

"Ah!" Gabriela dug her nails into his shoulders and moaned. So full. She felt so full of him. Every nerve within her was abuzz with ecstasy.

"That's it, female," Broxen growled, quickening his thrusts.

She became lost in a frenzy of movement, of sensation, and the torrent of need that had built within Gabriela burst against the force of his attentions. Intense pleasure consumed her, fragmenting her conscious thoughts. Only feeling remained.

Her cry was a hitched, broken sound as spasms wracked her. She fell upon his chest and buried her face against his neck to muffle the escalating moans tearing her from throat as her pussy quivered around the thick length of his cock, and her anus constricted around his tail.

Broxen removed his hand from her ass cheek to slip his fingers into her hair and catch the strands close to her scalp in his fist. He tugged back, lifting her face, and captured her mouth with his in a crushing kiss. He took possession of her mouth as surely as he had her body.

His entire body tensed, and he snarled against her lips as he came, clutching her to him. His molten seed flooded her mercilessly, the blast so hot and powerful it rocketed Gabriela into another intense climax.

When their bodies had ceased their tremors, and the tide of

passion had finally calmed, they lay together, Gabriela sprawled atop him, and basked in the glow of their lovemaking.

Broxen kept one arm around her waist while he soothingly combed his claws through her hair. Gabriela smiled and flattened her hand on his chest, fingers splayed, feeling the pounding of his heart beneath her palm. It matched the rhythm of his throbbing cock, which remained deep within her.

He slowly withdrew his tail from her ass. She winced slightly, hissing softly through her teeth.

Broxen smoothed his palm down her back and gently kneaded her bottom. "Are you hurt?"

"No," she said, taking in a deep breath and releasing it in a sigh. She'd never considered trying anal in her life, and this surprise...well... It had hurt initially, but after that, it'd been an amazing feeling. She wouldn't mind trying it again. Perhaps, eventually, with his cock.

Lifting her head, she folded her hands under her chin and smiled up at him. "Merry Christmas, Broxen."

His violet eyes glowed bright as they met hers, and his lips stretched into a wide grin. He stroked her cheek with his thumb. "Merry Christmas, my mate."

A rattle of the doorhandle and a loud knock on their bedroom door startled them.

"Mom! Broxen!" Ana cried. "He came! Santa came!"

Her excited voice faded as she hurried away from the door.

Gabriela looked back at Broxen, and they both broke out into laughter—which quickly turned to moans as his cock moved within her.

Thank God for locks.

TWENTY-ONE

Confident that the Ana's stocking would keep her busy for a little while, Gabriela and Broxen shared a shower during which the biggest frustration wasn't from a lack of space or hot water but because they knew they needed to keep their hands—and tail—to themselves. Fifteen minutes was reasonable for a shower. Much longer than that, and Ana was likely to be pounding on the bedroom door again, demanding they come out before they missed Christmas.

Once they were dressed and their hair was brushed—and after Broxen had pulled Gabby in for a deep, passionate kiss that left her reeling—they finally emerged from the bedroom.

"Mom!" Ana shouted, darting from the living room into the hallway like she had a jet engine strapped to her back. Her eyes were bright with excitement, and her smile was huge. She grabbed Gabriela's hand. "Come look!"

Gabby's heart melted, and the worries she'd harbored about this day vanished entirely. She'd feared Ana would wake only to disappointment.

She glanced back at Broxen for a moment as she let her

daughter drag her into the living room. When she turned her face forward, her heart stuttered, and she froze. Ana released her hand.

Ana's stocking was on the coffee table, its contents scattered around it, and Gabriela knew from a glance that there was much more there than she'd bought. She didn't recognize several of the items; she couldn't have afforded all of it.

But that was only the start. Because under the tree, there wasn't the single wrapped gift Gabriela had bought with the last of her money—there were dozens of presents wrapped in red wrapping paper with white reindeer and snowflake patterns on it. They were *all* in that paper except for the one gift from Gabby, and they all looked like they'd been packaged by someone who had no idea what they were doing. Each gift was decorated with a brightly colored bow, none of which matched the wrapping paper.

A couple of the presents even had holes in the wrapping that had been haphazardly covered by tape.

The air fled Gabby's lungs in a rush. Tears flooded her eyes, making the Christmas tree's lights look especially bright and sparkly. She looked at Broxen, who'd come to stand beside her.

"You did this?" she asked quietly. "This...this is why you were gone so long the other day?"

His smile was soft, but it was also heartfelt and passionate as he bent close to her. "I wanted my mate and kit to have everything."

She laughed, and the tears fell down her cheeks. She wrapped her arms around his neck. "But you've already given me everything I could ask for just by being part of our lives. You are all we wanted—all we needed." Drawing back, she met his gaze. "Thank you. Thank you for making Ana's Christmas wonderful."

"*Con mucho gusto.*" Broxen lifted a hand to tuck a few

loose strands of Gabriela's hair behind her ear, the backs of his fingers gently brushing across her cheek to wipe away her tears. "I love you, Gabriela."

Gabby pulled her lips into her mouth and tried to stem the flow of tears. This was a happy moment. She wouldn't let tears ruin it—not even happy tears. "I love you, too."

Broxen and Gabriela rocked slightly on their feet as Ana threw her arms around them from the side, squeezing them tight. "I love you both, too," she said, peeking up at them. "Can we open presents now?"

Gabriela laughed and reached down to hug her daughter, pressing a kiss to her forehead. "Yeah. You can open presents now."

Ana squealed and pulled away, running toward the mountain of gifts.

Gabriela and Broxen sat on the couch, his tail curled around her waist and his arm around her shoulders, as Ana tore open one present after another. Every gift was met with wide-eyed delight from Ana—and disbelief from Gabby, who kept looking at Broxen.

There were games—both video and board—dolls, stuffed animals, seemingly every product ever made with a unicorn on it, and a stockpile of sketchbooks, stickers, and art supplies. But there was also clothing. Shirts, pants, pajamas, dresses, hoodies, enough to pack Ana's dresser full, and three new pairs of shoes. Ana loved every bit of it, hugging every single gift while thanking Broxen and Gabby.

No one could ever have considered Ana a spoiled child, but Broxen sure seemed keen on changing that today.

"Mom," Ana said, pushing a pile of gifts toward Gabriela. "These are for you."

"What?" Gabby's brow furrowed. She glanced at the gifts

before turning her eyes toward Broxen. "But I...I didn't get you..."

"You have given me everything, female," Broxen said, running his hand up and down her arm. "Open them."

Excitement filled Gabriela as Ana placed a wrapped box in her lap. Other than the sweet little homemade gifts Ana had given her over the years and gift cards sent from her parents, she couldn't remember opening a present like this since she was a kid.

She tore open the wrapping and lifted the lid of the box within. Her eyes widened. There were several articles of clothing inside, but not just any kind of clothing—these were the satiny, revealing sort of clothes typically reserved for use in bedrooms during intimate moments.

Ana giggled and lifted a pair of lacy teal panties out of the box. "Preeeetty."

Gabriela snatched the underwear away from her daughter and stuffed it back in the box, her cheeks turning red. "These, *mija*, are not for you." She replaced the lid and set the box aside, giving Broxen what she hoped was a pointed but playful glare.

With a mischievous grin and fire in his eyes, he rumbled, "They're for me."

Now it wasn't only Gabby's cheeks that were warm. Fortunately, Ana had returned to the presents. The tip of Broxen's tail brushed over Gabriela's upper thigh as she and her daughter opened the remaining gifts.

Most of Gabriela's gifts were clothes—not just lingerie, though there was a little more of it, but real clothes. Blouses and slacks, t-shirts and jeans, dresses, pajamas, shoes, and even a stylish new coat. She didn't know if it would all fit, didn't know if any of it would fit, but she didn't care. Because he'd bought it all for her. He'd thought about her, he'd done what so many men seemed unwilling to do, and he'd braved clothing stores to get her gifts. Not just what he must've thought she'd look sexy in, but what he thought she'd be comfortable in.

There were also candles, a few boxes of gourmet chocolate, and a DVD of Gabriela's favorite movie, The Terminator.

Had that been why he'd written it in that paper in his room?

But there was something else in one of the boxes, something that brought fresh tears to her eyes.

A nativity set.

She'd told him about the one she'd lost in the fire, the one that her mother had given her. Now, he'd given her a new one to cherish.

Gabriela turned and pressed a lingering kiss to Broxen's cheek. "Thank you."

When all the gifts were opened, a huge pile of crumpled wrapping paper and bows had accumulated on one side of the room. Ana lay on the floor in front of the fireplace, playing with some of her new toys, and Gabriela sat tucked against Broxen on the couch with her head resting on his shoulder. He had an arm wrapped around her, holding her close, and his tail lazily flicked back and forth over the top of her thigh.

Gabriela looked around—at the mess, at the gifts Broxen had bought for her and her daughter, at the crooked tree and its lovely, mismatched decorations, at the low-burning fire and the two stockings still hung on the mantle.

Even without the gifts, this had already been the best Christmas she could recall.

"You really didn't have to do all this, Broxen," she said, finally looking at him. "Thank you so much. For everything. You took us from disaster to...to paradise in a few days."

He chuckled. "Don't think anyone could call this place

paradise. But with you two...I think it is. There's one more thing, though."

Gabby lifted her head. Her lips trembled as though unable to decide whether they wanted to smile or frown. "You don't need to give us more, really."

Keeping that gentle smile of his in place, he disentangled himself from her, withdrawing his arm and tail, and pushed himself to his feet. He walked to the fireplace, carefully stepping over Ana's things that were strewn across the floor. He reached forward and plucked Gabriela's stocking—the simple red and white one—off its hook.

"You didn't check your stocking," he said as he returned to her.

"Oh, Mom! Did Santa get you something?" Ana hopped to her feet and scurried over to sit beside Gabriela on the couch.

Broxen stopped in front of them and dipped his hand into the stocking. Gabby turned her gaze up to him with a crease forming between her brows. Her heart sped just a little, and her stomach fluttered; it must've had something to do with the way he was looking down at her. What was he doing? What was this?

As Broxen withdrew his hand from the stocking, he sank onto one knee. His hand emerged holding a jewelry box that looked so tiny in his big fingers. His tongue slipped out to wet his lips. Draping the stocking over his thigh, he took hold of the box's lid and pried it open.

There was a necklace inside—a silver unicorn with a mane of glimmering stones, wrapped around a larger pink teardrop gemstone. Broxen held it out to Ana. "Ana...will you be my daughter?"

Ana looked from the necklace to Broxen, eyes rounding and shimmering with tears as her features crumpled. She nodded and threw her arms around his neck, squeezing him tight. "Santa really did grant me my Christmas wish. I love you."

Broxen's arms engulfed her in an embrace, one of his big hands cupping her head.

Gabriela covered her mouth with a hand and met his gaze, recognizing his love and affection for Ana in his eyes. She knew that her daughter could want for a no better father.

Ana turned her head, kissed his cheek, and drew back wearing a big smile. Broxen released her.

"My dad," she said.

He grinned as he removed the necklace from the box and carefully wrapped it around Ana's neck. His thick fingers fumbled with the delicate clasp for a few seconds before finally getting it closed. When it was in place, he looked up at her. "My daughter."

Gabriela's chest constricted.

"This is the best Christmas ever," Ana said, pecking another kiss on Gabby's cheek before stepped away and lifting the unicorn pendant off her chest to stare at it in wonder.

A gentle touch on Gabriela's leg drew her attention back to Broxen. His tail stroked her thigh before trailing down to wrap around her ankle.

"I'm not done yet, female," he said. He slipped his hand into the stocking again, keeping his eyes locked with Gabriela's all the while. Drawing in a slow, deep breath, he took out another jewelry box, this one slightly larger than the first.

"Broxen," Gabby breathed.

Broxen set the stocking on the floor, rested the little box on his palm, and took delicate hold of the lid. "Gabriela, my mate" —he slowly lifted the lid—"you are mine in all ways but this. Will you be my wife?"

The ring, tucked in its dark velvety cushion, had an elegant white gold band with tiny diamonds inlaid upon it and a single, larger diamond at the center that sparkled brilliantly.

Gabriela looked up at Broxen, grinned, and threw herself at him. He caught her, but her momentum carried them both to the floor atop the pile of wrapping paper and bows. His arms banded around her, holding her on top of him.

With a laugh, she lowered her lips to his ear. "You were in my butt. Of course I'm saying yes!"

Broxen's laughter was deep and rolling, thrumming into Gabriela through her chest. "Every way, female. I needed you to be mine in *every* way."

"Guuuuuys," Ana whined. "No tongue sucking!"

"Look away, Ana," Gabriela said with a chuckle. She brushed the long strands of hair from Broxen's face, tucking them behind his horns, and caressed his cheek. Her heart was overflowing with love. Lowering her head, she pressed her lips to his. "Merry Christmas, Broxen, my mate and husband-to-be."

He hummed, his violet eyes aglow, and turned his head to kiss her palm. "Merry Christmas, Gabriela, my everything."

Thank you so much for reading *Claimed by the Alien Bodyguard*! We hope you enjoyed it.

We meant to release this a lot sooner, but after Rob and I ended up with Covid-19 in November (we're doing fine now, no worries!), we fell a little behind schedule, and of course this story ran longer than we planned (no surprise!), but it's here, it's out, and we hope you all loved Broxen, Gabriela, and Ana. We had so much fun writing them. They are such a sweet family.

And if you loved it, please, please, please leave a review. **Puppy dog eyes**

...did it work? Haha!

So! Fun (or maybe not so fun?) fact about the fire in this book: it's actually based on the house fire that destroyed my parent's house in 2009.

My parents were not home at the time (dad was working, mom was at the gym), but my brother was there, having moved back in with them. He said he was taking a shower when he smelled something burning. He got out, dried off, opened the door, and saw smoke all over the ceiling. He threw on some boxers and rounded the corner to the hallway and saw the fire, which was as high as the ceiling and had spread from the dining room (where their Christmas tree had been) to the living room. The smoke detector went off then. Thankfully, he was able to go out the back door.

So here it is, middle of winter, snow on the ground, and my

brother is standing barefoot outside in his boxers. He calls my dad, then calls 911. I get a call from my other brother and he's like, "Parents' house is on fire."

Thinking he's just being his typical wise-ass self, I was like "Nuh, uh." Cause, you know, that just *wouldn't* happen. It couldn't...right?

Him: "I'm serious."

Me: "What? No way? For real?"

Him: Yup.

And then all of us, me, my dad, my two brothers, and my sister were trying to get hold of my mom, who was ignoring our calls while she was on the treadmill (most likely playing a mobile game). We're just blowing up her phone. Finally, thinking it has to be an emergency with that many missed calls, she answered. She said we should have texted her first, and she would've answered sooner. LOL! Oh, mother.

The cause: A surge protector (that wasn't currently on) had started an electrical fire around the Christmas tree. And that fire devoured everything so fast.

The good news: Their insurance was REALLY good to them, and even though it was a difficult, upsetting time, everyone made it through safe and healthy.

This happened in December, just a couple weeks before Christmas, so I really connected with Gabriela in this book.

Anyway! Thank you all again for reading.

Silent Lucidity

ALSO BY TIFFANY ROBERTS

THE INFINITE CITY

Entwined Fates

Silent Lucidity

Shielded Heart

Vengeful Heart

Untamed Hunger

Savage Desire

Tethered Souls

THE KRAKEN

Treasure of the Abyss

Jewel of the Sea

Hunter of the Tide

Heart of the Deep

Rising from the Depths

Fallen from the Stars

Lover from the Waves

THE SPIDER'S MATE TRILOGY

Ensnared

Enthralled

Bound

THE VRIX
The Weaver
The Delver
The Hunter

ALIENS AMONG US
Taken by the Alien Next Door
Stalked by the Alien Assassin
Claimed by the Alien Bodyguard

STANDALONE TITLES
Claimed by an Alien Warrior
Dustwalker
Escaping Wonderland
His Darkest Craving
Yearning For Her
The Warlock's Kiss
Ice Bound: Short Story

ISLE OF THE FORGOTTEN
Make Me Burn
Make Me Hunger
Make Me Whole

<u>**Make Me Yours**</u>

VALOS OF SONHADRA COLLABORATION

<u>**Tiffany Roberts - Undying**</u>

<u>**Tiffany Roberts - Unleashed**</u>

VENYS NEEDS MEN COLLABORATION

<u>**Tiffany Roberts - To Tame a Dragon**</u>

<u>**Tiffany Roberts – To Love a Dragon**</u>

ABOUT THE AUTHOR

Tiffany Roberts is the pseudonym for Tiffany and Robert Freund, a husband and wife writing duo. Tiffany was born and bred in Idaho, and Robert was a native of New York City before moving across the country to be with her. The two have always shared a passion for reading and writing, and it was their dream to combine their mighty powers to create the sorts of books they want to read. They write character driven sci-fi and fantasy romance, creating happily-ever-afters for the alien and unknown.

Sign up for our Newsletter!
Check out our social media sites and more!

www.ingramcontent.com/pod-product-compliance
Lightning Source LLC
Chambersburg PA
CBHW020343220726
48290CB00013B/545